**EXTRAORDINARY
PEOPLE**

to Anita,
best wishes,
Paul

6 · 11 ·91

EXTRAORDINARY

PEOPLE

A NOVEL BY

PAUL GERVAIS

HarperCollins*Publishers*

I would like to thank a few people who have backed me with their kind assistance and faith: Amanda Urban, Alice Quinn, Marie Behan, and Craig Nelson.

P.G.

A portion of this book originally appeared in *Confrontation*.

FIRST EDITION

Designed by Cassandra J. Pappas

Library of Congress Cataloging–in–Publication Data

Gervais, Paul
  Extraordinary people / Paul Gervais.
    p. cm.
  ISBN 0-06-016618-5
  I. Title.
PS3557.E744E96 1991
813'.54—dc20   90-56361

91 92 93 94 95 MAC/HC 10 9 8 7 6 5 4 3 2 1

For Gil Cohen

CONTENTS

ONE

1

SUITE FOR A MOTHER AND

TWO SONS

My mother was bragging about having driven, all by herself and at the age of twenty-four, from Maine to Florida, where my father was stationed in the army. "You know, girls my age didn't drive like that in those days," she told my brother, Cliff, and me, raising a single eyebrow at my father who'd just said he didn't like the idea of her taking us to New York City all by herself.

She often got her way with these things though. She wanted to show us some city life before school started, and since my father, as usual, couldn't leave the store, just the three of us went: my mother, Cliff, and I. It was late August 1958.

We had a suite on the top floor of the Sheraton Russell Hotel, a huge suite with three bedrooms and a separate living room that looked out onto Park Avenue. Thick damask curtains fell from ceiling to floor, and there were landscape paintings in gold frames over the beds. We hadn't planned to have this suite, which cost much more than my mother was willing to spend, but when we got to the desk at the Sheraton McAlpin, the man said they had no reservation for "Beeler, a mother and two sons," repeating my mother's exact words. Suddenly, tears came to her eyes, and in a second they rolled down her high, flushed cheeks. Her lower lip quaked. "All right. All right," the man said, winking at the other desk clerks, who all stared at her, listening. "Let's just say it's our fault," he said. "How about a nice suite? Would you like that, Mrs. Beeler?" It hadn't taken this guy two seconds to fall in love with her—it took lots of men even less. My father called her "Face" for a reason. All at once, I knew we were going to have a great vacation; Face would get us whatever we wanted in this town, our heart's desire.

In a matter of minutes our car was off to the garage and we were in a cab on our way to the Sheraton Russell Hotel, where they gave us four plush rooms for the price of *one* at the McAlpin. It was thrilling to stay in the kind of suite only celebrities could afford. (Eddie Fisher rode up on the elevator with us, in fact, wearing bright yellow pants.)

I couldn't sleep. It was hotter in Manhattan at midnight than it was at home in North Tewksbury in the middle of the day. I'd been to New York lots of times, but just the same, all the noise—the battling horns, the odd shout, then a siren rising up out of the street to find its way through my open window, the elevator gong, heavy footsteps on the thick hallway carpeting that gave off a smoky, lemony scent, and the hooting, jiggy laughter of people on vacation—all these sounds kept me up half the night. Every once in a while I'd go to the bathroom sink and run cold water over my wrists (a way to beat the heat suggested by the cabdriver).

The next morning, we walked out the front door and ran into four hillbillies. They were in overalls and high felt hats, and they had holes in their faded blue work shirts and pieces of straw in their mouths. Three of them were barefoot, and one wore boots whose thin soles flopped loose on the hot New York pavement. They were all very busy fiddling with a weird-looking machine, like something out of *Twenty Thousand Leagues Under the Sea.*

"What are they doing with that thing?" I asked my mother.

"Making moonshine," she said. "It's a still."

I watched one of the hillbillies apply water-soaked bread to bubbling valves. "How come?" I said.

She took my hand when I lost balance, jostled by a hurried businessman. "I don't know," she said.

Once, playing in the barn, I found a brown, earthenware jug, left behind by the Burrs, the family of farmers who'd owned our house before us. My father told me it was a "moonshine jug," or "like a moonshine jug," then showed me how the hillbillies drank from it, sticking their thumbs through the ringlike handle and laying the jug on their bent elbows, raising it high.

"What's moonshine?" I asked my mother.

One of the men (the one with the boots) glanced at me, then at her. "Cheap whiskey," she said, laughing so loud it put her right into their act.

The way the hillbilly smiled at her, I could tell he was no hillbilly at all. He was just a normal kind of man in a hillbilly costume—but this is what was so much fun about New York for me: all the ruses, actors on every corner deceiving you, giving you thrills you wouldn't get at home.

All day long, we walked around the city in heat that made you sick, almost. We had lunch at Longchamp's, then afterward went looking for beatniks in the Village. Cliff hated beatniks, but I was crazy about them. My mother once broke my heart when she said I could never be a beatnik because I was too fair. Today she bought Cliff a shrunken head and me a tiki god.

When we got back to the hotel late in the afternoon, the three men were still working on their sour mash. There were corncobs thrown all around on the now sticky, spotted sidewalk and there was a bittersweet smell on the hot breeze: spilled beer and lemonade. When we came near, the hillbilly with the boots said to my mother,

"Wanna sample the brew, ma...dame?" He held up a glass of yellowish liquid with little clear flecks (maybe the broken, transparent skins of corn kernels) floating on the surface. It didn't look anything like whiskey to me.

My mother hesitated and blushed, but she went up to him, took the little glass, put it to her lips and drank.

"Ick," Cliff said.

"Purtty legs on that there filly," said one of the hillbillies.

"Darn right, Clyde," another one said, "'bout them legs o' hers."

There was a crowd by now. I watched my mother's throat move up and down the way it always did when she drank, and as the glass came away from her mouth it seemed to leave behind, on her lips, its circular, smiling shape.

"Hee-haw!" said the guy with the boots. "Look at that city gal gulp down the mash!"

They don't really talk this way, I thought; they're faking it.

The one they called Clyde stared at my mother. "That there's a million-dollar baby like we heared about, Mott," he said. And then he made a sound like "whooh" and shook his finger as if he'd just burned it on the gas flame of the still.

"You don't say!" said Mott. "That what that is?"

"Sho' 'nough," said Clyde. "Look at them eyes. Cost a purtty penny make them shine. Them ain't shinin' fo' no po' hillbilly like you an' me. She got a rich city man home keepin' her happy."

I knew this wasn't true. My father wasn't keeping her happy like they said. Sure, she might have been all smiles now, in New York— she loved the city, the "splashy people"—but it wouldn't take her long to go gloomy once she got back home again. Soon she'd be wearing her oldest clothes, moping around, bored as usual, and then at night, after a few drinks, she'd be complaining to my father that there was nothing to look forward to.

When I was little, we were rich enough to go to Florida every winter and stay in Daytona at Ocean Sundeck Apartments. We'd drive on the beach, and we'd visit Marineland, and my mother would get black as pitch, the way she liked to be. But these past few years, when she'd say, "We're going to Florida this March, aren't we, Daddy?" he wouldn't answer.

My father had a liquor business, and a few good years with it, but eventually, things went bad. "Times change," is what everybody said. There was enough money, at this point, for dinners out and for drinks, enough to rent a cottage for a couple of weeks up at Rye, or on Lake Winnipesaukee, but not enough for Florida, not enough for trips like rich people take, not nearly enough for all the things my mother wanted.

Inside the hotel lobby, I glanced at my mother's face; she was suddenly off somewhere, busy with thoughts she'd never share with us.

"What was that yellow stuff you drank?" Cliff asked.

"Beer," she said.

"Are you crazy?" Cliff said.

"Who are you talking to?" my mother said, mad.

Cliff did act like he was her father, sometimes.

I was fascinated with the transom over the door to the hall, which the maid sometimes left open. I invented a game. I got an extra roll of toilet paper from the bathroom; standing on a chair, I held on to the end of the roll, heaved it up over the transom, watched it tumble across the rippled glass, and imagined it skipping off down the hall past the doors of all those hooting, giggling hotel guests who'd kept me awake half the night.

The telephone rang, and I heard my mother answer it. "Yes?" she said. "Oh...yes. Good, and you?" she said, in the proper voice she used for people she didn't know well—I liked this voice of hers best of all.

I jumped down and sat in the chair facing the door, a white streamer in my hand.

"Well...I suppose I could," my mother said, and then she listened a minute.

I leaned forward, opened the door, and laughed when I saw the end of my toilet paper roll way down the hall by the entrance to the emergency stairs.

In a minute my mother stood beside me. "Sam," she said, "for heaven sakes!" I looked up at her and she was smiling, her lips freshly red. She could tell I was having a good time on my vacation, and I understood that it was O.K., as far as she was concerned, that it was great, even, if here in New York we all went just a little crazy.

She had on a black, sleeveless dress, and her arms were still coppery brown from sitting out on the lawn in the wooden chairs she'd painted "bright red" early in the spring. "I'm going to the lobby for a drink," she said. "If you want me, that's where I'll be, all right?"

After she left, I found Cliff in his room, flipping through *On Screen.* "Let's go down and watch the people?" I said. Cliff loved movie magazines; he had a whole stack of them next to his bed at home. Once he'd got his face in an article about Connie Francis, there was no moving him, so in a little while I cleaned up the toilet paper and went downstairs by myself.

When I saw that my mother was sitting with one of the hillbillies, the one with boots on, the one whose name I hadn't heard, something in my throat rose up fast so I had to swallow hard.

"This is the baby," she said as I came to stand beside her. "There's sixteen months' difference." She looked at me and smiled proudly.

"The baby?" I said, hurt.

"That just means the younger one," my mother said.

The hillbilly's hat was on the table next to his glass of whiskey and ice. I was looking at his bare head for the first time, and I could see it wasn't a hillbilly haircut he had but a neat one, done by a real barber. "He's not a hillbilly," I said to my mother, "is he?"

"This is Mr. Law," she said, and then they gave each other looks, like the looks my father and mother would exchange, keeping things from me. "He's a Rotarian. The Rotary Club's having a convention."

"We're from Albany, West Virginia, son," said Mr. Law. The collar of his worn-out shirt was wide open and a patch of Brillo-thick hair coiled out. "This hillbilly stuff is a little routine we're doing," he said. "For the fun of it, see?" He wasn't talking like a hillbilly anymore, but like a normal person from the South. In a way, I was disappointed. I wanted him to prove me wrong, to end up being a real hillbilly after all. That would have been fun. Instead, he was an ordinary guy, and I wondered what my mother found so appealing about him—she was gushy, in fact, all charm and pretty grins.

"Anyway," said Mr. Law, "I was saying she's got very high principles. She does her duty to the kids and me and she never complains." His voice was deep as Arthur Godfrey's, and smooth.

"I'm a complainer," said my mother.

"I don't buy that," said Mr. Law.

"You don't, hah?"

"That angel face of yours?" he said, playing up. His eyes sparkled and narrowed, and his face went red.

"Gerald gets fed up," she said. "I can't behave."

"Lois is a cleaner," said Mr. Law. "You got to walk around on your tippytoes. She's good for me, though; I'm a slob. I open my briefcase wherever there's a phone, and my papers are all over the place."

I was trying to picture him shaved and dressed like a businessman, but I couldn't.

"I hate housework," my mother said. "You should see my closet; you have to duck when you open the door."

He laughed, and so did she. Then she brushed the palm of her hand slowly over my fresh-clipped whiffle.

"It's true," I said. "You should see the floor of the *bathroom* closet if you think hers is bad. There's an old enema bag—"

"Oh shut up," my mother said.

The cocktail waitress came.

"You want another one?" said Mr. Law, pointing to my mother's empty glass.

"Oh why not," she said. Her voice was already changed the way it got when she'd had a drink or two. Her words were getting clipped, and she was clearing her throat every two seconds, whether she needed to or not. "I'll take a fresh one. This is my vacation," she said, as if she didn't drink every day.

"And he let you out of his sight?" said Mr. Law, squinting, turning his head quickly as if he had a bug at his ear. "If you were my wife," he said, "I'd have to say no to everything. I wouldn't buy you a car. I'd say no. I'd keep you shut in so I'd be sure where you were all the time."

"You're fresh!"

"I'm a selfish, jealous guy," he said. "Some women find that sexy. I don't know."

My mother blushed and looked at me.

"I'd take all the precautions I could," said Mr. Law, "to keep you from running into characters like this one!" He pointed to himself.

"Oh hush and finish your drink," my mother said. "Are you cuckoo?"

The waitress came and he ordered another round, plus a ginger ale for me.

"How many men did you have before you married him?" he asked. "Do you mind if I ask you an extra question or two?"

"No," said my mother. "I like it when people ask me things."

"I bet you had dates lined up weeks ahead," said Mr. Law. "How many men did you get serious with before you married your husband?"

"Sidney Poole was the only other one," she said. "My mother loved him. 'Why don't you go and marry that duck,' she'd say. 'What's the matter with you?' He was a dentist. I went out with him for three years when I worked at the Wyandotte. I should have married him, by gosh! He's got his offices on Marlborough Street in Boston now. Imagine how he lives? But I'll tell you something funny; you'll get a boot out of this!" She looked to the side at me, then back at Mr. Law. "Gerald was surprised the night of our wedding. He hadn't thought I was a virgin, but you know something? I was."

Mr. Law laughed and shook the ice in his empty glass before tipping it high.

"You wanna bet!" my mother said. "I was a virgin on my wedding night. It's the God's honest truth."

*   *   *

Cliff wanted to see a television show, and so she took us to Radio City. As we stood in line to get tickets for *Tic Tac Dough* a young woman came up and asked if we'd like to participate in previewing the pilot episode of a new TV series.

We sat, like a panel, at a big table, maybe twenty of us, and they gave us each two boxes, one with a red button, one with a green. While we watched *The Invisible Man* we were supposed to push the green button during the parts we liked, and the red button during the parts we didn't like. Cliff hardly ever pushed green, but neither did I, for that matter. Afterward, Cliff told the group how much he hated the show. "Tough critic," the moderator said; I could tell she liked him.

When we got back to the hotel, Mr. Law and the others were making moonshine again. The one they called Clem had no shirt on under his strappy overalls, and the back of his neck was sunburned and flaking off; and the one they called Mott was lighting a corncob pipe with a piece of straw he'd just run through the flame under the copper canister. "Afternoon, ma…dame," said Mr. Law, the hillbilly again. Then he stepped close to my mother, held her by the neck, and whispered something in her ear.

It must have been a dinner invitation, the thing he whispered, because that night we went to Danny's Hideaway (my mother's choice), where they had the biggest steaks I'd ever seen. While Cliff and I were putting on our ties my mother dabbed herself with perfume and said to us, "You just can't go into some of these places without a man. It's nice of him to take us out." Now, at dinner, she repeated this to Mr. Law, calling him Dave. "A woman alone, Dave, or with kids, can't get any service in a place like this. You're a good egg to have us."

Mr. Law had shaved his full face for dinner and his lips looked pinker without the grayish stubble around them. There was something wrong about his suit, though, like the shoulders were too wide or something, and I laughed to myself thinking that we still weren't getting a look at the real Mr. Law but at a guy in yet another costume, doing another routine "just for the fun of it."

"God knows I ought to be used to it by now," my mother said, "but I still feel silly, for instance, ordering a drink for myself." She finished up the one she had.

I stuck my finger through the hole in one of her ice cubes, fished out the cherry, and popped it all into my mouth. Cliff's eyes wandered, studying; he knew something about everyone in the room by now.

"Gerald and I came here when we lived in Elmhurst during the war," she said. "That was years ago, when we still had some fun together once in a while. Jeesh, I'll never see those days again. Danny would send us complimentary stingers after dinner and then he'd sit with us. Danny liked Gerald." Her gaze drifted off a minute. "In spite of all I can say that's wrong about my husband," she said, "he does have a little class, you know." It was like she wanted to convince him of it.

"Oh sure," said Cliff, sarcastic. He hated my father, but my father couldn't bear Cliff either, for that matter. He'd always felt Cliff was a mama's boy.

"Mind your business, Cliff," my mother said, still looking at Dave. "Gerald's good in a restaurant, with the bartenders and waiters."

"Look," said Dave. "I'm not gonna sit here and take that all through dinner."

"Take what?"

"Take all that punishment with your Gerald this and Gerald that. Can't we leave him home for once? You got in the car and you drove here all by yourself. Come on now. You're in New York. This is your vacation."

"Well *you're* the blowhard," said my mother. "All the cleaning your Janesy does. What is it? Lois? I think I'd hate her."

Mr. Law laughed real loud and covered my mother's hand with his own. "Supposing I told you my Lois was a pretty plain-looking girl, after all?" he said. "What if she was homely, in fact, heavyset and what not?"

Cliff looked at me and smirked. He didn't like Mr. Law—he'd told me so—but he didn't like most men.

"Is it true?" my mother asked.

"Well I'll tell you something that *is* true," he said, trying for a cute smile. "There's nothing wrong with *you*, Meg. And that's a fact! You got a damn sight more going for you than any Lois of mine does. And I know another thing that's true: Whether you admit it to me or not, there are things a guy like me could give you that your *Gerald* never will."

By the time we got to dessert, my mother had drunk four Manhattans and Mr. Law, four Cutty Sarks and water. In a while they grew silent, dreamy.

At one point, they exchanged tender looks. "Wish I had a code," Mr. Law said, softly. He ran his eyes past Cliff and me.

"Now you behave yourself," my mother said.

"But I'd like to know something," he said. "Ever want to…you know, cut him out of the picture?"

"Oh look!" said my mother, changing her voice and pointing fast across the room to a waiter with a tray. "Those are the lamb chops, Cliff!" she said, and then she said something else to Dave, under her breath.

I went to the men's room, and when I got back to the table I said, "The walls are papered with pictures of women bare!"

I was so surprised to see my mother laugh. She wasn't horrified the way she ordinarily would have been, say, if my father had been there with us, my father who once whipped me with his belt when he found out I'd seen *The Sins of Rachel Cade*. She didn't make me feel like a sinner because I'd gone to the men's room and got a look at all those beautiful women wearing only cowboy boots, holding lariats. Perhaps it was because we were away, in the city now, that she was so relaxed about things.

"I was thinking of making a visit myself, son," said Mr. Law. "Show me where it is."

Cliff slid in close to my mother as I went off to the men's room with Mr. Law to show him the walls covered with *Playboy* centerfolds, and really, to get another look for myself.

"How come they've got those up?" I asked.

"Because this is what gives a man pleasure, Sam," he said. "Women excite men, and then, when a guy's excited, he wants to touch that woman all over. He wants to kiss every part of her body, kiss her all over. This isn't dirty stuff, son. This is about love. Children come of it."

Walking back to the table alone, I thought about something that happened once. We'd been to the Beelers' house, my cousins, and when we got home my father said, "There's nothing I would have wanted more than to have had a big family like theirs. I think that's great, a big family, six children. It's the most wonderful thing in the world!" My mother got furious when he said that, answering back in a mad voice, "It takes two to tango!" My father went red and stormed off in silence. Remembering this now, I imagined my mother and father doing the tango. I watched them, in my mind, with their cheeks pressed together, their bodies close, their hands clasped way out ahead of their step. This was something I'd never seen in real life. I'd never seen them touch tenderly, and hold each other close.

Leaving the restaurant, it wasn't like going outside at all, but like stepping into another, bigger room of the same building we were in, this room filled with people strolling, enjoying the atmosphere of it, an atmosphere that seemed to heighten all our feelings.

Back at the Sheraton Russell, they wanted a nightcap in the lobby lounge.

"Look how sleepy," my mother said of me. "He can hardly keep his eyes open." But I thought Mr. Law seemed more beat than any of us, the way his eyelids drooped, the way his head seemed to hang. He held his glass on his knee and it was always just on the verge of spilling.

My mother finished her stinger. "Well, this was darn nice of you, Dave," she said.

"You need a *man* in New York," he said. "You're right about that. But I'll tell you something: I was lonely. I'm a selfish guy. It's a two-way street."

"You're a good sport," she told him. "Honest to God, Gerald's an old poop sometimes."

Cliff laughed; he thought my father was an old poop *all* the time.

"Why the devil did you marry him?" Dave said in a low, tired voice.

"He was handsome," my mother said.

I found my father's face hard to look at: too angry, too cold. But maybe it hadn't always been like that, his face. Maybe it got changed somehow, somewhere along the way, and who knew why or when it happened.

"He was the handsomest man in Lowell, people said."

"Who said?"

"Everyone in Lowell said that. I never heard the end of it. 'Meg is *so* lucky to get a man like Gerald. He could take his pick, you know!' Talk like that."

"So what?"

"What?"

"Where's your handsome guy ended up?"

"Owning a liquor store," said my mother with a laugh that seemed to mean, You're right, that's nothing.

"Is that what you wanted?"

"I thought he had a lot of money," she said. "I thought he inherited an extra buck when his father died. If he did, I never saw it. But I hardly knew Gerald. We went together for only two months before getting married. Two months, imagine that! Sometimes in your life you have to make a fast decision, and you just make it, that's all. Gerald had to go into the service and there was no time to think it over. We had our wedding in a rush at six a.m. We had a breakfast reception, and you know something? I wore a suit. A gray suit."

I must have dozed off a minute. When my eyes opened, my mother and Mr. Law were standing up beside the cocktail table in front of me, and Cliff was walking toward the newsstand. "Sam," my mother said, as if she'd already called my name a couple of times and was doing it again, louder this time. "Sam!"

"Yes?" I said.

"Wake up!" she said. "You and Cliff are going to the room. Cliff has the key."

"What about you?" I asked.

"I'm having a drink upstairs with Dave."

"Upstairs where?"

"Up in his room."

"Why?"

"Because," she said. "O.K.?"

"How come?" I said. She was jiggy enough already, it seemed to me. "How come you have to go up to his room to have a drink? Why don't you have more drinks here, with us?"

"He wants to go up to the room, Sam. He just wants a little company, that's all. He's lonely. It'll be all right. You and Cliff go on to bed, and I'll be there soon, O.K.?"

"O.K.," I said.

We went to the elevators. Across the lobby, Cliff was buying a magazine. "Wait for him," said my mother, getting into an elevator with Mr. Law. When the doors closed, I watched the needle over the elevator point to ever larger numbers, and I felt abandoned and afraid, afraid that this elevator of theirs would never stop at the floor where Mr. Law's room was, but would carry them on up through the roof, out into cold space, to a place where there were no feelings, no feelings for me, and where I'd never find my mother again.

Cliff came and stood beside me. "I'm telling Daddy on her," he said. "I am. I'm telling."

I thought about the time the Cushman's bread man kissed my mother in the front hall of our house, and how Cliff told my father, and how mad he got. "Do you think he's kissing her?" I said.

"Course he's kissing her," Cliff said. "Course he is, and I'm telling too!"

I was wide awake now after having dozed a bit in the lobby. I got into bed but I couldn't sleep; it was boiling in my room. When the elevator gong struck, I waited for the sound of a key in our door, but all I could hear were unfamiliar, whispering voices, then heavy footsteps out in the hall. It was almost three o'clock.

I looked in on Cliff. His light was out and he was sound asleep. In the living room, I took a piece of stationery from a folder on the desk; I made an airplane out of it, then launched it across the room. The window was wide open. Leaning on the dusty, cracked windowsill, I stuck my head out and looked down on the yellow taxi roofs and the dark tops of heads coming in and out of the hotel doors. I got my paper airplane out from under a chair, went to the window again, and launched it toward the blue-black sky. In a minute it caught the light of the moon. It took off in air currents and soared higher than the height of my window, higher than the hotel roof, as it tried new layers of atmosphere, one by one. Edging my way out, I followed the plane with my eyes till it disappeared in darkness, up above the skyline...

"Sam!" my mother cried, clutching my ankles, pulling me back inside. "Sam!" she screamed, holding on to me, shaking.

When my bare feet hit the soft, carpeted floor again, I turned around and looked her in the eye. Her makeup was worn off, and I could tell she'd been crying. She wasn't jiggy anymore, and this was the strangest thing of all: it was as if she hadn't had a single drink all day. She threw her arms around me and drew me in tight till I felt light-headed and weak, the night air squeezed from my lungs.

Once, when I was little, a warm feeling prompted me to say to my mother, "Let's kiss like lovers." I remember her answer: "No," she said, "that's nasty!" But now, so relieved to have me safe and close, she said my name again and again, and kissed my face all over, everywhere, even on the lips, the way I'd always imagined lovers do.

2

BIG CHICKENS

Gerald was working late, as usual, and so Meg had an early dinner with Cliff and Sam at Green Apple, a nightclub out in the Highlands. They ate fast; at six the cover charge went on and all kiddos had to go.

Pauline Gurren, the owner's wife, pushed her way through a green, tufted door with an apple-shaped window in it, and by the time it stopped swinging, she'd slipped into the booth next to Meg. Pauline had a blond ponytail that shimmied in a nimble, sporty way, and her eyebrows were vaulted and plucked. "Listen to me with your ears!" she said. She was from Detroit and had a different accent from other girls around; she said "extrey," for instance.

"Listen to me with your ears!" she said again, running the palm of her hand over Cliff's brushy haircut. But then she went quiet all of a sudden. "I'm no fun tonight," she said.

"How come?" said Meg.

The waitress came by to see if Pauline wanted anything. Meg lifted her Manhattan with one hand, then gave Pauline a little push with the other. "Oh have one," she said. "Rye and ginger, go on!" She waved the waitress off quick.

"No...well...all right," said Pauline. "I need it. I'm ready for the gloop!"

"The gloop?" asked Sam.

"You look bushed," said Meg. "Take a sip of mine." She pushed her glass Pauline's way. She was wearing her dinner ring.

"Carl's been working like a dog," said Pauline. "The harder he works, the harder he is to live with." She tossed her car keys down on the tabletop, where silver and gold boomerangs floated in green plastic. "I swear to God," she said, "I was better off when I had a job."

"I'm getting a job," Meg said. "I'm sick of it. I wasn't made to stay home alone with the kids. Does Carl need a hostess here? I wouldn't mind that. I look good enough, don't I, Pauline? Does he have any hostesses who look as good as I do?"

"Course not, Meg," said Pauline. "But don't you dare go back in there and ask him, O.K.? That's all we need!"

"I'm going to, one of these days, by gosh," Meg said. "You bet your boots I am, Pauline. Have my own money I can do what I want with! Are you kidding?"

Pauline lit a cigarette. Meg hated smoke, but she liked the angles Pauline's hand made holding the cigarette high, and the white underside of Pauline's wrist. Meg once tried smoking a pastel orange cigarette with a gold filter—Sociables was the brand—at one of her New Year's Eve parties. She was wearing false fingernails covered with globs of glue. That was the night Pauline's husband, Carl, kissed Meg under the mistletoe, a hard kiss that seemed to fill her lungs the way water does when you drown.

"I worked at the Pentagon, you know," said Meg, "back when Gerald was stationed in Washington. I haven't always been good for nothing."

"I know you did," said Pauline, pinching Meg's chin till her dimple closed to a pencil-thin crease.

"I was General Pearson's secretary," she said. "He was darn nice to me. If he'd see me walking to work in the morning, he'd have his driver stop and pick me up, give me a ride in his splashy Cadillac, and I'd sit in the back with him like Garbo. That's what my brother Armand used to say—'She looks like Garbo riding along with the general.'"Meg laughed at her own story. She hated blowhards, but even she could brag, when she was bored, say, or when she felt her whole life was behind her at that point.

"Have another one, Pauline, go on," said Meg. "I'm having a stinger. Let's get that German waitress Janesy over here." She waved to her. "What's her name? I know everything about her except her name. She married an American soldier after the war, you know. *You* know that. I got a look at him one day. He's black as the ace of spades. Oops!" She covered her mouth. "Handsome guy, though. You know I don't mean anything by that. Don't you want a stinger, Pauline?"

"Two stingers," Pauline shouted; her voice rang in the cymbals of the drum set which stood, unmanned, on the still-dark stage.

"Whenever Pearson had big shots," Meg said, "and they had to go around the Pentagon, he'd get me to take them. I was the only one who never got lost in that place. 'Meg'll take you,' General Pearson would say. I could get a job right this minute, if I wanted, a darn good one. Bet you a buck I could, Pauline. I can say I've done something."

In a while their stingers came, full to the brim. Pauline's long neck curved like a swan's as she bent low, sipping. In a minute her eyes grew heavy.

"Are you all right?" asked Meg. "Come on, perk up! Let's have some fun!"

Cliff made a marbleized soup of his second helping of Jell-O topped with whipped cream. Sam was miles away.

Pauline said, "Meg, you're damn lucky you can stay so full of pep; that's all I can say."

"What do you mean?" Meg narrowed her eyes. Her mouth got rectangular as she drank.

"I can't, that's all," said Pauline. "I run out of gas."

"Oh for heaven sakes," said Meg.

"Like what you did Halloween," Pauline said. "I just thought that was marvelous, Meg. The witch's getup. The raisins in your teeth and the Chiclet warts on your nose. I could never get away with a stunt like that. How'd you get up on my roof anyway? I'll never forget it."

"A ladder," Meg said.

"I'm not myself these days," said Pauline. "I'm changing into someone even I don't like: the last person you'd ever want to go around with."

"That's the silliest thing I've ever heard," said Meg, growing loud. "You think I'm happy-go-lucky all the time, not a care in the world? You're not the only one who's married to a man who works nights!"

Just then, Carl Gurren came out of the back room. He was in a dark suit with shortish sleeves that showed a lot of white French cuff, and when he came near, Meg's gaze fixed on his big lapis ring. His eyes were deeply shaded beneath thorny black eyebrows, wiry and thick.

"Hi Meg," he said, with a little nod, and then a leer in her direction. Meg thought, That's a dirty look if I ever saw one!

Meg had always wondered if Carl disliked her. Tonight she was suddenly sure how he felt. He hated her. She knew it. He hated her, and he hated her going around with his wife. Suddenly, she felt scared. She was positive he had a gun holstered in his armpit, like all the nightclub thugs did.

Carl looked at his watch. It was getting late. He'd be booting the kids out soon (a job he liked a lot, it seemed to Meg). A couple of customers appeared at the door. They stopped and turned their heads, gazing into the corners of the empty green dining room, then down at the apple blossom carpeting. A guy in a white sport coat went around to the eighth-note-shaped music stands, passing out the evening's program.

"Let's wind this up!" said Carl, with the rudest tone to his voice; it was like an act of violence. Meg almost shook with humiliation as she reached for her bag.

Pauline leaned wearily forward, her chin practically resting on the edge of the table. Carl put the palm of his hand against Pauline's forehead, pushed back her head, and peered into her half-shut eyes. She'd got plastered quick tonight and you could tell it irked him to see her like this. With a disgusted look on his face, he jerked the unfinished drink away from her, leaving a trail of liquid beads on the green tabletop. Meg guessed what he was saying to himself: The party's over, dear!

"Let's wind this up!" he said again.

Meg wondered how Pauline could ever sleep with him.

When Meg, Gerald, and the kids moved, several years before, to North Tewksbury on the outskirts of Lowell, Meg didn't know anybody except Gerald's brother and sister-in-law. They were good people, but not a lot of fun to go around with, and so Meg, without a close girlfriend, was lonesome much of the time.

Meg was originally from Connecticut, but she and her family had been living in Waterville, Maine, for almost six years by the time she met Gerald and married him. He was manager of the new Jefferson Store up there. Lowell, Massachusetts, was his hometown though, and in a while he wanted to go back. It was hard for Meg. It broke her heart to leave behind friends she loved: impulsive, fun girls, like herself.

In Lowell Gerald took over his late father's package store, then joined the Elks, just as his father had done, mostly for the right to furnish liquor to their monthly dinner dances. These were affairs to which members brought their wives, and it was where Meg met Pauline Gurren: just the person she'd been hoping to find. "Statuesque" was Meg's word for Pauline. And so was "stunning." Pauline had long hands and long red fingernails Meg envied— Meg's nails always broke and fell off, and she never polished them since color just called attention to the problem. Meg told Gerald, "Well, it's about time. Thank God there's at least one girl around here besides me who's got a little style!"

The Gurrens had a nice summer home up in New Hampshire, at Rye, above Hampton. It was on Cable Road, just a five-minute walk to the beach. That year, Meg managed to convince Gerald to rent a cottage there for half the season. It was a plain white house whose marine-blue wooden shutters had silhouettes of sea gulls on them, punched out as if with a cookie cutter.

The girls had some fun at the beach. Their husbands were seldom around, and so, when it got to the point where Meg and Pauline couldn't face another night at home with just the kids for companionship, they'd hire sitters and go out together, the two of them. With their sweaters buttoned at the neck and their side windows up against the bite of a cold wind out of Quebec, they'd speed across the causeway to Seabrook in Meg's convertible—Meg never worried about cops; she knew them all, and they knew her. Those nights, Pauline and Meg had the courage of young girls who'd never made a wrong turn, never made mistakes.

Even if the girls had been out all night, their kiddos—Brenda Gurren and Meg's two boys—would get them up at the crack of dawn to go bottle hunting on the beach. Meg and Pauline, in shorts, would trail along with shopping bags as the kids scooped around in the sand wherever they saw a trace of bottle glass peeking out, and by the time they'd made it from one end of the beach to the other, the shopping bags would be full and heavy, and Meg and Pauline, hung over, would groan, huffing, their arms aching at the sockets. "Who do you kids think we are?" Meg would say. "Two Man Mountain Deans?"

Finally, the girls would have to haul the sand-coated bottles all the way to Carberry's for the kids to get their deposit money just so they could buy Tootsie Pops and ice cream sandwiches, stuff Meg and Pauline would have bought them anyway. But it was something for the kids to do. It made them feel clever and enterprising, and Meg and Pauline enjoyed being together even for things as stupid as this, liked being the two beautiful, madcap blondes who'd turn men's heads wherever they went—even at Carberry's with bursting bags of Coke bottles in their arms, pushed around by towheads with salt-streaked, sun-browned bodies.

Meg and Pauline loved getting invited for drinks by Everett Clarkson, the young bachelor who lived in a palatial house on the oceanfront, who had a new Roadmaster and a yacht he kept up at Portsmouth. They loved sharing the compliments he never let up with. And they liked getting whistled at by the boys on the road crew who hung out at The Sea Dog, and by the man in the Moxie truck. The girls had fun names for all of them.

Meg especially liked the waiter at the Hotel Farragut pool, where she and Pauline sometimes went to drink foamy collinses as the kiddos took a freshwater swim.

"How do you get suds on the drinks like that?" Meg once asked the guy, who was a ski bum at Bromley in the winter.

"They bubble up soon as they see *you*," he said.

"Oh that's cute," said Meg. "Honest to God. Pauline, wasn't that cute?"

Pauline laughed. She was a nose wrinkler; there were little white lines on the bridge of it where the sun didn't hit.

One day, the waiter asked Meg, "Don't you own a bathing suit?"

"Course," said Meg.

"How come you never wear it, then?"

"Pain in the neck changing all the time," she said. Her figure wasn't quite so good as Pauline's. Pauline always got herself into a tight swimsuit there at the Farragut, but the most revealing outfit Meg ever wore was a pair of shorts and a sleeveless blouse, clothes that hid her round stomach (which all those drinks had made). Meg relied on her pretty face for attention, but that was always more than enough to get her what she wanted.

They found out the waiter's name: Jude. "What a cute name you've got," Meg said. She flashed her perfect teeth, baking soda white.

"Look, Mrs. Beeler," Jude said, "if you get down to a bathing suit next time, the drinks are on the house."

They never went back.

It was the day after Carl clamped down on the girls up at Green Apple. Gerald was home for lunch. Meg served him Scotch broth in the living room on a tray table they'd got as a beer premium—they never ate in the breakfast room, and ate in the dining room only on Sundays.

"I felt like two cents," said Meg. "Carl says, 'Let's wind this up,' like some kind of a bouncer in a cheapo joint. Can you imagine that? I could have pushed his face in."

"You know what I say, don't you," said Gerald, the know-it-all in him coming up.

"No, what?" said Meg.

"I think you've been playing in the wrong backyard," he said. He lifted his brow and gave her a priggish, sidelong smile.

"Oh is that right?" said Meg, angered, her hands on her hips. She hated it when he got paternal.

"He *is* some kind of bouncer in a cheapo joint," said Gerald, bending forward as he ate, holding his tie back away from the streams of soup falling off his spoon. "I never liked either one of them, if you want my honest opinion. I never thought she was for you."

"What are you talking about?" Meg blustered. She stood in the kitchen doorway with a pot holder in her hand, a dishcloth over her shoulder. She'd got splashed at the sink and there were wet spots on her shabby white blouse. "Pauline's a darn nice girl," she said. "She's cute as anything. What are you saying, not for me?"

"You know what I'm talking about," said Gerald. "She's fast. I never liked the idea of you seeing her, to tell you the God's honest truth."

"Fast?" Meg's voice jumped up an octave, but its volume fell to something just above a whisper. Her eyes searched about. "What are you saying? Where do you get such ideas, Gerald Beeler!" She laughed. "Listen to you talk!"

"I hear things around," Gerald said. "And I'll tell you something. If I weren't an easygoing guy, if I were anything like Carl Gurren and the type of pain-in-the-neck husband he must be, I'd have told you to get off that Pauline kick a year ago."

"Oh you would have, would you?" said Meg. Mad now, she charged back into the kitchen. Fast! she said to herself, then laughed out loud. She was good as gold, Pauline Gurren. Meg thought about the time, up at the beach, when Touey got his tail bitten off by another male cat. Meg went to save Touey's life and he scratched her arm from shoulder to wrist, making deep slashes. And who took me to Dr. Campobasso's? Meg thought to herself now. Who was there when I needed help? Not you, Gerald! You weren't *fast* enough! "Well I've heard everything," she said to the empty kitchen. "I've...heard...everything!"

"What, dear?" said Gerald, in the other room.

In a second she was standing beside him as he ate, watching the television news. "You tell me something now," she said. "Just what have you heard around? Tell me that! Just what have you heard about Pauline?"

"Oh what difference does it make," said Gerald. "For the love of God! Forget it!"

"Makes a difference to me," said Meg. "You can't just sit there and say such things about a friend of mine if you haven't got reasons for it."

Gerald turned, peering at her over his lowered glasses, and his eyes seemed to say, O.K., you asked for it! "What have I heard?" he said. "I'll tell you what I've heard. She's easy. That's what the story around is! And you can tell me anything you want about what a nice girl she is, but I'm going to tell you she's easy, O.K. That's what *I'm* going to tell you. There! You satisfied?"

"Oh you're such a gosh darn *saint* sometimes," Meg said, her face all hot and red. "Honest to God!"

Meg would always remember how angry Gerald once got when she brought home the *Enquirer*. "You know where that's going, don't you?" he said as he snatched it out of her hand, tore it to bits, and threw it in the garbage. "What are you thinking of anyway," he said, "buying that rubbish?"

The second time she did it, Gerald got so furious she had to make up a lie. "I *didn't* buy it," she insisted. "Mrs. Hugh Waldo gave it to me at the cleaners."

"Mrs. Hugh Waldo my fanny!" said Gerald, even in front of the boys. That's just how angry he was.

He was so "saintly" he even hated making love in their bedroom now that the boys were older and apt to be awake evenings, now that they were old enough to wonder what the noise of bedsprings was all about, and the whimpers and the odd groan one of them might let slip. Their bedroom door had no lock on it, and Meg was always after him to install one, but she knew that he would be embarrassed, that he'd blush, tongue-tied, when Sam or Cliff, seeing him drill holes in the doorframe to screw the bolt in place, expected some kind of explanation.

They had a place where they went parking, far out of sight and earshot of the kids, way down on Bailey Road, practically as far as Shattuck's Farms. There was a turnout in a field, and that's where they would go to do it, after they'd had dinner together at Worth's. Sometimes there would be another car, young lovers, teenagers, but luckily, they wouldn't be so near that Gerald would feel self-conscious or silly, or afraid of getting recognized by neighborhood kids. And fortunately for Meg, he was always good and jiggy by the time they got there.

One night after pigs' feet and German fries at Worth's, and four or five Löwenbräus each, they drove out Bailey Road, but when they went to pull into their parking spot, they found it chained off. Behind the chains, in the glow of their headlights, were massive piles of construction materials: cement blocks and loads of lumber. It turned out that the archdiocese was building a new church on that site, the church that would eventually become, once the parochial boundaries were redefined, their new parish, St. Jerome's. Years later, on Sunday mornings, Meg would chuckle to herself, thinking about where their elderly new pastor, Father Flynn, now stood to celebrate the sacrifice of the Mass. But she was sure Gerald wasn't chuckling along with her, these mornings, as tingling bells accompanied the consecration. Saints didn't have any fun in church.

Pauline stopped calling Meg. She used to call two or three times a day, checking in, but not anymore. Who knew what kind of tough-guy tactics Carl was using on her? Meg finally got up her courage and called Pauline—she'd been terrified of doing it, sure that Carl, in one of his rare moments at home, would answer the phone and tell her off. Pauline's voice was cool and distant. She went on for a while about her "gorgeous" new dining room wallpaper with peacocks on it, but when she'd exhausted that subject, she said she had to go. Meg thought about stopping by her house for a face-to-face talk. She wanted one question answered: Did Carl hate all Pauline's girl-friends, or just Meg? But she was scared to death to go there, sure Carl would pull into the driveway behind her just as she got out of the car. "And bet you a buck he'd have that gun with him," Meg told Gerald. "I wasn't born yesterday. He's crazy as a coot. Who knows what he'd do if he got good and mad at me!"

"Oh Meg, for goodness sakes!" Gerald said to the sports section of the *Lowell Sun*. "Forget the darn Gurrens!"

"I can't," said Meg.

Gerald laughed himself sick when one day the oven door fell open with a loud bang, and Meg ducked into the living room saying someone had shot at her through the kitchen window.

He suggested she join a ladies' organization, get her mind off Pauline and Carl, get out and meet women more like herself, Catholic women for a change.

She joined the Ladies of Good Works at the hospital. She served on the ways and means committee, and wore hats and gloves and a mink stole to their luncheon affairs. But she didn't like any of the Ladies as much as she liked Pauline Gurren, and so there was still that big, nagging emptiness in this lonely life of hers with a husband she rarely saw and kids who were, of course, just kids.

Before long, it came back to Meg that people in the organization felt she was "just a dumb blonde." In tears she told Gerald she'd had it. "Just a dumb blonde," she said. "Can you imagine that, Gerald? I'm sick and tired of that damn bunch of old biddies!"

Gerald convinced her it was a lot of nothing; they were just jealous of her good looks. That was it.

One day she invited one of the Ladies of Good Works, Olivia Webb, to play golf with her at Brightacre, Gerald's club. Meg hadn't had any silly fun in ages, and so, little by little, she worked her way into hilarious hazards. Giggling, she took fifteen strokes blasting her way out of a sand trap, and Olivia, downwind, turned up the collar of her shirt and sucked in her shoulders. "Jeesh Meg, for Pete sakes!" she said.

When a foursome came up on their heels at the next tee, Meg ribbed them for being so serious. "Look at the getups!" she said. She took a couple of practice swings, laughing at herself, at the way her choppy follow-through picked her up off the ground so both feet were in the air; then finally, over her ball that wouldn't stay put on its tee, she called out "Fo-wah!" and said, "Here we go now, one, two, three! Count with me, here we go, one ..." And then she topped the ball—"Whoops!"—and it skipped off, in slow motion, and came to a stop hardly three yards away. Claiming it counted as a single stroke, she scooped her ball out of the rough with a strainer on a rod designed for water rescues.

Even though Meg felt that Olivia was a poker face, she would have given her a chance to redeem herself, gone to lunch with her at the Princeton Lounge or something, but Olivia was always quite unavailable for any other dates Meg proposed.

"She always has lipstick on her teeth," Meg told Gerald when he asked why she hadn't seen her new friend again. "And not only that," Meg said. "She's got halitosis something awful."

Carl and Pauline didn't come to the Beelers' New Year's Eve party, even though Meg felt daring enough to call and invite them as she'd always done. She was hurt when Pauline begged off in an icy, faraway voice. Meg had hoped that at least by New Year's things would be back to normal and she and Pauline would be friends again, just as before. She told Gerald, "If she weren't married to that horse's...she'd come, and she'd stay late too, till the last gun was fired, like everybody else. Bet you a buck!"

It was a big surprise when Pauline, her face full of apologetic excuse, came stealthily by at about six, before any guests arrived, delivering the plate of deviled eggs she'd made. It was raining, half-freezing rain, and she had no lipstick on and a babushka on her head—that's what Meg always called it anyway: a babushka. "It's the Lithuanian in her," she'd told Gerald, in the midst of a recent stew, missing her. The babushka went with all the housecleaning she did, and the gardening, and all the manual labor she seemed to love. Driving past the Gurrens', Meg would catch Pauline out in the rain, in her babushka, at the edge of the road with a hoe, building little dams in the mud, and straight canals to the sewer grate. That was "real old Lithuanian stuff," Meg figured: bothering with how the water flowed on the side of the road. Lately Meg would remember Pauline's bragging too much about how expensive her wallpaper was, or Pauline's telling Meg all this stock market statistical stuff that she knew Meg didn't understand. Meg would say to herself, or to Gerald if he was in the mood to listen to her troubles, "And she's really nothing but a buck farmer, you know, when you come right down to it," or else she'd say, "Pauline didn't have a pot to pee in before she married Carl, and now all she can talk about is her *gorgeous* wallpaper. Everything she has is all of a sudden so *gorrrrrgeous!*"

But when Pauline came by that evening with her plate of deviled eggs sprinkled with paprika and carefully carried in a bakery box, Meg's heart went soft. She entered right into Pauline's mind and body as she'd boiled those eggs, peeled them, spooned out the hardened yolks and beat them up with mayonnaise; she felt Pauline's weariness when the job was done.

Missing her, Meg's evening turned into a series of sad reflections. After a few drinks, tears fell, not just for Pauline's absence but for

Meg's distant brother Brian, the colonel, and then for a memory of her parents as they were when she was young, when Meg hoped and prayed that she would die before they died because she knew she could never take the loss. Tears fell for those weekends at West Point when Brian would fix her up with another cadet for a military ball; tears fell for Waterville, and for her old friend Janet Bigelow.

By eleven she'd pulled her scrapbook out of the piano bench and shown everybody pictures of Janet Bigelow and herself, in jodhpurs and leather helmets, on the front page of the *Waterville Sentinel:* Meg and Janet posing beside Janet's little plane which had done three somersaults before its belly scraped the runway and it screeched to a slow stop. "'Oh what a thrill,' says Meg May after the crash." That's how the headline read, even though Meg never said such a thing at all. She was scared to death, in fact. But she sure missed Janet Bigelow now and her two sisters; they were a fun crowd. She wanted to be living back in those days again, back when she had a job, and so did her friends, and they could get away with anything and everything, back when they were free to choose for themselves, according to their own ideas about life, and not their husbands'.

At midnight Meg, jiggy and sentimental, tried hushing those around her as she dialed the phone, calling Green Apple where Pauline and Carl were supposed to be. She sat there on the little telephone chair in the corner of the living room, her slip showing, her makeup faded, listening to the phone ring in the receiver, barely audible through the background of piano playing and their exhausted, pie-eyed friends' crooning of sad old songs they all seemed to know by heart—"songs of yesteryear," Sam once called them.

Nobody answered over there. Having too much fun, Meg figured. Lowering the receiver, giving up, she said to herself, "Happy New Year, oh sure!" In a moment drunken tears filled her eyes again, so that she couldn't read a thing as she scanned through her phone book for Janet Bigelow's number in Waterville.

That week, two feet of snow fell, and then it thawed. Meg's car fishtailed and plowed up muddy puddles in the circular driveway.

After dark, the roads were glare ice, but she couldn't stay home alone with the kids another night. She wanted to see Pauline; she didn't care how anybody else felt about it. She wanted to have just one drink with Pauline and maybe a laugh that might make her feel good about herself again. She decided the heck with it; she'd take the kids to Green Apple for dinner. It would be all right, she assured herself. Pauline had brought her the deviled eggs. Maybe this meant Carl was loosening his grip on her. Maybe he wouldn't mind if his wife saw her old friend *once* in a while, provided they didn't get so close as they used to be.

Cliff and Sam watched their mother dress. They lay on their parents' unmade bed, on top of the pink satin puff, staring at her in her bra (hooked crooked in back) and the long rubber girdle she'd just powdered, with its dangly garter clips. In nylon stockings, she stood way up on her toes as if she were already in heels, then did that thing with her mouth, made her "mirror face," which sometimes Cliff, having fun with Sam, would imitate—he could reproduce, precisely, every move his mother made, every sound. Cliff and Sam would laugh themselves out of control. Then Meg stepped into her black dress, and attached her pearls. She gave her thick, dark eyebrows one last pinch together, as if wanting to squeeze their wildness into fine, subtle curves. Her hands lifted her blond hair, reshaping its casual waves, arranging the locks against her forehead. She reached for one of the three or four tall, lidless cans of Helene Curtis hair spray that always stood on the night table beside her bed, beside the full-length mirror where she dressed, and all at once a cloud of mist fell to her shoulders, and the room filled up with its bitter smell.

But it was all for nothing. Pauline wasn't there.

At about six, Carl came out of the back room wearing a coat and carrying a briefcase. Meg knew he saw her; he had to have seen her there, in the corner of the empty dining room, but he never really looked her way, never raised his chin.

Back at home, Meg was alone in her room getting ready for bed, when the phone rang. She took off an earring and reached for the receiver, knocking over one of the half-empty cans of hair spray.

"Meg?" she heard. "Is that you?" It was a man's voice.

"Yes?" said Meg.

"Meg?" he said. "Carl Gurren here."

"Yes," said Meg, clutching the receiver, trembling, her voice caught.

"Meg," he said. *"Stay out of it!"*

The rhythm of Meg's heartbeat broke, and her shoulders fell, and her head bowed, and the only thing she wanted to do was run and hide, hang up and hide, go and get a motel room in a place where Carl would never think to find her, somewhere in Shawsheen maybe, far out of town, way away from Lowell.

"Look," he said, "just...don't bother us, O.K.?" That was all he said; then he hung up.

Months went by. In time, Meg got over her fear of Carl. Though she still thought about Pauline all the time, she hardly ever mentioned her name to Gerald; she knew he hated hearing it.

She and Gerald met a bunch of people at the parish Theology Club get-togethers. Soon almost everyone dropped out of that boring group, but Meg and Gerald stuck with these new friends who would take turns inviting each other to their homes for Michigan rummy and roast beef sandwiches once a week. The wives were nice; not beautiful women, or glamorous, but nice enough, if not a lot of fun. There was one who would shut herself up in the closet and play the saxophone once in a while when things got dull, and Meg could giggle at that.

Meg was so happy when her mother and father moved down from Maine to a newly built house across the street from the ball field on Hayes Circle, near Tewksbury Center. "I'm a new woman," Meg told Gerald. To that, Gerald said, "Thank God," but even though it seemed he was only kidding, real tears filled Meg's eyes.

She and Gerald hadn't been parking out on Bailey Road since the archdiocese started construction on the church, and Gerald had never suggested that they find another place, that they try the field out by the Wang factory, for instance. Meg had grown melancholy by now, and maybe Gerald didn't find that sexy in a woman. Little by little she moved into the guest room; one night a week, then two. In a while its closet was filled with half her clothes and the window seat was stuffed to the brim with her ruined nylons and yellowed girdles.

And her mother and father, old now, didn't provide the companionship they once had. No matter how much Meg loved them, loved them, in fact, the way a little girl loves her parents, by now they just meant more duty instead, more errands and bother. If she didn't call them every twenty-four hours, Meg's father would phone and say, "Where the hell have *you* been?" and that made her feel bound up in more and more dull obligation.

She and Gerald didn't take the beach cottage this year, and so every Sunday Meg would have to entertain her parents for dinner in the afternoon. She'd have to get out the barbecue grill, and hose it off, and dump in the charcoal, and squirt the devil out of it with that starter fluid, and singe her eyebrows when it shot up in flames like out of a refinery chimney. Gerald was no longer good for the kind of chores most men did. He'd just sit around in the living room, with his slippers on, watching TV. When the in-laws showed up, he'd put on smiles like the ones he wore when he dated Meg, smiles that were pretty scarce by now. Meg, doing all the work, ended up getting herself stiff in the kitchen with stolen shots of whiskey, thinking about Pauline up at the beach with Brenda, wondering if Pauline had a new girlfriend she liked as much as she'd once liked Meg.

She had every right to take the kids up to Rye for an afternoon at the beach if she felt like it. It was a hot day in July; the kids were getting too big for their little wading pool full of floating, half-dead mosquitoes and bumblebees.

Meg found Pauline on the beach, in her usual spot, brown as an Indian. Brenda, pretty grown-up by now, stood by dripping after a swim.

"Taking on a few curves," Meg said to Brenda.

"What's that supposed to mean?" asked Cliff.

"She's got a little shape to her," Pauline said. "See it?"

Pauline was lying there beside a lonely stack of *Look* magazines, a little nest of cigarette butts next to her in the sand. Seeing her after all this time, Meg felt as if she'd come to the edge of a cliff, and that her own body was the enemy, that even a move so slight as the quick blink of an eye could pull her into a spinning fall. She wondered if Pauline's heart beat with the same uncertain speed as hers.

But then Pauline's face picked up. She jumped to her feet and gave Meg a hug that wouldn't quit, and in a moment Meg's fear seemed to pass.

That evening, Brenda Gurren stayed home with the boys while Pauline and Meg went to The Sandpiper for boiled lobsters and cole-slaw. Meg wore a paper bib. "Face it, Pauline," she said as her fingers dripped with drawn butter, "we married a couple of darn little Ipswich clams!"

Pauline's fluid, familiar laugh came back out of the blue like a prodigal son.

At one point, a pair of hands blacked out Meg's eyes. "Give me a hint," Meg said.

"It's the guy who looks like the Cushman's bread man," Pauline said. "Only this one has a yacht."

"Everett!" Meg said.

It was Everett Clarkson, the bachelor with the big house on the beach. He had his brother-in-law with him and that fellow who owned a brewery in Haverhill; they were all real gentlemen, types Meg liked. The first thing you knew, a tray of stingers came by, and they reached for them. The piano player came on singing a Belafonte number, and soon they were all dancing the limbo, stingers in hand, spilling. Around eleven Pauline and Meg took turns dancing slow with Everett, cheek to cheek.

They walked back along the beach, barefoot. "There isn't a breath of air!" Meg said. The sand was damp with dew, and there was a still, heavy cloud sprawled out over the Isles of Shoals. They passed the cottage Meg and Gerald once rented, and Meg wished she had the key to it in her bag right now, wished that tomorrow she'd be waking up in its knotty pine bedroom to hear, first thing, the lingering beat of waves in sets of three, and the kids' eager voices out on the porch.

When they got to the head of Cable Road, where a big rock stopped you from driving out onto the beach, they noticed a car parked in front of Pauline's. Its headlights were on and they shone brilliant against the white clapboard house. "That's Carl's car," Pauline said.

They put on their shoes and walked along the dirt road, dusty and littered with stones and pebbles. Meg's pace had no pattern or order. She thought about the kids. Did he have them hostage? Able to focus only sporadically, she tried to calm herself thinking, How can Pauline tell that's Carl's Lincoln, and not just somebody turning around in the driveway?

As they came close a yellow light, inside the car, shone on Carl's face, and then the door opened and he stepped out, looming and black. The car was running; exhaust fumes, white as steam, rose up out of the tail pipe, and tumbled a moment in the cool evening air before they disappeared. Carl took a step, reached to the ground and picked something up, something dark and heavy. Tall and stiff, he stood there, holding this thing in his hand.

Brenda Gurren appeared in the front doorway of the house, and in a second Cliff and Sam squeezed in beside her.

"Look, Carl," Pauline said, "for the love of Mike ..." Her voice had the timbre of his, not hers. "Come on, Meg," she said. Taking wide, quick steps, she bolted past Carl, heading to the house, disappearing for a moment in the car's exhaust. When Meg went to follow, Carl stepped out in front of her. Light, deflected off the house, threw shadows sideways across his face, played tricks on the object he held in his hand. A half-moon hung yellow in the sky like the last potato chip on a plate.

Meg stopped short, two yards away from him. All at once, she was a cat, tense before its unknown adversary. As seconds ticked off, her feet dug into the dusty road, and a force built up inside of her. Carl raised the object high. Cliff, meeting up with Pauline, let out a scream and started to run, but she grabbed him by the arm and held him tight. "Carl!" she yelled.

It was a stone Carl had, sea-smooth and black in the dark. He laughed as he threw it. It wasn't a hard throw. He just lobbed it so it fell at Meg's feet with a single bass thud, stirring up the white dust. He laughed. "Get it?" he said.

Meg rushed him. Grabbing on to his sport coat at the biceps, her hands were like pincers. "*You* ..." she shouted out, shaking him, thrusting, pulling back, shaking herself with the force of it. The whole time, Carl just laughed out loud, letting her go at him. When she was all but ready to drop, he squeezed her against himself and kissed her on the mouth, driving in his tongue like a cold spike to pierce the bone of her skull.

Stepping back, freed, Meg felt as though Carl, with his kiss, had killed off something in her, some part that doesn't regenerate. Suddenly, she knew Pauline better than she ever had. She knew of Pauline's internal injuries; they were like the ones Meg now suffered, the ones that had her spitting up black, bloodlike drops— drops that covered the white sand beside that dark, cast stone.

Meg saw Pauline one last time before Carl Gurren filed for bankruptcy, closed Green Apple, and moved his entire family away. They went to Detroit, Meg eventually heard from someone who was in touch with Carl's mother.

It was in the spring. Meg was out in front of the house picking lilacs from one of the great overgrown bushes that lined the driveway, when she heard the phone ring. She rushed inside and answered. It was Pauline.

"I cut myself ..." Pauline managed to say. Meg let her bouquet of lilacs fall. Her eyes closed tight as she listened. "Cut it on a glass...Come quick! Quick!" Pauline said. "Hurry...I'm bleeding! Hurry!"

Pauline was waiting out in front of her house, sitting on a rock beneath the spindly birches growing beside her mailbox. Shivering, she looked at once half dead and girlishly pretty, with a new, short

hairdo. She was bawling like a child. She got in the car beside Meg,
clutching a blood-soaked dish towel around her cut hand, and
quickly they headed to St. John's.

"What did you do?" Meg asked. They were in the passing lane on
Andover Street.

"I was drying a glass," said Pauline, squinting in pain. "I stuck
my whole gor-ram hand in it, stupid me," she said, and then she
passed out, bleeding onto her shorts. Blood ran down her leg and
onto her sneakers.

At the hospital, Meg stayed near Pauline the whole time—all the
doctors and staff knew Meg, knew her as the volunteer.

It was a bad cut, having come quite close to arteries. Pauline had
lost a lot of blood, but she would be all right. That's what the doctor
in the emergency room said.

Meg sat for a long while at Pauline's bedside watching her face
move in almost undetectable ways. Time flew by as she remembered
things: July afternoons, Pauline and herself lying on woolen blankets
in the sun, drinking Tom Collinses till they were giggling like a couple of girls. And she remembered those secret nights, up at the
beach, when the two of them would hire sitters and sneak out
together and have lobster Newburg at Rye On The Rocks, where
they met guys younger than their husbands, younger than they
themselves, guys who called them "a couple of lookers," who asked
them to dance, and who danced so well, pressing their almost
smooth, young cheeks against theirs. Those were special moments.
Who knew then how things would have ended up? No one could
have predicted the future they now lived, with the pain of its loneliness, with so much love held in check, and so many feelings kept
locked away as if they were terrible secrets.

Pauline, half conscious, opened her eyes. "Meg?" she said. "Is
that you?"

"Sure," said Meg. She sat bent forward in a slippery vinyl chair.

"I've never forgotten your number," Pauline said, in a harsh,
sleepy voice. "Two-oh-two-two-oh. Course, it's easy. You don't
mind, do you?"

Meg snickered. "You kidding?" she said. "Course I don't mind. Don't be silly."

"I figured you owed me one," said Pauline. She winked.

"I owe you a bunch of things," said Meg. "When you come right down to it. I do."

"Remember the time Touey got his tail bobbed and he took it out on your arm?" Pauline's laugh was like quick, hard breathing.

"Course I do," said Meg.

"Well, you owed me one," said Pauline. "There!" Then she laughed again.

"You're right," said Meg. "I owed you one. I'd never thought of that."

"I didn't think you should get let off the hook," said Pauline. "You had a debt to pay."

"Course I did," said Meg.

Pauline closed her eyes and sighed. "You never knew I was such a chicken, did you, Meg?"

"What are you talking about?" said Meg. "Listen to you go on! Try and get some rest, Pauline. Stop it now!"

"I fooled you, didn't I?" said Pauline. "For a while anyway."

"Shush," said Meg.

Pauline turned her head. Her eyes were closed, but tears leaked through and fell to the pillow. "Why are we so afraid all the time?" she asked. "Will you answer me that, Meg?"

Meg felt herself blushing. "I don't know what you mean," she said. She was crying too now.

"We're so much alike," Pauline said.

"Course we are," said Meg.

"Neither of us would ever be alone, would we, Meg? That's one thing you could say about both you and me. We're two peas in a pod as far as that goes."

"What do you mean?" said Meg.

"Say, if you didn't have Gerald. Say, if he died all of a sudden, you'd have someone else, soon, wouldn't you? It wouldn't take you long. You'd find someone fast, I know you would."

"I don't know," said Meg. "I've never really thought about it."

"Well I have," said Pauline. "I've thought about this stuff a lot. We're both big chickens. You or I could never make a whole life just around girlfriends. We need someone there, you and me. If I didn't have Carl, I'd have somebody else. And it wouldn't make any difference if he drove me nuts either, and he probably would drive me nuts, but I'd have to have him. And it wouldn't matter if he worked nights and days nonstop. I wouldn't go ten minutes without someone. That's just who I am. And you know something?" Pauline said. "That's who you are too."

"Maybe," said Meg. "Maybe. I just never thought about it that way."

"Not maybe," said Pauline.

"No," said Meg. "Of course not. You're right, Pauline," she said. "Of course you're right."

Pauline raised her head, shifting position, and it seemed to make her dizzy. "I'm tired now, Meg," she said. Her face went white, but only for a second; soon she was sound asleep and color found its way to her cheeks.

Meg looked at her watch. It was almost lunchtime and Gerald would be coming home from work, hungry, wondering where she was. She stood up and grabbed her bag, then remembered the leftover lobster stew in the refrigerator. But maybe she'd suggest they go to the Towne Inn for lunch instead and have steak sandwiches in the bar and listen to the piano player. She could wear her new blue linen dress with white piping on the sleeves. They hadn't been out to lunch together in a long, long time, and Gerald would enjoy it. She knew he would. Gerald liked a nice change every now and then.

PINE TREE LODGES

Dwight and Natalie Hildebrand, my parents' old friends from New York, were vacationing at Pine Tree Lodges in New Hampshire one August. They invited us to come up for the weekend, and so we did; we spent three days with them there in a pine wood at Lake Winnipesaukee.

Cliff and I swam all day long in the still, fresh water, which was a nice change from the ocean with its buffeting waves that never let you alone. My father and Dwight played golf, and my mother and Natalie husked corn and snipped the ends off beans. Drinking beer and Tom Collinses, they gabbed their way through the afternoon, sitting on the dock, calling out, every now and then, to Cliff and me, "Watch that boat coming in!" or, "Don't go out too far!"

We had such fun we decided to join up with the Hildebrands again next year, and so my father reserved a cabin there for ourselves (even though, to my parents, Pine Tree Lodges felt "awfully Protestant").

Dwight Hildebrand took pictures as we unpacked the car. Cliff and I were wearing identical lightweight plaid jackets that zipped up the front: "spring jackets," we called them. The weather wasn't very nice that year.

"We've come too late," my mother said, looking at the last of the summer's corn we'd bought at a farm stand along the way, each ear with its husk pulled slightly back showing deep-yellow kernels, far bigger and closer together than she liked them to be. "It doesn't pay to come up north in August," she said. "Summer's over by now." It was too bad.

But Dwight and my father played golf just the same, even in the worst weather—eighteen holes a day—and we wouldn't see them until late in the afternoon when the rain had stopped, at least for a little while, and the two of them, with pine needles stuck to their shoes, would walk out onto the dock, into the wind whisking off the lake, and stand beside the aluminum chairs where Natalie and my mother sat drinking icy rye and water. Cliff and I would be bailing out the speedboat my father rented at the Wears, the boat we hardly ever got a chance to use because we couldn't start it up without my father. Early in the morning, when he was around, it was often raining or the wind was so fierce that out in the middle of the lake there were swells as big as ocean waves, and small craft warnings were up.

At the water's edge, several yards beyond the dock, was a house, not a cabin at all but a real house, and this was where a family named Wailes lived, father, mother, and three sons. The father, whose brother-in-law, Wallace Rand, owned Pine Tree Lodges, always wore a bathing suit, even in the rain—a small, swimmer's bathing suit of the type my mother hated—and it wasn't until late in the evening that he'd get dressed and put on creased white pants. My mother called him "Body Beautiful" because of his muscles.

Body Beautiful didn't play golf. Instead, he was always with his sons. I'd see him and the two younger ones fishing at the water's edge near their house, and I'd hear his very serious voice, like the voice of a scoutmaster, boom out across the surface of the lake as he explained, in a TV-like accent and with words unfamiliar to me, how to get the most out of a cast and how to reel in with short tugs so the lure slipped through the dark water like a real minnow.

I was shy with strangers, but gradually, I worked my way over to where they fished till I was close enough to hear the click and hiss of bearings as the line ran off their reels, close enough to notice the beautiful fishing equipment they had.

"Come and have a look, son," said Mr. Wailes.

I walked over and he introduced his boys, and they shook my hand like grown-ups. "Nice to meet you," they said. The smaller boy's name was Flippy and the other one was Thad. There was a soapy smell in the air, coming from their sweatshirts. Both boys had clear, crystalline eyes and patches of red on their cheeks, and their hair was blond and long enough to comb into straight parts, pale strips of scalp—I felt like a baldy with my head practically shaved.

"Thad," said Mr. Wailes, "let the young man try your spinning rod."

"Yes sir," Thad said. Then he handed me the rod so the handle came at me first. I was uneasy holding it; it seemed like such an expensive thing.

"Never fished, son?" asked Mr. Wailes.

"Nope," I said, comparing how I sounded to the way Thad and Flippy spoke, suddenly wondering if I seemed coarse.

Mr. Wailes crouched down and put his arms around me and showed me how to cast. He showed me where the antireverse lever was, and he showed me how to look after the line guide and the pickup arm. I cast out a few times, and reeled in the way Flippy had done. When I handed the rod back to Thad, he said, "Pity you didn't catch anything," and I laughed a little, thinking that was funny, because I had such a nice time anyway. Catching a fish was the farthest thing from my mind.

I heard my mother's voice. She and Natalie were setting up their aluminum chairs at the end of the dock. They were wearing raincoats and holding tall drinks with lemon slices floating among the ice cubes. Cliff, in his spring jacket, long pants, and Hush Puppies, was right beside them as usual, and they were all in a giddy mood. By the time they were settled and my mother had ripped open the paper bag full of green beans which she held on her lap, the lake was suddenly streaked with whitecaps, their peaks carried off in the wind, and a little rain began to fall. My mother motioned "come here" with her finger, and so I left Mr. Wailes and the boys and walked out onto the dock. When I was standing beside my mother's chair, she said to me, "Getting friendly with Body Beautiful?"

Natalie laughed and glanced over at Mr. Wailes, who was pulling a white sweatshirt over his head. "That's how you know it's *really* cold," she said.

"Cliff's been making us laugh doing imitations," said my mother. "Why don't you stick around for a while, Sam."

"Imitations of who?" I asked.

"Marilyn Maxwell," said Natalie.

"Who's that?"

"An actress," said my mother. "Cliff, show Sam how Marilyn Maxwell walks."

Cliff walked, in his normal way, down to where the dock met the shore. Out of the corner of my eye, I could see Mr. Wailes watching us as his boys went on fishing. Cliff, with one arm outstretched and a hand on his hip, came strutting our way, his shoulders alternating leads, his pace glamorous, his lips in a haughty pose. When he got almost to where we waited, watching, laughing, he tripped over himself and fell, rear end first, into the deep, cold lake, screaming out above the noise of a big splash (he was a heavy boy). "Help!" he called, at the top of his lungs.

My mother panicked (she couldn't swim, and was scared to death of water), and shouting for help herself, she made a run for a life preserver on the deck of one of the docked boats nearby. Cliff was doing the dog paddle, but in just a few seconds he'd attached himself to the ladder and was back up on the dock, standing in a puddle, in the wind, out of breath, furious with himself, soaked. He reached in his pocket, pulled out his wallet, and opened it. There was money inside. "Sopping wet," he said, holding up a droopy dollar bill with his arched, plump fingers as if it were a piece of slimy bait he couldn't bear the sight of.

My mother glanced over at Mr. Wailes, who was cutting a jumpy perch off Flippy's line. "He couldn't have cared less when I called for help," she said. Then she looked at Natalie and, I think, smiled. "Can you imagine?" she said.

The rain let up for a few days, but it turned colder. I was watching Flippy fish off the dock one afternoon with his other brother, the biggest one. When Flippy cast his line, the reel made a soft click-click, and then a peaceful purry sound.

Suddenly, there was a big splash. Flippy's reel had fallen off his rod into the lake; the pole mount must have come loose. He got a hold of the line and tried to pull it up, but the reel was caught under a stone on the lake floor and wouldn't budge.

"You know what this means," his older brother said, "don't you, Flippy?"

"No," Flippy said. "What does this mean, Tim?"

"Means you have to go in there and get it, Flippy. Now!" It was really cold and starting to get windy. We all had jackets on, and sweatshirts underneath. "*Now!*" he said.

"You jest, Tim," said Flippy. I thought it was neat, the way he said that.

"Flippy! Do you hear me?" said Tim, firm about it. "Do you know what's happening to that reel right this very minute as you stand here like a goof?"

"What, dearest brother?" said Flippy, biting his lower lip.

"It's getting rusty, that's what's happening. It's getting rustier by the second. Now dive, Flippy! Do you hear me?"

Flippy shivered, then took off his jacket, very slowly. He took off his sweatshirt, and the shirt he had on underneath it; then he took off his belt, his shoes and socks. With his pants still on, holding his nose, he jumped in. It gave me a chill just watching his body move around against the pea-green floor of the lake. His legs were bent and wide apart, and chains of bubbles came away from his face and rose to the surface. A second later, he was up. He got out shivering, but he'd done it. He had it in his hand, and he was grinning. He'd rescued the reel.

As I watched him dive I imagined that it wasn't happening to

Flippy at all but to me instead. I imagined that it had been my reel that had fallen off into the lake, and that Tim had been my big brother who'd said to me, "Now dive, Sam," and I'd dived and come up with the reel in hand like a hero, like a Wailes.

That night, my parents and the Hildebrands were having drinks at our cottage. They were in a panic because they'd used up all the ice from both refrigerators. Natalie said to my mother, "Meg, go down to Body Beautiful's and borrow a tray. I'm sure they never use ice."

My mother laughed as if she thought they were kidding. But they weren't. She finished her drink, then went to the little pine-walled bathroom, leaving the door open as she touched up her lipstick and ran a comb through her wavy blond hair. She put on her raincoat, buttoned it all the way up, and without even looking back or saying goodbye, walked out the door.

A minute later, the door opened again, and her head appeared. "Come on Sam," she said to me. "You come too. They're *your* friends."

In a minute we were standing on the Waileses' porch. Yellow lights overhead shone through the white railing and laid a ladder of shadow on the surface of the lake. It was like being on a ship; where the painted floorboards ended, all you could see was water, now flat as linoleum in the dusk.

My mother rang the brass boat bell overhead and a woman came to the door, a big woman in a plaid dress with a cardigan sweater over her shoulders and some sort of clasp at the neck to keep it in place. Her forehead held a series of creases which followed the contours of a deep peak of graying hair in the center of her brow. She almost scared me, yet I was drawn to her somehow.

"Good evening," said my mother, in a smiley tone but giving her voice that certain polite quality it had when she talked on the phone to, say, Mrs. Hugh Waldo, people she really didn't know very well. "I hate to bother you ..." She put her hand on my shoulder and the woman looked at me. "I'm Meg Beeler, from Lowell," my mother said. "We have the cottage just up above, and we've run out of ice. Would you happen to have a tray of ice you don't need?"

The woman smiled, just faintly, and pushed open the screen door. "Come in," she said.

In a moment we were standing in a matchboard-paneled hallway with a steep old staircase in the back. "Just a second," said the woman. Waiting there, I followed her with my eyes as she walked through an archway, through the living room, then finally through a door beyond, into the kitchen.

It was such a quiet house; through the screen door I could hear waves (the wake of a distant motorboat) as they stroked the shoreline. There was no party in progress here as there was in our cabin every night. No one was drinking, cutting up. It was so peaceful, so serious. It occurred to me now that this was a kind of quiet I'd always longed for, always had an idea about, even though I'd never seen it take real form before, and I suddenly felt very angry with my parents, angry that they were not the Waileses, that they were very different from them, different even from me.

Stretched out on the living room couch was Tim, the oldest boy, reading a paperback book, its cover folded back in his hands. Lifting his eyes, he glanced at us standing beyond the arch that separated the living room from the entrance hall. He wore khaki pants, an Indian beaded belt, and moccasins, and his blond hair fell long over his ears. His cheeks held a deep blush like Flippy's and Thad's. He smiled and said hello, but then went on with his reading. What was in his book? I wondered. My parents didn't read books; they read only wide, unruly newspapers and *Time*.

All at once, I was deeply unhappy. I wanted everything Tim Wailes had. I wanted a book like his, a quiet house, those neat clothes he wore, his shiny, long, sun-bleached hair. I wanted his father and mother instead of mine. I wanted his brothers. Really, I wanted to *be* Tim Wailes; I'd had enough of being Sam Beeler.

Mrs. Wailes came out of the kitchen carrying a tray of ice, and she handed it to my mother with an odd, grand gesture, raising it high with a kind of flourish before placing it into my mother's outstretched hands, as if it were a pretty, decorated cake we would all have a loud party with up in our little log cabin under the pines.

"Oh thanks so much," said my mother. "You're a lifesaver!"

The next day, I broke out of a deep sulk and asked my mother a question. "Can I let my hair grow long like the Wailes boys?"

"You can't just let your hair grow long," my mother said. "It has to be trained. Your hair isn't trained like theirs is."

"Well then how do you train it?" I asked.

"You hire a hair trainer," said Natalie, laughing. She was eating yogurt, and my mother and Cliff were making faces about it.

In a little while I said, "Why don't you try taking a swim today, Mummy. It's clearing up." Then I laughed. I'd never seen my mother swim, ever. Each summer she bought new bathing suits, but she never got into them. Her suntan ended in the form of a V just below her throat.

"Come on, Mummy," I said. "Come swimming!" I'd been trying for years to get her in the water, but she would always say, "Tomorrow I'll do it, tomorrow …" I knew that if she ever did go swimming, she'd be doing it just for me and for no other reason.

"You know what I'm going to do?" said my mother.

"What?" I said.

"Some evening, when it's just getting dark and nobody's around, I'll put on my bathing suit and go down there and paddle. I don't want anybody to see me. And then when I've had a little practice, I'll swim out to the raft with you."

I laughed. "Oh sure," I said.

The next day was hot and sunny; summer wasn't really over after all; it had just been suspended for a while. On a little peninsula just beyond the Waileses' porch was a flagpole. As I stood gazing up at the bright stars and stripes laid against a backdrop of blue sky, watching the flag improvise its moves, never repeating, in the wind, Thad appeared. "My father's taking me out in the boat," he said. "He wants to know if you'd like to come along."

I blushed, surprised. "Sure," I said, and thought, They've come to get me. Now they'll take me off and I'll be with them forever, grow to be more and more like them each day till our being together, always, wipes out the last few differences between us.

I asked my mother if it would be all right.

"Well, it wouldn't hurt Daddy to take you out in *our* boat once in a while," she said, with a sour face. "That's what we rented it for, I thought."

Just when it seemed she was going to say no, she said, "I don't get what you see in those Waileses, but go ahead."

Flippy was in town with his mother, and I didn't know where the older boy was, so it was just the three of us going out: Thad, his father, and me. Mr. Wailes had a nice little speedboat. It was all shiny wood and had clean, new yellow cushions. His engine started right up when he turned a key, just like a car.

When we were out in the middle of the lake, far away from shore, Mr. Wailes cut the engine. "Sam," he said, "come forward to the helm here and take the wheel." I was excited and nervous. The one time we went out on the boat with my father, he didn't let Cliff or me drive; he said we were too young. But I knew it wasn't true. I'd seen lots of little kids driving boats with their fathers sitting beside them.

I stepped up front and Mr. Wailes gave me his seat. He pointed out a few things: the throttle, the engine stop, the tach, the fuel gauge. And then he asked me if I knew the difference between port and starboard. I said I didn't. "Remember this," he said, "starboard is right, port is left. Got it?"

"Yes," I said. I would never forget it.

Mr. Wailes went back to the bench where I'd been and sat down beside Thad. "Let's move out," he said.

I pushed the lever forward and saw the bow rise and heard the motor grow loud and I could smell its fumes, a smell I liked. The water was like mercury in the sun. It sprayed off the bow and in a minute my face was covered with a chilly film, and it felt as if we were flying and I was the pilot. We were speeding along now, even faster than Mr. Wailes had gone. I kept thinking that he was about to put his hand on my shoulder and ask me to slow down, or that any minute he'd reach out and draw the throttle back. But he never did. He seemed to trust me, like he trusted his own sons.

On the Hildebrands' last night, my mother and father had a party for them at our cottage. They filled and refilled their glasses and told stories in loud voices, and there was a lot of banter and laughter. I'd brought along my set of bongo drums, and my father and Dwight took turns playing them. My father sang a calypso song and danced, and then Dwight did a beatnik act. He sat cross-legged on the floor gripping the drums between his knees. Banging out a little rhythm, he gazed very contemplatively at the ceiling. "The moon...is mud!" he said, softly. We all laughed and snapped our fingers, being cool. He paused, then drummed again. "The night...is hay."

My mother put a dish towel over her head and sang "Indian Love Call." Right in the middle of a long-held note she stopped. "We forgot to return the ice tray to that poker face," she said. "You know, Body Beautiful's gal."

"Oh gosh," said my father. "Why don't you do that *right now*, before we forget. Suppose they want a pop?"

My mother went behind the counter into the tiny kitchen and came out holding Mrs. Wailes's ice tray, carrying it straight out in front of her, carefully, because she'd filled it up with water. "I thought I'd be nice and return it to them full," she said.

Everybody laughed and howled. Dwight banged on the bongos. "Meg," he said, "there are only two of you and you're both of them!"

Cliff and I roared.

"Oh do it," said Natalie. "They'll get a kick out of it. Go on!"

Dwight drummed.

My mother was laughing so hard the only sound she made was a sharp, high whine. Water spilled out of the ice tray, a little bit, onto the pine floor.

"Come on, Sam," she said, clearing her throat in a way that

always irritated me. "You come too. Let's have some fun with them. Come on."

I went sour again. I couldn't imagine taking such a joke out of this household, taking it to people who wouldn't get it the way we got it. Suddenly, I hated this joke. I didn't want any part of it. "No," I said.

My mother put on her white button earrings, then got into her raincoat. "Oh come on, Sam," she said. "They'll get a big boot out of it."

"I won't go," I said. In a minute I'd be crying.

"He's so serious," my mother said to the mirror on the bathroom door. Standing up on her toes in her sneakers, she puckered her lips and picked up her chest.

"Go on, Sammy," said Natalie. "Give us the report."

"No," I said. "Never!" I shouted.

"Who are you talking to?" said my father, his face all red with anger.

"O.K. then," my mother said, stuffing a rumpled handkerchief up her sleeve. "I'll go without you." She was mad at me now.

With all the hard looks everybody gave me, I felt disloyal, strict and small, unappreciative of my mother, unloving. I knew I had to go. I put on my jacket and walked out the door behind her.

Outside I could tell she was pretty drunk, the way she weaved her way through the trees carrying the ice tray, very carefully, down the slope to the lakeshore. I felt so ashamed to have a mother who was drunk, a mother who made silly jokes, who made fun of people who were different from her, people like the Waileses who were worth so much more than my family was.

There were lights on in all the Waileses' windows, golden lights, but the porch light was off and so we climbed the wooden steps in shadows. At the front door we heard voices. "Ring for me," my mother said, holding the ice tray, still full of water. I rang the bell and, feeling scared, looked away, toward the sound of a boat out on the lake. Through the bluish mist I could make out its tiny colored lights.

The porch light went on and Mrs. Wailes appeared at the door.

She was wearing lipstick and a string of pearls, and she brought her face close to the screen and peered through. "Who's that?" she said.

"It's just us," said my mother. "Returning your ice tray."

"Oh yes," said Mrs. Wailes, pushing open the screen door. "We're having dinner, but do come in for just one moment."

Mr. Wailes appeared, wearing a plaid tie and cotton sport coat. His cheeks were rosy like his sons', and his eyes fell on mine as I walked into the house ahead of my mother. The owner of the place, Wallace Rand, was now there in the hallway too, and so was his wife, holding a cloth napkin. They all watched my mother as she lost balance, stepping up off the porch, coming through the door. In a minute their eyes lowered to the ice tray, the water dribbling out onto my mother's outstretched hands, her wrinkly joints and stubby, broken nails flecked with shards of old red polish.

Looking at the ice tray and then at their blank faces, I tried a laugh to help my mother out, but I felt like a circus MC seeking applause for an act that hadn't gone over. My mother's joke was a dud. My laugh fell apart and then was gone, irretrievably, and I no longer knew what to say or do. I looked back at the ice tray dripping in my mother's hands, which had now begun to shake, and then I looked at her face and I found an expression there, an expression just like those on the faces of the others in the room: an awkward, uncertain smile that barely masked a terrible fear, like the fear a fish must have when he's pulled out of the lake on a line, and when he feels the dreadful, unknown air against his body as he's swung back to shore.

There was moonlight; it dappled the pine needles underfoot. My mother stopped halfway up the hill, out of breath.

"I feel like a damn fool," she said. Her face was in shadows except for a medallion of light on her chin, which was ruddy and crimped, and so I knew she was crying.

I kept thinking about that look she had on her face when she stood there with the ice tray in the Waileses' hallway. Though it was a fearful look, it was somehow a very pretty one. It made me conscious of my love for her.

I was feeling bad now, so sorry about what had just happened. I put my hand into the pocket of her raincoat and there was an apple in there, a green apple. I took it out and smelled it. It smelled tangy and fresh and it made me feel good and so I held it up to my mother's nose. "Smell," I said.

"Have you ever seen such poker faces?" my mother said, taking the apple out of my hand.

"No," I said. "Never."

"But you like that, don't you, Sam?" she said. "You like people who put on the dog that way."

"No I don't," I said. "I like people who have fun. People like Dwight and Natalie and you."

She put the apple back in her pocket, sat down on a rock, and held her face between her hands. Her finger was swollen around her wedding ring. "Sometimes, when you look at me," she said, "it's like you think I'm an old hag."

I was seeing the moon in the tears in her eyes, and in a moment I was crying too. I was so sorry I'd abandoned her, even if I'd only really done it in my dreams, and if it hadn't been something that no one in my family ever, ever did, I might have told her that I loved her.

The Hildebrands left the next day. "Leave a deposit," Dwight said to my father. "Make your reservations for next summer before you check out. Two weeks beginning on the seventeenth."

We were all sad as they drove off. I hated to see our vacation end, dreaded the thought of school starting soon, of trees losing their leaves, of the cold coming on.

"I'm going in to talk to Rand," said my father when the Hildebrands' car was out of sight. "Be down in a minute."

My mother was making a pie for our last dinner. My father came in, looking droopy, as if he'd just played eighteen holes of golf. He took off his straw Sam Snead hat and put it on the kitchen counter beside an ashtray that held a couple of golf tees and his pipe tobacco.

"Rand claims they're full next year," he said, in a failing voice.

My mother stopped what she was doing. Her fingers were covered with applesauce. The look on her face was a daytime look, not an evening, jiggy look but a serious one. "They're full?" she said.

"They're full," said my father.

She stared at him, keeping silent, then looked away. "Do you suppose—?" she said.

"I don't know," said my father, interrupting. "I don't know."

My parents were quiet all day, testy with each other, and with us. In the afternoon, Cliff and I went with my father to the Wears to bring back the boat, and later on, my mother met us there with the car.

When we got back to Pine Tree Lodges, I watched the Waileses drive off in their station wagon, the boys' blond heads barely visible above stacks of neat luggage. They were headed home to Pennsylvania where they lived, but they'd be back next year, and probably when Tim and Thad and Flippy were grown-up and married, they'd come to Pine Tree Lodges too, with *their* children. As they rounded a curve, into the shade under trees, I felt more than a little sad to be left behind.

That night, after dinner, I took a walk in the moonlight, all by myself. There was a cabin cruiser anchored out on the lake, and they had piano music going. I went up to the office and got a cold Coke out of the machine, and when I came back over the crest of the hill, I saw a figure, someone walking through the pines, heading toward the water. It was my mother. I sat down at the trunk of a big pine and leaned back against the sticky bark and drank my Coke, watching her, at the water's edge, take off her raincoat and stand there, in her bathing suit, looking off. And then I saw her step into the water and crouch down. The way she moved her arms on the dark surface of the lake, it was like she was really swimming.

4

EXTRAORDINARY PEOPLE

It was a Saturday morning in February. Cliff and I were at home in North Tewksbury, up early, hanging around the room we shared.

"Let's go downtown," Cliff said. "I've got fifty-six dollars!" He crowed like Mary Martin in *Peter Pan,* then leapt and took to the air as if wired to a rig in the ceiling. When he hit the ground with his husky weight, I felt it in my chest like an extra heartbeat.

"Hah!" I said. "Fifty-six dollars! Baloney!"

Our room filled up with the sun of an unseasonably good day. We were still in our pajamas, but it was time we got dressed and out.

Cliff's smile made his full, low cheeks dimple in a couple of places on each side. He looked at me with his lazy eye. "Fifty-six," he said, "fifty-six."

"Hah!" I said.

"I've come into some money," he said. "Let's just say Michael Anthony knocked on my door and handed me fifty-six dollars from John Beresford Tipton."

"John Beresford Tipton gives away a *million* dollars," I said, "not fifty-six. Fifty-six dollars isn't anything. A million dollars, that's something!"

Downstairs, my mother worked at a crossword puzzle in the

Boston Globe, stopping once in a while to shout at cats who pounced on scattered newspapers and slid across the room stiff-legged. Four or five kittens added to the scratches on her bare ankles and calves. Blood dribbled out of a reopened wound, but she had no idea. Behind in her housework, she was cranky. My father's ashtrays were full. The enormous coffee table my grandfather built was a shelter for homeless objects. Spoiled cat food fouled the air.

Cliff and I put on our red toggle coats, exactly alike, and my mother dropped everything to drive us to the bus. Chauffeuring her two sons was a duty rural life assigned her, but she was happy to take an occasional run out of the wilderness.

We lived up on Mill Hill, far away from downtown Lowell. You couldn't walk anywhere from there. Cliff went to Tewksbury Junior High School and so he picked up the school bus every morning at the foot of our driveway. But there was no bus for me. My mother drove me to the Immaculate every day in her Buick Special convertible, then came and got me at three. On Saturdays she took us both to the stone watering trough on Hood Road where we caught the bus for downtown.

Today Cliff wanted to go to Record Lane.

"If I could buy a record," I said, sitting beside Cliff on the bus, "it would be *The Music from M Squad.*"

Cliff scoffed at that idea. He didn't like instrumentals. He liked Eydie Gormé, and lately, the Supremes. "Why don't you figure out a way to make some money," he said, "so you can get a couple of things?"

"I might," I said.

"Why don't you serve a wedding for somebody rich and get a big tip? Then you can buy Andy Williams's new album."

"I might," I said. "But anyhow, if I had money, I wouldn't buy Andy Williams. He makes me sick, all those dumb songs. I'd buy the Kingston Trio, that's what I'd buy."

"Ugh!" said Cliff.

"I'd buy Joan Baez," I said.

"Heck with 'em."

"How come?" I said. "You can buy a whole bunch of those for fifty-six dollars. Go on. What's stopping you?"

"Changed my mind," he said. "Heck with 'em."

"Hah! Michael Anthony. You wish."

"I've decided to save my money," he said. "You know I'm a good saver."

It was true. I remembered once getting a look at his old bankbook, the one he used to guard secretly in the locked drawer of his night table. When he closed out the account, I read around in it; there were years of deposits but only one withdrawal, on the last page. He bought Christmas gifts with that money. He bought my mother a sweater with kittens and balls of yarn on it and my father, a Tyrolean hat with a cocky fur brush stuck in its band.

We were going to the movies. My mother gave us the money. *To Hell and Back*, with Audie Murphy, was at Keeth's again, and that was what I wanted to see. Cliff wanted to see something else, a musical at the Strand. "Go ahead, Sam," he said. "Go see what you want. Meet you after. Meet you at the bus station." He owed the world a visit now that he was in junior high. When we were downtown together, it was normal for him to stray, losing me, leaving me out of his private fun.

There was this new side to Cliff. For the first time in his life, he brought home friends, boys from South Tewksbury who were quite different from Cliff and me. They were not dead-enders, but wore tight pants and had up-to-no-good looks in their eyes. It was a well-kept secret how they spent their time together.

Other things bothered me too. For instance, there was a man who passed our house every afternoon, on foot. My mother called him "the Strange Boy." He wore a straw hat, and smoked a pipe. He had a big nose and a large, bulbous chin, and walked, bent forward, with his hands clasped behind his back. One day Cliff showed me where the Strange Boy lived: downtown, in a wooden tenement house off Central Street. He told me that the man was all alone now that his

"Oh, ick," Cliff said, then he did an imitation of Joan singing a song he made up, exactly the kind of song she woul sung, though—about muddy rivers and cuckoos. His voice w like hers, a liquid soprano, and as he sang he made a gest pulling the long, tangled black hair away from his eyes. H loud. Heads turned all around. Even though I hated it when Cl weird this way, I laughed so hard I had to sink low in the bu sliding down the red vinyl. "She's such a scag," he said.

"She is not a scag," I said.

"Is too."

"Is not," I said.

"Yes sah."

"No sah."

"Hootenanny shit!" Cliff said.

Lowell was an ugly place, a gray mill town. There wasn't mu it. There was Bon Marché, and there was Cherry's. There was a tory outlet and Rhynn's Sporting Goods, where I bought arr There was the Dutch Tea Room, and there were two movie theate

This morning, Cliff went through the records at Record Lane. pulled out a Rosemary Clooney album and *Flower Drum Song*. few minutes he had a whole stack. "Hey creepo," he said, "I'm ting these."

"Hah!" I said. "You and what bank?"

"Me and no bank," he said. "Me and my fifty-six dollars."

"Oh sure," I said.

He was reading the album covers, thinking, maybe multiplyi $5.98 by six. All of a sudden he put them back, all the records toge er, in the wrong place, in the movie sound tracks section, and gave the bin a hard shove so the records shuffled into position, like neat stack of playing cards. "Let's get out of here," he said, a mood hopeless look in his eyes. It was as if he'd carried this bluff about th money too far. He was depressed now, empty-handed.

"What about your records?" I said.

mother had just passed away. Cliff knew too much. It didn't seem right, to me, that Cliff should know so much about the Strange Boy.

I spent a lot of time in my laboratory then: a tiny room, the size of a walk-in closet, that never got used till I put my chemistry set in there and hung a sign above the doorless jamb; "Sam's Lab," it said. Even though the room was small, it had a big window with an unpainted frame and a view of the barn. Tonight my father and mother were out to dinner at Lavaggi's with friends. When I got sick of sitting alone in my private space, leafing through old issues of *Scientific American* (given to me by Hattie Burr at the dairy up the hill), I went downstairs into the living room to see what Cliff was up to.

He wasn't there. But coming into the center of the room, I noticed something strange: a fine wand of fluorescent-blue light beneath the breakfast room door.

There were lots of things that never got used in our house—the back door, permanently locked; the cold half bath off the kitchen; the back entry hall no one ever passed through, where winter coats nobody wore hung on cast-iron hooks. And no one ever used the breakfast room. One wall was covered with cabinets, where *anything* was apt to get stuffed away, even an old pink satin boudoir robe my mother just wasn't the type to wear.

I climbed over the big stuffed chair that for years had kept us from using the breakfast room door, then pushed my way in. There was Cliff. He jumped back, startled. He was standing by the breakfast table wearing my mother's satin robe. But he wasn't wearing it the way it was intended to be worn. He'd made it into a huge gown-like skirt by tying the sleeves back around his waist; the whole span of it billowed out in front of him, full and light as an inflated raft on water.

The door swung back and forth, noisily, behind me, then stopped in place. I stood there, puzzled and flustered, not knowing what to say. Cliff blushed; then he grinned. His premature double chin fell. His lips drew in tight, like he was about to whistle. But nothing happened: just air came out—he'd never been able to whistle; he didn't have the lip-tongue coordination.

"What are you doing?" I said, looking down at his quilted pink skirt. There was a yellowish stain along one side of it where a cat once peed.

He went back into character as Anna in *The King and I*, dancing, gesturing. "Whenever I feel afraid," he sang, "I hold my head erect, and whistle a happy tune ..."

"You're weird," I said.

"You're a creep," he said. "You're ugly."

Cliff loved dressing up. One night, before bed, he came downstairs in his thermal long underpants and no shirt. My father was reading the paper and my mother was watching TV, when Cliff ran into the living room like a stag, his arms outstretched, his blunt fingers aflutter. He was a ballet dancer. He did a Nureyev leap over the coffee table, then landed beyond with a graceless thump, flat on his face. My mother doubled up with laughter, so hard it was silent. But my father was furious. "Get some clothes on!" he hollered. "What the heck's the matter with you? That's Dilla Marie stuff!"

"Oh Daddy," my mother said when she could finally talk again. "He's just having fun."

Once, when they were away for the day, I caught Cliff dressed up in a strange outfit.

Dicky O'Neil's mother had driven me home from school and dropped me off. When I got inside, Cliff was coming down the stairs, naked except for a kind of breechcloth, handmade out of a torn-up sheet. A piece of clothesline, tied around his waist, just barely held things in place. He stopped quick when he saw me, then grabbed the banister as if to push off and run for cover. But he didn't run for it; he stayed put. I threw my book bag down on the dining room chair and stood there looking up at him, my eyes trained on the piece of grayed sheet gathered between his chubby legs like the diaper Baby New Year wears. His dick and balls, bunched up, were the size and shape of a half walnut shell.

"Not again!" he said.

"Not again what?" I said.

The old radiators clanged and hissed as he skipped down the stairs. He was barefoot, and half his ass was hanging out like Tarzan's. Soon his soprano laugh came on, and I stood there staring at his two front teeth which overlapped a little. "I was just in the living room dressed like this," he said, out of breath, giggling, "and when I came out into the hall, there was this face in the door. The furnace guy! He's knocking on the door and here I am in my jungle shift." He laughed and laughed. "My fustanella!" he said.

"What'd you do?" I asked, so embarrassed for him I laughed to vent it.

"I let the grease monkey in," he said. "What do you think I did? He'd already caught me in the very act."

Cliff was a tattletale. He loved to see me get punished for things; he delighted in it, really. It all had to do with his jealousy. He felt I got more than he did, more of everyone's attention, more of everything. Maybe this was true, maybe it wasn't.

When I knew something about Cliff, I kept it to myself; I never told my parents on him. I didn't get a kick out of my father yelling and slapping Cliff around, the hours, the days of unhappiness that would follow. If my father had found out the furnace guy saw Cliff in a breechcloth, he'd have killed him; but I never told, and Cliff knew I never would.

And he knew I'd never tell about this other thing, either—something much more serious. Really, I can't imagine why this thing had stayed a secret, why my parents never found Cliff out; sometimes it seemed they didn't have eyes in their heads. But it did stay a secret as far as I know, since Cliff went on doing it, night after night, for years.

There was a small house next door to us. It was the size of a summer cottage, and it was set low in an overgrown garden. A young couple lived there. Their name was Wright. She was pregnant for the first time, and stayed home taking it easy. Her husband, Dick, worked a regular schedule at Raytheon, and didn't get back till close to six.

At about six o'clock every evening, Cliff went into my parents' bedroom, closed the door, and turned out the lights. Funny I was the only one who seemed to notice he did that.

"Do you have a type?" he said to me one time before he went in there.

"What do you mean?" I said. "A *type*?"

"The type of guy you'd like to see without any clothes on," he said.

I'd never thought about that before. "I don't know," I said. "Do you?"

"I like Dick Wright," he said. "He's a type."

"He is?" I said, thinking about Dick Wright, who wore a white T-shirt around the house and had a heavy, round belly. I'd never looked at the guy closely enough to be able to complete a mental picture of him, or describe him even now. I couldn't imagine wanting to see him without his clothes on.

"Yeah," said Cliff, "he's one. Don't you have a type?"

"Sure," I said. "Ralph Hoar." He was the ugliest, fattest, most repulsive guy we knew. Cliff laughed and laughed when he heard this.

One day, poking in my parents' bedroom, I noticed that my father's army field glasses were on the windowsill. I sat down on the window seat, picked up the field glasses, and looked out, scanning. I saw, magnified, the base of my mother's aluminum clothesline standing in a round pool of hardened cement; I saw the cap to the underground swill bucket; I saw the veiny red leaves of the Wrights' Japanese maple; I saw their bathroom window with its shade half drawn, a circle-pull dangling on a string.

And then I figured it out.

That night, I waited till Cliff had been up in my parents' bedroom for about ten minutes or so, then threw the door open quick to catch him in the act. Cliff was kneeling at the window seat with the black, foot-long binoculars to his eyes, and when the room filled up with light from the hall, he jumped and looked my way, squinty-eyed. I closed the door and went to him in the dark. "What are you doing?" I said.

"Peeping," he said. "What do you think I'm doing?"

"Peeping at what?"

"Shush," he said, focusing in again.

"What's there?" I whispered, knowing all the time what he was up to, and hating him for it. How come I had to have a weird queer for a brother, a Peeping Tom?

"Dick Wright," he said. "He takes a shower every day after work, and he leaves the shade up for all the world to see."

I leaned over and peered out at the Wrights' house sitting in shadows beyond our thick lilac bushes. Their bathroom window was a square of light—yellow in the middle and pink along the edges where gauzy curtains tinted it. "I don't see him," I said.

"Shush," he said. "He's there."

"Let me see."

"No."

"Come on," I said. Grabbing the binoculars, I knelt down beside him at the window seat. I set my elbows deep into the soft pile of my mother's balled-up winter sweaters, old girdles, ruined nylons; put the glasses to my eyes and looked. The Wrights' bathroom window was at the tip of my nose. It suddenly embarrassed me to be peeping in on them like this, to be seeing the gathered trim of their curtains, their steamy wall tiles beyond, every detail of their bathroom none of us were meant to see.

Just then, Dick filled the image as he stepped out of the tub. Naked, he was no longer our neighbor; he was an alien creature. I felt a flash of fear seeing him like this; I felt almost sick.

"There he is!" said Cliff.

Dick was drying his armpits with a yellow towel. All of a sudden he stopped, stooped down, and looked straight into my eyes. I dropped the glasses into the pile of old clothes and slid back quick on my knees. "He saw me," I said, standing up, brushing the dust kitties off. My eyes were still on their bathroom window; even though it was so much smaller now, I could still see Dick stooped over, looking back at us.

"He can't see you," said Cliff. "It's dark in here. When it's dark in a room, you can't see in. I've already checked that out."

All at once, Dick pulled down the shade and the show was over. But just for tonight. Cliff would be there for the next performance, and the next and the next, never getting tired of it. At six o'clock on week nights, I always knew where he was; but if anybody asked me, "Where's Cliff?" I just said, "Haven't got a clue."

"Wonder what I'm going to do with my fifty-six dollars," Cliff said, a finger on his chin.

It was Sunday night. We were in our room together, getting ready for bed. "Might take myself to dinner at the Princeton Lounge and have the charcoal-broiled sirloin," he said.

I turned back my bedspread; it was russet-colored with sailboats, riding whitecaps, tipped in the wind. Cliff was simpering in such a way that I almost began to believe all this stuff about the money. Maybe he really did have it.

"O.K.," I said. "Let's see it, Cliff, if you want me to believe you really got it. Show me the money."

"Why should I?" he said.

"Well, don't go on talking about it, then," I said, "if you can't prove you really got it."

"I got it," he said, pouting the way he did yesterday when he changed his mind and didn't buy the records. Maybe it was crime that made him rich. Maybe evil had crept so deeply into his life that there was no getting free of it now; he could forget about this evil only for a moment, then all at once he'd remember, and his face would fall into a sad frown.

"Show me," I said.

He went to the bookcase in the corner of the room where there was a stack of board games, in their boxes, on a shelf. Sticking his hand in behind them, he pulled out a manila envelope, a little one, only big enough to hold a pack of cards or something just as small. I watched him lift open the flap—still shiny, having never been licked and sealed—and take out a roll of bills. I felt my eyes growing big, the way actors' eyes get big on TV when they're surprised. I was amazed; all that money! He really did have it. He unfolded the bills and counted them out loud. "…fifty-five, fifty-six!"

"Wow!" I said, excited. "What a bankroll!"

I heard my mother out in the hall, passing by our door. She must have been in the bathroom. Quickly, Cliff folded up the money, stuck it back in the envelope, and squirreled it away.

Our bedroom door was hard to open now that my father had changed all the doorknobs and put on cut-glass ones, but I saw the knob turn and the latch bolt recede and my mother's hand leading her into our room. "What's this about a bankroll?" she said, clearing her throat in that pointless, habitual way of hers. She scratched something beside her nose. She was a little drunk, and she looked pooped; but this was nothing strange. On Sundays they started drinking before lunch instead of at five as on other days.

"Talking about money," I said. "Cliff's money."

"What money?" she said.

I looked at Cliff. I wanted him to tell us both about the money, tell the truth, but he kept quiet and turned his back to me. He bent over the bed getting his pajamas out from under the pillow.

"Where did you get it, Cliff?" I said. "Fifty-six dollars. That's a lot." And then I thought, Maybe I shouldn't have said the amount like that.

My father's face appeared above my mother's shoulder. He had only a little hair on the sides, and so his whole head was white skin. He was standing out in the hall, breathing heavily after the hard climb upstairs.

"Where did you get it, Cliff?" my mother said.

Cliff didn't answer.

My mother's nerves were up the way they often were at night, when even insignificant things would set her off and she wouldn't speak to any of us for a whole day or even longer. I was beginning to get worried for Cliff. My mother was growing red in the face, taking quick breaths. She would get to the bottom of this at any cost.

"Where did you get the money?" she shouted. "Did you take it out of my pocketbook?"

"No, I didn't," said Cliff. He followed this with a kind of laughing snort meant to dismiss the whole thing as something silly, not worth anyone's trouble.

I was waiting for my father to step in, but it didn't happen. He stayed back in the dim hall light, as if there was something else on his mind, something much more important than Cliff and his money.

My mother stared at Cliff, but her eyes didn't seem to focus. Her lips thinned to nothing, and all the muscles in her face went taut. "Don't you lie to me," she yelled. "You went into my pocketbook!" She made a sudden, determined move, going for him.

"No," Cliff cried. Terrified, he headed for the closet.

"Mummy!" my father called. The walls gained ground as he came in. The ceiling pressed down. My father was a man whose mind was made up. He never hesitated to find Cliff guilty. He put a hand on my mother's shoulder, holding her back. I was frightened. I felt hot; it was as if I were the one he'd touched. "Cliff didn't steal that money," he said. "It's his."

Cliff leaned rigid against one of the bedposts. My mother took a step and turned around. In the immeasurable silence we all looked at my father.

"His?" my mother said. She squeezed her eyes almost shut. "Fifty-six dollars?" There was just a trace of the morning's lipstick at the edges of her mouth.

My father's face was wan and slack. He had no courage. He shook his head and lowered his eyes.

"Then what *is* this?" my mother said, anxious again. "You two are in on it together, and you can't say? You can't tell me what this is all about? Well all right then!" she yelled. "I'll mind my own business. I'll shut up. You two can have your secrets. This is great, isn't it? Conspiracies and secrets!" She rushed out, pushing my father into the hall, then slammed the door behind her.

In just a second my father was back in our doorway. "Cliff," he said. "Get out here."

"No," Cliff said. He turned away, scared.

"Move," my father said.

Cliff knew he wouldn't be told again. He went out. My father slammed the door shut as if to say, This is none of your business, Sam.

In my stocking feet I crept quietly to the door and looked through the big old-fashioned keyhole—it was just like the one on the bathroom door that Cliff stuffed with toilet paper. Cliff and my mother were sitting on the stairs. I saw their backs, side by side, formed in the same rounded way. My father, just in front of them, leaned over the banister, gazing down into the stairwell. He was explaining something, softly. Holding still, I watched and listened.

"Where is that?" my mother asked. Beneath her loud voice I heard Cliff crying. He lowered his head. His hands came up to wipe away tears. His shoulders rose and fell.

"Shush!" said my father. "Keep it down."

"Where?" she asked, quietly. She was looking up at him.

"The one behind Woolworth's," he said, not quite whispering. "Cliff started to go down the steps, and this man appeared and said, 'Don't use that one. It's flooded, and not only that, it's dirty. Come on. I know where there's a better one you can use ...'" My father's words seemed to come from his throat, and some broke off, unfinished. "Cliff followed and the man took him up to a bathroom on the second floor of that building where there's the hardware store, Spock's. Upstairs there. And then he...the man forced his...intentions on him. "

My mother's head fell. She made the soft sound of a drawn-out whimper that seemed to come from a high place in her chest. She was sobbing, the lingering sob of deep suffering. Cliff turned and looked at her. I saw the tear tracks on his cheek. He grabbed hold of her arm, leaning against her; but it was as if she was stuck in that position, her head lowered, her shoulders pulled in. It was as if she didn't want Cliff to be touching her.

I don't know why, but I thought about a strange man we once met in Washington Square Park. He told us he was a poet, then wanted to explain to Cliff and me what hormones are. I remembered the way my mother jumped in to change the subject, not wanting us to hear. I didn't want to be listening now. I didn't want to know about these things my father explained, and yet something—it was a physical thing—kept me anchored there, bent down at the keyhole, concentrating on the story my father told.

"Cliff found a policeman and they got the guy, and then they called me at the store and I went down to the station. We could have dropped the whole thing right then, but they convinced me—the police—that we should prosecute, because this guy's a bad actor, obviously, and maybe we could prevent some other kid from going through this too, if we brought him to court and got him off the streets." His voice was much less nervous now. He stood up straight and took a long breath, then expelled it through his teeth.

Cliff's crying tapered off almost to silence. He sat there beside my mother with his elbows on his knees, his chin in his hands. My mother gripped the railing beside her. She looked up at my father, her face full of anger.

"The trial started two weeks ago," he said. "It went on for three days, and Cliff had to be there every morning, and he *was* there—"

"What about school?" my mother said. "I watched him get the bus."

"I didn't want to worry you about this," my father said. "I had him get on the bus at the end of the driveway as usual so you wouldn't know. He'd get off over at Burr Road and I'd meet him there and take him to court. At the end of the trial, the guy was found guilty and he was sentenced. The court clerk gave Cliff fifty-six dollars. It's a kind of fee they pay the prosecutor in criminal proceedings. For three days in court, that's how much it came to. I wasn't going to let him have it, but then I figured he ought to get some kind of reward. It hasn't been an easy period for him. I let him hold on to the money, but I told him to keep it quiet. I didn't want you to know about all this. It didn't seem like something you deserved to know about."

I stepped quietly back to my bed. My whole body felt prickly and fragile, as if it were made of glass, and for a moment I was afraid that if I touched something, accidentally or even on purpose—anything around me—my body would shatter.

I put on my pajamas, turned off the overhead light, leaving only the desk lamp on for Cliff, then got into bed. Through the wall behind my head, I could hear their voices. I could no longer make out what they were saying, but I could tell that my mother was still crying, at times hysterically, and that my father was still explaining things.

Half an hour or so later, Cliff came into the room. He put on his pajamas, turned off the desk lamp, and got into bed. When my eyes adjusted to the dark, I could see his round shape under the bedspread with the boats on it, and I could see his body shiver with silenced crying, his face buried in the pillow, turned toward the wall.

Before he came into the room, I was thinking about the way my father explained what happened, the words he used. This thing about the man having "forced his intentions on him." I didn't know what these words meant. When I tried to imagine the man and Cliff together, the way it happened, I saw them in a bare room, an empty room, standing at a measured distance from each other, staring into each other's eyes which were full of fear and dread. And that's as far as I could go with it.

I was wondering how Cliff felt now, as he cried, alone in bed. Was he ashamed? Why didn't he keep the secret my father wanted him to keep? Tonight I had no answers to such questions. But someday, years into the future, something would prompt me to think about these things again, and at that moment I'd suddenly understand why Cliff wanted us, all of us, to know what happened to him that day downtown: he needed the attention that ordinary, everyday mothers and fathers, brothers and sisters just give out naturally, never having to think about it. This was what Cliff wanted, and that was how he asked us for it.

I woke up early to the sound of snow hitting the windowpanes above the window seat beside my bed. It was the kind of snow that sounded almost like rain, yet I knew it was snow by the way it hissed, deflected. I put on my bathrobe and went downstairs.

The story my mother heard the night before brought a strict look to her mouth, an iciness to her eyes. She barely spoke to me when I came into the kitchen. She was busy feeding the cats. The whine of the electric can opener excited them, and they stretched up, reaching for the countertop.

She had the radio on. "No school in Lowell," said a comforting, fatherly voice, "all schools, all day. No school in Tewksbury ..."

"Yippee," I said.

Cliff, dressed, appeared in the kitchen door behind me. His curly hair was combed out flat as he could get it. His eyes were my eyes in a very different face: from my father's side of the family. I wanted my mother to forget the cats for once. I wanted Cliff to be her pet today, to be the first thing she took care of this morning. I wanted her to turn away from the electric can opener and go to him, to tell him everything was all right, and would be all right, because she now understood certain things she hadn't understood before. But my mother's daily duties were set. Cliff got only a cool "Good morning," from afar, before she bent down with a can of cat food and, holding it over a bowl still full from yesterday, shook it till its cylindrical contents fell and the cats gathered round, purring.

By midmorning the house, inside, was awash with white light. At the rear of the living room was a big picture window, and I stood there for a long time with my feet tucked under the radiator below it, looking out at the snow falling to Kenwood, to the hills of Dracut and southern New Hampshire, and to the old peach grove behind our house. Later, I made a batch of fudge that failed, and afterward I read the Tom Swift book I'd asked my father to get for me in New York.

Cliff mostly stayed in our room all day. He set up his stereo on the floor in the corner and he listened to records.

Late in the afternoon, I knocked on our door, then opened it. A weepy-voiced Connie Francis was singing a love song. "In this world of ordinary people, extraordinary people, I'm glad there is you..."

"The snow is beautiful," I said to Cliff. "It's deep. Have you looked out?"

Cliff was cross-legged on the floor, surrounded by albums. "No," he said, his head down.

"We're going skiing," I told him.

"That's what *you* think," he said, and then he snickered.

"That's what I know," I said.

I got out our ski boots, our coats and gloves and hats. I put his parka around his shoulders and placed a knit cap on his head, and finally, he agreed to come.

At the front door I told my mother we'd be walking around on the lawn in our skis, but when we got outside, I changed my mind and headed off, Cliff following, to the open hillside. At the end of our driveway a car passed wearing chains that jingled, tossing snow pellets through the red glow of taillights. Carrying the army skis my father had given us for Christmas, we walked, for a while, in the car's fresh tracks, then turned into Burr's pasture, where the road got steep going down past the barn.

It was clearing up, and the sun, about to set behind a distant scrim, drew a shaft of tawny light on the wind-hardened snow. Where this shaft of light stopped at our feet, we laid out our skis, far too long for us (made for soldiers, in fact). Cliff had trouble with his bindings. I got down on my knees at his feet, and giving him a hand, my fingers grew red and numb. I knew he would always be clumsy with these things. Today I was grateful for this; there was comfort in these small tasks assigned me by all that was left unsaid.

I pushed off with my poles. "Come on," I said, gesturing with my curved arm like a guide.

Halfway to the crest of the slope, I turned my head and looked back.

Cliff wasn't there.

*   *   *

It was dark by the time I stood my skis up in a snowdrift on the front porch, laying them, next to Cliff's, against the gray asbestos shingles of the house.

We'd had stuffed pork chops for dinner, and now my parents were downstairs playing cribbage. They'd be there till close to midnight, drinking boilermakers and having outrageous fights—my father cheated by changing the rules as he went along.

I was heading to the bathroom when Cliff, in shrunken cotton pajamas, came prancing down the hall, swinging a small suitcase (really, it was a portable bar, a whiskey premium). Giving his shoulders one final wag, he stopped in front of me, put down the suitcase, and sat on it posing, his plump legs crossed knee over knee, the top one bouncing. "Pardon me, boys," he sang, "is this the Chattanooga choo choo ..."

But I couldn't laugh with Cliff tonight. I stood there kind of bewildered and still, regretting the fact that just when I thought I loved him, he'd go and do something to make me change my mind; regretting that that was the way it was, and that was the way it always had to be.

In a minute I turned away in silence and headed for the bathroom.

"Poker face!" Cliff said.

After I'd brushed my teeth and peed one last time, I went to our room. Cliff was sitting in the chair next to his bed, gazing down at something small he held in his hands. He looked up at me and smiled. "Hi creepo," he said.

I paused, taking off my shoes, to watch him pull his folded wad of money out of its waxed manila envelope.

"Fifty-six dollars," he said, grinning, shaking his money in the air like a program vendor at the circus. "Fifty-six!" he said "Fifty-six!"

TWO

5

THINGS WE CAN HARDLY
BEAR TO TOUCH

"The way she's been going on," says Cliff, "you'd think the BVM's
boy himself were checking in!"

"The BVM?" my mother says.

"Blessed Virgin Mary," Cliff says.

She gives in to a laugh that doesn't quite sanction his irreverence.

My father shakes my hand. "Sam-boy," he says.

Cliff snorts, blushing. "*Sam-boy?*" he says, mocking him.

There was a time when my father would not have stood for such
teasing, but he's grown more tolerant now with age. He even puts
up with Cliff's red nightshirt, Cliff's pink, plump knees peeking out
below its hemline.

"All I've heard from this one," says Cliff, pointing to my mother,
"is 'Sam's coming home! Sam's coming home!' She's done nothing
but clean. Things have to be piss-elegant around here all of a sudden!"

"Oh shut your face," my mother says. She has earrings on, and
fresh makeup.

It's Christmas vacation and I'm home from the college I go to in

Vermont. It's been almost a year since I've spent any time with my family. Last summer, I didn't visit them at their rented cottage on Rye Beach; I stayed up at school and worked for Dr. Underhill as a lab assistant.

Things are not so perfect here as Cliff, in his complaints, makes them out to be. My mother has had more than a few covert shots. I blame my father for her drinking; he's driven her to it with his distance, with all the silence. Every night he brings home a "jug" from his liquor store, and most of the fifth goes down her hatch on the sly. There's always an emptied shot glass hidden behind the Ivory Liquid, waiting to be filled again when nobody's looking. How many times have I walked in on her with her head back, shaking the last amber drop out of a jigger, scowling? "I'm having a little whiskey before bed," she always says, as if it were a glass of warm milk, "you want some?"

Her drinking habit is like the bad smell in this house: it's been around so long none of them seem to notice anymore. But I notice. I notice she's given up those domestic duties that used to get her through the day. I notice that the sheets and pillowcases all have laundry tags on them. Who knows when she last dusted? I become asthmatic when I stay here. I sneeze in sets of ten or more until my father, jokingly, says, "That's enough now, Sam! Cut it out! Quit it!"

"Cripes," says Cliff, "all I've heard is 'Sam Sam Sam!' Honestly, she thinks you're God's gift ..."

The warm, motherly look she gives me hurts. I feel bad that I don't have the kind of unqualified love for her most mothers deserve just because they are always *there* for their children. My mother has not always been *there*. She's been jiggy. I turn my head and gaze, instead, at her Pfaff sewing machine in the dining room to my right. It was meant to change her life. She was going to make all her own clothes, new curtains and bedspreads for every room. Now, closed up and piled high with odd, vagrant objects, it looks like any small, convenient table, and not the expensive, sophisticated machine she's never understood and, so, never used.

Through an archway, in the living room to my left, I see that furniture has been rearranged to accommodate an ugly gold couch. I take off my parka and throw it on a dining room chair. My mother's shadow follows her into the hall, then gets swallowed up by buttery kitchen light.

"Where'd that couch come from?" I ask.

"Got it from this guy who comes into the store," my father says. His tone makes it sound as if they took it in like a stray dog, out of pity. "It's not new," he says.

"Could have fooled me," I say.

"Don't be fresh," says Cliff.

I think about "this guy who comes into the store." As a little kid, I often wondered if it was always the same guy who effected so much weird change in our lives, or if there was, in fact, a whole string of guys who sold my father whatever old stuff they needed to unload.

Walter Cronkite is coughing his way through the news. My father has resumed his place in front of the TV; it's a new one with a huge screen. He's wearing slippers. The heels of his daytime shoes stick out from under the skirt of another stuffed chair by his side. The newspaper is draped across his knees like a woolen robe, as if to warm them. He's given up smoking his pipe after thirty years of never appearing without it, but I can hear his wheezy breathing (Half and Half's lasting effects) even above the loud TV.

Cliff sits down in the chair that hides my father's shoes. He drops his Weejuns on the floor, toes pointing to the television, then brings his bare feet up under himself and stretches his nightshirt over his knees. He has a new job in Boston, and takes the train to work. It's a long day for him. Apparently his evening routine is to put on this nightshirt first thing, then come downstairs for the news and the dinner my mother has fixed. He wants to be living on his own, to share an apartment in Boston with his friend Ken, but as yet he can't afford it. He claims he'll move out as soon as he's saved enough money, but I know he finds it easy living here. My mother runs his errands and irons his shirts. He can use her car whenever he wants. Weekends, he's out.

No two chairs in this room face each other for conversation. I take a seat on the gold couch, just back behind my father and Cliff. I see the rear left quadrants of their heads. The couch is hard as granite.

"How are things upcountry?" my father says. His head turns slightly my way, but his eyes never lose contact with Walter Cronkite's.

"Cold," I say. "Kids wear knit face masks to go from building to building. Too cold to ski. When you get on the chair lift, they throw these frozen tarpaulins over you. They're like ice packs."

"How's Maria?" Cliff says.

"Who?" I say.

"Trapp."

"Haven't seen her."

My mother appears in the archway. "The hills are alive la da da da da da ..." she sings.

"Oh there she is!" says Cliff. "Say, Baronessssss!"

She bends forward in laughter, one leg kicking out, excited to have me home. Somehow, her hairstyle looks wrong to me (she's taken to having it done by a hairdresser). It's too high, and too smooth. And she's gained weight since I last saw her. A lot of weight.

Hurriedly, she sets up tray tables in front of each of us, then stands a fourth, for herself, before an empty chair in the darker end of the room. Cliff jumps up to refill his glass of rum and Coke. We're given a brief look at his white underpants.

My mother serves us dinner: chicken with pimentos awash in cream sauce. There are two vegetables plus whipped potatoes. "You wouldn't find anything this good in the cafeteria," I say.

"You're skinny as a rail," she says.

"Can't eat their 'mystery meat'" I say.

My father's wheezing grows loud as he chews, trying to keep his mouth politely closed. I can imagine how much this must bother him. He's always prided himself on good table manners. He used to nag Cliff something awful for talking with his mouth full, and me for never switching my fork over to the right after cutting.

"Did you hear about Dickey?" he asks me.

"No," I say. Dickey is the French Canadian guy who works for him in the store.

"Had a stroke," he says. "I thought you knew."

"I didn't," I say. "And so how is he?"

"Not so well," he says. "It'll be a long recovery." He wipes his lips with a paper napkin, then refolds it neatly and lays it on his knee.

"Oh gosh," I say.

"And it's Christmastime," says my mother. She's seated more than three yards away from the rest of us, beyond the broad coffee table. "There's still Herb helping out once in a while," she says. "He'll go in tonight and give Cliff a break. But Herb's not enough. Daddy's bushed. Doesn't he look exhausted to you, Sam?"

"You do," I tell him.

She picks at her dinner; she's always too full of drink to eat. "Cliff's been going in weekends ..." she says, with the boggled diction whiskey gives her.

"I hate it," says Cliff. He looks at me with a scowl, rolling his eyeballs, but then his dimples show up and I know he gives my father his best.

"Well, he's been a darn good kid to do it," my mother says, "even if he does squawk. He works enough hours already. It's not fair. But you can help out while you're here, can't you, Sam? Go in a few nights when he needs you? Hah Sam? Go on, be a good kid."

I haven't been here fifteen minutes yet, and already they're trespassing against me, demanding that I be one of them.

I don't want to sulk, but I hate the liquor business. As a kid, I prayed my father would change careers. It's never too late to start something new, something better; one of our neighbors went to law school when he was in his fifties, and now he's got a good practice. My father's a bright guy, a graduate of Notre Dame. He never should have settled for this business he inherited from his stepfather. I don't want to learn any more than I already know, from Cliff's stories, about the derelicts, drunks, and whores my father has devoted his life to serving. I hate having to say, "Sure, I'll go in." But I do.

"Attaboy," my father says.

"He's a good kid, that Sam," says my mother.

For a while, I had two very close friends up at school, Lester and Inez Underhill. I'd prefer to be spending this Christmas with them, but it's my duty, I guess, to come home to North Tewksbury and make the best of it. Besides, the Underhills never would have invited me. Last summer, our friendship fell apart.

Lester, who's my father's age, is head of the science department. He's an amateur viticulturist and wine maker. As a freshman, I would trap him with my questions after biology class, after all the other students had gone. This is how we got friendly. Taking on the job of his unofficial aide, I did everything but carry his books to the car.

His wife, Inez, is Italo-Peruvian, and has a long black braid she ties up on the crown of her head. Her skin is clay-colored, almost glazed. Lester is a big man. Though his voice has a peaceful, giving tone, the word "imperial" came to mind when I first saw him and heard him speak in class. He drives a red Jeep, brand-new. They live out in West Castleton and have two Appaloosa horses, trained English.

Lester and Inez are in complete control of their lives. The sterilized empty wine bottles in Lester's cellar stand up in orderly rows, capped with white paper held in place by rubber bands. Their learned journals and periodicals are boxed in complete volumes. Lester never fails to find time in his busy work schedule to do the things he loves most, such as travel. Last summer they went to India. Inez brought home a flat round basket made, in the ancient way, of woven, spearlike leaves. When she offered it to me in her outstretched hands, it was a deep greenish brown, yet still soft with the leaves' own moisture. "Asian humidity," she called it.

"But if only you'd seen this a week ago," she said, "when they gave it to me with three Indian sweets on it. It was green and tender as a maple bud."

Now, whenever I look at that dish-shaped basket in its place of honor in my room up at school, I see it in just that fresh state. And whenever I think about our friendship, I think of it as it was in the beginning.

It's Saturday morning. I'm standing at the kitchen counter, where grimy, odd objects have reduced the work space by two thirds. Dust has been sponged away only up to the toes of a china shepherdess who stands with her back to tin canisters, beside a jar of mustard, a salt box, a spice rack, a cocktail shaker, and dozens of other things, all bunched against the wall as if in a magnetic pull. My mother makes coffee in a battered aluminum percolator, while her good electric pot—a Sunbeam, stainless steel—sits, enveloped in a yellow film, high up on a shelf, out of reach.

"Are you going to be grumpy the whole time?" my mother asks.

"I hate having to go in there," I say. She should know the truth.

"Oh come on," she says. "It won't kill you."

Cliff emerges. "Hi creepo," he says to me, then, "Morning Aretha," to my mother. He is still in his nightshirt.

"It isn't the work," I say. "I don't mind working. It's the ... the atmosphere. And those *people*."

"Oh," says Cliff. "You don't like that atmosphere, Sam? What do you want, an old biddies' tearoom? My, aren't we elegant all of a sudden!"

"Sam," my mother says, "you're not going to give me any trouble now, are you? Come on, just for once. You've never helped Daddy out at the store. It's about time you did."

I make a face.

She gets mad and throws down her dishcloth. "Well, *I'll* go in," she yells, her lower lip trembling. "Jeenen crow! That settles it then. I've had it. *I'm* going in."

"Oh I can just see you," says Cliff, tittering. "Pink pantsuit. Big picture hat! 'Did you say Miller High Life? Here's your change, dear: four sixty-five, seventy-five, five, and five is ten. Thanks for calling, honey.'"

She is still mad, but can't help being amused by Cliff. One by one, over the years, my mother's girlfriends have abandoned her. She claims not to know why. Cliff is, by now, her best friend, her closest companion. He never hassles her for drinking secretly. It irritates him, but he lives with it as if, all things considered, drunkenness amounted to little more than a harmless habit—like knuckle cracking or grinding your teeth in the night.

Cliff gets himself a Coke with lots of ice in it, then leaves the room. My mother's mood goes bad again and she pouts at the sink, her back to me. I wonder if she is crying now. She sets out mugs of odd shapes and colors. "Daddy's not as young as he used to be," she tells me, pouring coffee. "You know that, don't you?"

"I know," I say.

"He went to the chiropractor again last week. He can't lift the cases anymore. I feel sorry for him. You didn't hear what happened last summer up at Drake's Island, did you?"

"I'm not sure," I say. "What?"

"We were visiting Bill and Mary. Daddy had some kind of attack. He was white as a sheet, and he passed out. It was awful. Happened all of a sudden. I took him back to the cottage in Rye and he went to bed and didn't move for three days. He put down his pipe and hasn't touched it since, and that means something. He was scared. I think it was his heart."

"You didn't take him to the hospital?" I say. "Didn't he see a doctor or anything?"

"You know him," she says. "He hates doctors. By gosh, I'm sure that's where Cliff got it. Can't take either one of them to a doctor—are you kidding?"

"But he got over it," I say. "I mean, it couldn't have been a real heart attack."

"Oh Sam," she says, pleading. "You can help him out, can't you? Fill the refrigerator at least. Do it for me. He needs you. Really. He bought you that ski parka, and it was a darn expensive one."

"O.K., O.K.," I tell my mother. "Don't worry. I'll go in. I'll give him a hand."

"Well, be nice about it too," she says. "Can't you be nice about it?"

"O.K. Sure," I say. "I'll be nice."

Whenever she wants me to do her a favor, she uses my down parka as leverage. These days, it's greasy at the collar and thinned out, having given off hundreds of feathers at the seams. But I loved it new, and still love it old. My father bought it for me one parents' weekend in an unprecedented moment of fatherly pride, while my mother egged him on, missing me.

It was my freshman year, and they were both in a great mood. We went out to dinner at the Castleton Inn with my roommate, from Washington, and his parents. My father paid for it (he's generous socially, always has been; and he's really quite elegant when he pulls crisp new bills, always crisp, always new, out of his neat leather money clip, when he drops a huge tip as if he had millions to spare). That night, he wore the suit of his I liked best, the Brooks Brothers suit he'd got a few years back at my suggestion; dark blue, with a pinstripe. Before that, he'd worn it only once, the evening he brought it home. "Too stuffy," he'd said. "I feel like I'm laid out." It had hung in the corner of his closet for three years, until he had it cleaned and pressed for the trip to Vermont. He'd brought it along just for me. He knew I liked him in that suit.

Something happened to my father that weekend; his attitude about me changed a bit. For the first time ever, it seemed he had warm feelings toward me. Perhaps he finally stopped to think about the fact that I was in college, that I wasn't a flunky after all, the hopeless nonachiever he'd always felt I was. I deserved his appreciation for the good work, he seemed to feel, and that's why he bought me the parka, and that's why he wore his Brooks Brothers suit. It was his way of thanking me for not having let him down. There was still the chance, he must have believed, that I'd grow up to be just like him, and just like his nephews whom he loved far more than he'd ever loved Cliff and me. There was still the chance that I'd grow up to be an honest, Catholic man who makes an honest, middle-class living, who talks the way he talks, the way his nephews talk, who harbors the same dreams they all do, dreams that can be related in practical, familiar terms.

Faint winter light filters in through foggy storm windows. My father, with a necktie in a frayed collar, positions himself before a tray table and his bowl of cornflakes. Cast-iron radiators fizzle at their valves. Cliff's pink, hairless legs make a zigzag on the gold couch. He drinks his Coke, watching a kids' show on TV.

"Have you seen the pictures of our trip?" my father asks. He points to a padded, blue leatherette book on the coffee table.

"No," I say, going for it. I sit down and open it on my lap.

Last February, they cruised the Caribbean on the *France*. Afterward, my father put together this album, an effort I might have imagined him too tired, too weak to make. There are captions in the white borders of the pictures, which are pasted up in arrangements of four to a page. He has attached mementos here and there: a ship's cocktail napkin, a matchbook, a packet of sugar.

In one photo, my mother stands against a backdrop of hanging, handmade baskets. She has a vaguely lost look in her eyes. Her lips are redder than the hibiscus.

My father, in his pictures, looks like a retired career man: checkered sport coat, open collar, suntan. I wonder if he believes that he's brought the important concerns of his life to a neat, closing-time resolve, that he's done his duty to my mother and us, and to himself. He faces the camera with his arm resting awkwardly on my mother's shoulder as if to say, Yes, we are still together after all these years, still in love.

I'm sure he's never cheated on her—it would be the easiest thing in the world to do these days, since most nights she's drunk and passed out in bed by nine thirty. My father made his vows of fidelity twenty-five years ago, and they were final. But I wonder what his feelings about my mother really are at this point. If I asked, would he answer? And if he answered, would he ever tell me the truth?

"We liked Martinique best," he says. "The kids go to school all in white. See them? They're immaculate."

I look, instead, at an embarrassing shot of my mother, seated on a couch in their stateroom, taking a mock slug out of a bottle of Canadian Club, tipped high.

Now that I live in Vermont, I have no idea how much worse my mother's drinking has become, how much more ground she has lost in the battle, halfheartedly waged, if waged at all. I never call home after five, when she is sure to answer, muddle-headed and gloomy. I did it once when I was a freshman; it was the one and only time.

"Who are you having dinner with here?" I ask, pointing to a photo of my parents seated at a table with a young, attractive couple. My mother looks seasick. My father offers the camera a smooth, social smile. The other man wears a black dinner jacket, not a white one like my father's. His wife sits high in her chair, her eye level above my mother's head, her arms thin and tanned. She and her husband look disappointed. There is something about this cruise that isn't quite right for them; they're sharing a table with the ruin of their vacation.

"That's a French couple," my father says. "You don't just eat with anybody you want, you know."

My mother appears in the archway. "She was a pain in the neck," she says. "God, she put on the dog!" She throws her nose up, sniffing.

"Piticazzutti," Cliff says, "wasn't she, Aretha?"

"She was a horse's ..." my mother says.

We just had a Saturday-night-style dinner: slices of boiled ham my mother rolls up and sticks with toothpicks, Boston baked beans, potato salad with chopped onion. I declined the franks.

Cliff is upstairs taking a shower. He's going to Boston in my mother's car to spend the evening with friends. I saw his clothes laid out neatly on his bed: yellow Brooks Brothers shirt, yellow Shetland sweater, yellow socks.

My father and I are leaving for the store. He puts on his topcoat and Irish wool hat, then rolls his newspaper into a narrow log and sticks it under his arm. I put on my parka, zip it up to the neck, cinch it at the waist. Outside, heavy rain has turned to sleet. Grainy splashes dot the porch steps.

I am thinking about a day my father and I spent together back when I was in high school, the time he took me skiing at Temple Mountain in New Hamsphire. My mother pushed him into doing it; I knew it couldn't have been his own idea.

In a funny way, I dreaded the idea of spending so many hours alone together. What would we talk about? I wondered. What could I possibly say that might interest him?

My mother packed a lunch for us, and we left early in my father's pink Plymouth. He brought along a wineskin, full of Chianti, that a customer of his at the store had given him as a joke gift.

Temple was the closest ski area; that's why we went there. It was a crummy facility: not a mountain but a low, rocky hill. Its short, boring trails were always caked with blue ice. I hated the place, in fact. It was dark and gloomy. The base lodge was no more than a shack. A day at Temple was a consolation prize. When I'd suggested to my father that we drive the extra half hour or so to Sunapee, where there was some real skiing, he'd said, "No, Sam. No, and that's that."

The star lift at Temple was a rickety old T-bar. The two of us got on, side by side, and it slowly dragged us to the top through fine, wet snow which had just begun to fall.

My father wasn't a very good skier; he could do a low-grade christie when he got going, but most of the time he plodded along in an awkward, bottom-of-the-class snowplow, his poles dangerously extended, his palms up and out. When we let go of the T-bar at the top, he made too quick a right turn and skied into a lift wire that got him in the eye. He bolted back, in pain, then had to slip quickly out of the way of the next two skiers, who'd already begun their dismount; a second later, they'd have crashed into him.

We were off to a bad start.

"Fine," I say.

"God's country up there, isn't it?" he says.

"Come around here, Sam," says my father, gesturing with his finger. He has put on a caramel-colored work jacket, styled like a sport coat. He's got another one just like it in his hand. "Here," he says. "Slip into this."

Herb says good night and leaves. I put on the jacket. The sleeves are too long, and I roll them up.

My father is demonstrating the cash register as a man comes in. Cold air from outside, taking on the musty smell of his old winter clothes, follows him to the counter. "How's it goin', Gerald?" the man asks. The gentle voice doesn't go with his rough, swollen face, his battered hands.

"Oh, a little pain here, a little pain there," my father says. He knows what the man wants without having to ask. He goes to the refrigerator, takes out two six-packs, comes back, and sets them down on the plastic pad, one on top of the other. Pulling out a paper bag, he gives it a quick jerk so it blows wide open, a rectangular sheath; the six-packs fit so perfectly the bag's edges take on a knife-like sharpness.

"Got a trainee?" the guy asks, pointing to me with the roll of bills he's just taken out of his pocket.

"This is my son," my father says. He pulls a half-pint of apricot brandy off a low shelf and hands it to the man as is, unwrapped.

"You're shittin' me," the man says, sticking the bottle into his back pocket and hiking up his trousers. "I didn't know you was married."

"Twenty-two years," my father tells him. "I've got two sons."

"Well I'll be goddamned," the guy says. "All this time comin' in here I was thinkin' you was a bachelor."

I watch my father's hands as he takes the man's money. His fingernails are clean and clipped. He wears no wedding ring, and never has.

"Always thank the customer," says my father, once we're alone.

"Always count back the change the way I just did, and then say, Thank you very much, call again. And when a customer comes in, you say, May I help you? Say it like that, O.K.? Don't just say, Yeah, what do you want? Say, May I help you? Always be courteous. I don't care how much of a grub the guy might be."

I'm not sure my father really wants to know the details when he asks me what's new in my life, but I tell him I've applied to graduate school at U.C. Davis. I haven't checked with him yet to see if he'll pay for it (he's paid for all my education so far), but I'm somehow hopeful he will. He invested in mutual funds when I was a kid, setting aside money for Cliff's and my education, and from what I understand, he hasn't had to tap into it so far.

"I've decided enology is the right career for me," I say. "It'll give me the chance to travel. Besides, I'm just, you know, really into biochemistry. Dr. Underhill turned me on to viticulture and vinification. He collects wine, and he even, you know, makes his own. He's practically the only guy in Vermont into this stuff."

"Isn't it too cold up there for that?" my father asks.

"Warmer than upstate New York," I tell him. "Dr. Underhill's been growing French-American hybrid grapes for years. They're pretty cold-resistant. But now he's experimenting with viniferas, like Riesling. He's amazing. He's done all his own grafting with different American rootstocks, and he's come up with some pretty incredible findings that have come out in agricultural journals."

My father is sitting on a stool by the cash register. "I don't get much call for wine here," he says. He stretches, pointing to the wire basket on a tripod stand near the other counter. I go to it and pick out a dusty bottle. It's from a Burgundy consortium, and there's no vintage date. It's heavily sedimented. Its thin color looks off to me. "I couldn't guarantee this'd be any good," I say, holding it up to the light.

"What is it, a Bordeaux?" he says. "I don't like any of the Bordeaux. And I don't like any of the Burgundies. I don't mind a Côtes-du-Rhône, but I don't like any of the Bordeaux."

"I'm real interested in the California wine industry," I say. "Dr.

Underhill knows a lot about it. He's given me books. The American research is unbelievable."

"Well, you've already got the California accent," my father says. His lips thin out and turn down scornfully. I was wondering how long he could go without taking some kind of swipe at me. Cliff used to say, "He never should have had kids."

"I wouldn't object if it were the real thing," he says, "say, if you've been living out there or something. But it's fake. It's just like Maureen Sheehan's; it comes and goes. You should hear yourself. And you should hear how often you say 'you know'! It drives me nuts!"

"I don't talk Californian," I say, snapping back. "I just don't have the local accent. It's the ugliest way to talk in the world, the way they talk around here. I speak standard American English. That's a plus, the way I look at it!"

As a freshman, I stayed with the Underhills for three weeks when I came down with mononucleosis. Inez put me on a high-protein diet: legumes, and trout Lester catches himself in Hubbardton River or over the line in South Bay. Evenings, I'd lie, covered up, on the couch in Lester's library. Sometimes he would read to me, and as he read I'd study the way he moved his free hand as if conducting music, the way his lips set when finishing a paragraph he felt I should think about a minute. I would listen to how he pronounced his words in a way that almost seemed to define them. I know that when I speak now, if I don't sound exactly like him, I sound like Inez. I sound as if I've lived all my life with just the two of them.

Looking down, my father scans the items on a shelf behind him. "I used to have some Christian Brothers rosé," he says, now in a lower-toned, kinder voice. "Don't know whatever happened to that."

"There's a lot of big corporate money going into the California wine industry," I tell him, thinking he might respond to the business side of things. "They shelter it that way. They're developing some incredible plants."

"Why don't you just go out there and get a job in the field?" he says. "You'll learn the ropes fast enough."

"I don't know how easy that would be," I say, "without, you know, the right qualifications."

"You'll have a B.S. That's not a qualification? That's not good enough?"

"Frankly, no."

"What are you talking about?" he says, anger winning out. "A college degree doesn't mean anything anymore? You're going to tell me that now?"

"Do you want to know what percentage of my closest friends are going to graduate school?" I say. "Like, two thirds. You can't do anything without a master's anymore."

"Well, you want to know how I feel about it?" he says. "I don't believe in graduate school!" He has no idea how narrow-minded he sounds. He stands up quick and busies himself with slips of paper he keeps in a cigar box next to the cash register. "I don't even want to *hear* about it!" he says.

Every morning Lester practices Tai Chi on a covered patio off the kitchen. He learned it from an old man in a park in Formosa. When I had mononucleosis, I would sit at their kitchen table and watch Lester's hands in the window over the sink, watch the way his fingers seemed to curve around an imaginary piece of fruit, but never as if to pick it.

He gave me instruction, and I got good at it too. "It's as if you're holding a sphere," he said, "light as air. You can balance it on your fingertips like a circus performer, take great risks with it, yet no matter how new you are to the art, the sphere never falls out of your hands."

For Lester, this sphere is like the symbol of all things, physical or spiritual, we are made to suffer, to endure in our lives—things we can hardly bear to touch, let alone carry around with us in our hearts. In Tai Chi, all burdens take the form of this round object we manipulate without effort, like a skilled juggler. At least that's how Lester sees it.

One day, during lunch at the Underhills, I said something. I don't remember what it was, but Lester looked me in the eye and said, "You know, the children of alcoholics are often painful perfectionists. Look out for that, Sam."

I felt my body go tight. Suddenly, I wanted distance between us. Without a word, I went out onto the patio to do a little Tai Chi.

Lester followed me there. "Sam," he said, "you can't use Tai Chi like this."

All at once, the imaginary sphere I held seemed to grow heavy in my hands, and when I stopped the exercise to look at him, I lost balance and stumbled. "What do you mean?" I said.

"You hide behind it," Lester said. "That's not the idea, Sam."

I felt afraid. "I don't get it," I said.

"We have to face things, sooner or later," he said. "You should never hide from us, Sam, from the people you love. You've got to get over this diffidence of yours."

I was afraid to ask, What do you mean by "this diffidence"? Did he feel I wasn't really one of them after all? That I was just a Beeler and not an Underhill, just my parents' son, and that I would always be only that? I guess I was afraid to learn that he and Inez no longer loved me.

"I didn't think I was hiding," I said. "I just didn't want to talk anymore, that's all. Sometimes I just don't want to talk. What's wrong with that?" I felt hot inside, and then a cold film of moisture coated my skin.

"But you leave everything unresolved that way," Lester said. "Just as we get to the point where you should open up wide and tell us how you feel, you tune out. You've got a million active buffers going. You're not honest with us, Sam."

"I don't see how you can say that," I said.

"Our relationship isn't growing," he said. "You're not letting it grow. It's stunted. It's your fault, Sam, and no one else's."

I got angry hearing this. What did they want from me? I didn't get it. "Bullshit!" I said.

Lester closed his eyes and shook his head. "I don't know, Sam," he said. "I frankly don't see how we can do much more for you. I thought you would come out of this, but I don't know anymore. It's an awful thing to say, but…"

I wanted him to see I was crying, but he never looked at me again. He went into the house, closed the door, and left me alone there on the patio. In a moment Inez gazed out at me through the kitchen window. Her face filled my own reflection, but not as if to make one composite image; there were two distinct faces there, immiscible, like water and oil.

A very skinny woman comes into the store. Her hair is stringy. Her eyes are covered with a smoky veil. She's drunk. She has a stack of old magazines under her arm.

"You take this one," my father says.

I get stage fright as I go to her. Part of me wants people to think I've been doing this all my life, yet another part wants to overstate my awkwardness, proving that I don't belong, that I know as little about this business as I do about those who need its services.

"May I help you?" I say. The woman has sour breath. She is shivering; her coat isn't warm enough for a night like this. She doesn't look me in the face as she orders, but gazes at my chest, squinty-eyed.

"Pint o' Seagrams Seven," she says. "Qua't o' Hollahan's Ale. Two packs o' Salems. Two vawdka nips."

I look at my father. He moves to gather these things. The expert, he knows what each item is, where it is kept.

The woman suddenly lifts her eyes and smiles at me. She has a black tooth. She throws her magazines down on the counter. They're comic books. The one on top is called "True Love Adventure," and shows a woman dressed like Sheena of the Jungle, her ass tossed up in the reader's face. She's terrified of the snakes at her heels.

My father has completed the woman's order and placed her items on the plastic pad in front of me. He stands back to let me close the sale. I reach under the counter and take out a bag. I don't try to shake it open; I stick my hand in and push.

I've chosen too big a bag. Bottles fall over inside, clanging, as I slide the clumsy package across the counter. The woman has the exact change, in odd coins and wet, rumpled bills. "You keep the funny books, sonny boy," she says. "You like funny books?"

"Yes," I say, without a thought. "Thanks."

She flashes me the black tooth again, embracing her awkward bundle. When the door buzzer sounds, I pick up "True Love Adventure" and read the title of the comic underneath: "Love Choo-choo." The conductor is a woman with bare legs about to be surprised by a man clinging to the railroad car roof.

My father jerks the comics out of my hand. "You know where *they're* going, don't you?" he says. He throws them into the trash and gives me a scornful look.

In the fall, I almost got up the courage to go back to the Under-hills. I planned it in my mind to happen like this: From a distance, I would hear the sound of someone digging, Lester hard at work beyond rows of vines still thick with red, tissue-thin leaves. I would get a shovel from the shed, then, without saying a word, go to work across from him as I'd done since my freshman year, earthing up the plants to protect them from the cold.

Lester's face would brighten when he saw me there; then his eyes would focus on the hurt I'd felt. He'd stop digging, lean the shovel handle against his cheek, and stand there with his arms around it. "Thank heavens," he'd say, scratching his beard. "This is getting to be a lot of work for an old man."

As we'd dig, we'd talk. Something would have got into me all of a sudden: I wouldn't be holding things back anymore; I'd hear myself saying things I had never imagined saying out loud. We'd talk about everything, and by the time we had done a day's work, we'd be friends again. Not friends like before, but real friends.

Of course, it never happened like that. I never went back.

At about nine, my father starts me filling the refrigerator. Most of the beer is stacked in back rooms that are covered with wallpaper left over from when the building was a tenement house. There used to be two upper stories, but he had them torn off. It was a destructive peri-od for him. We used to have a barn at home till he let the local florist's son tear it down and use the lumber to build himself a house. To me it seemed like a weird thing to do; when they finished their work, we were left with a hole in the ground that gave off a rotten stench in July.

My father bends low and picks up a case of Schlitz. Blood courses into his white cheeks in rivulets, and his eyes water. "Wait, let me do that," I say, taking it out of his hands. He has trouble straightening up again. I hear a quiet pop, which must have come from his hip joint, and afterward I hear his wheezing, a peep coming from some-place high in his lungs.

While my father takes care of customers I stock the refrigerator with Budweiser, Narragansett, Pabst. My hands and ears are cold and my nose is red.

Later, he finds me in the back room. "That's enough now," he says. "Come out front a minute. Warm yourself up."

I go and sit on a stool behind the counter, in front of a Mr. Boston ashtray that always used to be full of his blackened pipe tobacco.

The phone rings. I hope it isn't somebody wanting a delivery.

"Broadway Liquor," my father says in a musical voice.

It's only my mother calling.

"Anything else, Face?" my father asks her. "Just whiskey?" He's quiet a minute but for his heavy breathing. "He's doing fine," he tells her. "He's a good kid. Big help."

He hangs up and goes straight for a fifth of Seagram's 7. After slipping it skillfully into a paper bag, he sets it down on top of his folded newspaper so he won't forget it.

I make my decision. Whatever the consequences, I will say what is on my mind. I'll address the problem with a tough question. I don't care if it turns him inside out.

I look him straight in the eye as he stands there beside me. "Was she loaded?" I ask.

He gives me a fierce, shallow stare. "What are you getting at?" he says. Urgently, he pulls down the knot of his tie and shifts his gaze

to the window, to the dark street, where sleet still falls and a few battered cars pass slowly by.

"Her drinking," I say. I feel so impassioned my eyes sting. My
body heat seems to set the air shimmering in waves around me.
"She's given up. She's destroying herself. It's serious. But really, it's
not just her problem, it's yours, too."

"Sam!" he says, in a familiar combative voice, the one he's always
used in responding to my mother's demands for all those things she
rightfully deserves, like his attention for instance, his time. He has
never been confronted by me in quite this way before, yet I know he
will silence me before I go too far. It doesn't really matter. I will
already have said what I have to say, and he will have heard my
thoughts. He will know how I feel. I will have done my half, told my
half of the truth.

With his thumb he fans the corner of the Yellow Pages, trying to
stay calm, but I know that he is terrorized, and that he will not be
able to stand this for long.

"You've always been the one who decided things in our house," I
say, "the one who said no, who put his foot down. You did that to all
of us. But what about this?" I ask. "Why haven't you said no to this?
You've never talked about it with her, have you? You've never tried
to help. What she needs to make this problem go away has to come
from you, but you just bring home the jug, night after night, and
turn your back."

The rage he contains is like a fire burning underground. I don't
see it, but I feel it there, growing immense. I listen to the noise of air
drawn in and out of his smoke-damaged lungs. I listen to him suffo-
cate.

"That's a sore subject!" he says. His voice sinks low with restraint.
"I won't discuss it with you, Sam."

As he turns away fast and goes out into the back room, piled high
with cases he can no longer lift, the words "I won't discuss it with
you" tumble around in my mind, and I hear them against the sound
of his fading footsteps.

*   *   *

I used to sleep out in the vineyard at harvest, with Lester and Inez, to help scare away raccoons—they love sweet fruit almost as much as the robins who one year ate so much Riesling they were too full to fly and had to be herded out of the vineyard, waddling like quail. We'd take turns shooting off Lester's shotgun, aiming into the dark bushes. But I wonder, now, how it would have been had we just talked all night long instead. I wonder if just the talk itself might have scared the pests away, even the raccoons, the cleverest bandits of all.

I follow my father into the back room, and find him standing in front of a case of malt liquor in bottles, much heavier than a case of canned beer, too heavy for an old man. He stoops down, his legs held mistakenly straight, not bent as they should be to take the pressure off his back. He slips his fingers under the carton and I see his dry hand grow stiff and whiten as if there were a source of light within the bone.

"Sam," he says, trying. His voice gives. It breaks under the weight of huge, nameless burdens he's always carried in secret, and always will. "I can't ..." he says.

I rush to him and take it. "Don't worry," I say. "I've got it. It's O.K."

6

THE BEST OF UNCLES

I was twelve years old when this happened.

It was Memorial Day, and what made the day memorable to me was that my mother was madder than I'd ever seen her before in my life.

She asked me to take out the garbage. I balked for just a second, and in that short length of time she'd already hoisted the two ruptured, grease-stained DeMoulis bags up off the kitchen floor and stormed out the front door with them close against her breast, as if they were still topped with new growths of pale green celery and not the yellow-brown rotting leaves that drooped wet and limp across her throat.

But she wasn't mad at *me*, she was mad at my father. He'd left the house early that morning; now it was almost dinnertime and he still hadn't come home. "I've had it," she kept saying to herself. "Honest to God, I've had it! I've had it! I've had it!"

"She's had it," Cliff said to me, clearing his throat just the way my mother unconsciously did. He poked his cheek repeatedly with the tip of his index finger, building on the imitation, and I chuckled with him, naughtily, while she was out.

In a while my father came through the front door with a rolled-up

Red Sox program under his arm. "Hello hello hello," he said to the empty dining room, as if my mother, Cliff, and I were seated there at a fully set table waiting for him to come and join us for a proper holiday meal together.

He was a very stern-faced man, my father, straitlaced and severe. The faint smile that accompanied his hello got shed long before he took off his gray soft hat and laid it on my mother's vacant dining chair.

No hello came from the kitchen. My mother, lips sealed, dumped wedges of cabbage into a pot where a chicken, some carrots, celery, and onions had been simmering far too long.

In the living room, my father changed the channel on Cliff to watch the tail end of a locker room interview with Ted Williams. "You don't mind, do you?" he said, knowing, of course, that Cliff hated anything that had to do with sports, hated it when players talked about their limbs as if they were national treasures—Sportscaster: "How are your legs running, Ted?" Ted Williams: "Good. Good. They were giving us a little trouble back in practice, but I think we're finally out of the woods with it."

There's a story my father often told, and I'm reminded of it now. He told the story dozens of times in my presence, to lots of different people, but he never told anyone what the story actually meant. I figured it out for myself.

My father had taken Cliff to the barbershop for his first haircut. Cliff cried and shrieked "as if he were getting his leg amputated," my father would say. And then he'd add, "That was it. First and last time. I swore I'd never do it again."

My father, when he saw the worst of Cliff that day in the barber chair—I'm sure Cliff made some awful scenes when he was little; he was generally girlish and fussy—turned away from him once and for all. He pushed him out of his life, and out of his mind, and he never really let him back in again, ever.

What my father never explained, telling his barbershop story Sunday afternoons, say, at my cousin's house on Curry Street, was that he swore off *both* his boys with that incident. From then on, he never did, with either of us, any of those things fathers normally do with their sons. He never taught us how to play baseball or football, or shared any of his interests with us. This is why Cliff had such an aversion to sports; this is why his personality changed when my father walked through the front door each night. "Don't be such a pill," my mother would tell him, using Cliff's own word, but he'd go on being a "pill" till my father was off to work again in the morning.

The TV set was a blond, spread-legged console, an RCA Victor, and my father peered at it now, intermittently, over the top of his horn-rimmed glasses, the way you watch a toddler who's always on the verge of getting himself into trouble. But he was really more interested in the sports page of the *Lowell Sun* that he held in his outstretched arms—Sundays, he'd give fifty percent of his attention to the *Globe*'s sports section, twenty-five percent to a football game on TV, and twenty-five percent to a baseball game on the radio. I can still, to this day, hear Curt Gowdy's excited voice calling plays through the static: "A high fly ball out to center field, and it's going ... going ... going ..."

My mother brought in a drink and handed it to him in silence.

"Thanks, Face," he said, so busy with sports media that he didn't even look her in the eye and see just how mad she was.

Perched at the edge of the couch, Cliff sorted through a stack of magazines. My father's profile cast an ominous shadow over him. When Cliff saw me glance his way, he threw my father the bird.

My mother always used to say that my father was "adopted." I'd picture him as a kid with ringlets and tattered knickerbockers, eating gruel out of a wooden bowl and skipping over rats in a dank orphanage like the one in *Oliver Twist,* and I'd think, Maybe that's why he is the way he is.

Eventually, I learned the truth. When my father and his brother, Neil, were very small, their real father died—it's whispered he drank himself to death. A few years later, their mother married a man named Herbert Beeler, and soon after that, he adopted her sons (this is why I'm Sam Beeler, and not Sam Connolly, as I might have been).

Herbert Beeler was an Englishman from Manchester, a machinist who came to Lowell in 1897 to fit out the Wynammit Textile Mills. In time, he quit that field and bought a package store, and then a bar, and then some real estate.

When my father was in his twenties, his stepfather died, and within six months, my grandmother followed. The estate was split between my father and Uncle Neil. But Uncle Neil was a gambler; he lost everything at Rockingham Park and ended up having to borrow money from my father to buy a gift shop on Appleton Street, where he sold Hummels and Infant of Prague statues dressed in rayon gowns.

We visited Uncle Neil, Aunt Jenny, and their six kids every Sunday afternoon at their huge white Victorian house in Lowell. As the grown-ups fussed with ice cubes and measured out their whiskey my cousins, Cliff, and I played hide-and-seek out in the yard. Vinny would hold one fist behind his back and knock against his chin with the other. "One patada, two patada, three patada, fowah ..." he'd say.

"What the heck's a *patada?*" Cliff would say, mocking.

After supper, Aunt Jenny would get us doing the hokeypokey: "You put your heaaaaaad in, you put your heaaaaaad out ..." Later, someone would sit down to play the piano, and we'd sing. "Peggy O'Neil." "Galway Bay." "Smile." My father had a beautiful voice, and knew all the lyrics. Sometimes, near the end of a song when the music swelled, everyone would go suddenly silent and let my father finish on his own. He was an Irish tenor; "a darn good one," everybody said.

One day, when I was ten years old, I got home from school to find my cousins upstairs in the hallway. Three of them were just standing there, as if waiting for instructions from someone. Three were coming out of the bathroom. Altogether there were six of them, two girls and four boys.

"What are *you* doing here?" I said.

My mother was in the guest room doorway, wearing a straight

wool skirt and pearls. She had a grave look in her smeary blue eyes. "They'll be staying with us for a few days," she told me. "Uncle Neil passed away." And when she said that, I got a glimpse of Uncle Neil, in my mind, at the Beelers' house on Curry Street. He was in a white shirt with no tie, on his way upstairs to take a nap, and the reddish skin of his face was wrinkled in such a way that there were little V's under his eyes.

I didn't know enough to feel sad. I hardly knew Uncle Neil, the man for whose absence everyone shyly apologized, since he'd usually go off to bed as soon as we walked in their front door on Sunday afternoons. As far as I was concerned, he'd always been out of the picture, so his being dead now really didn't change things at all. Or did it?

It did: all of a sudden, my father had a second family to raise.

From now on, whenever she'd see him, little Linda, in a pleated, mint-green dress, would run to her uncle as if he were her father miraculously come back to life. He'd put his hands around her smocked waist and pick her up high overhead. A grace, unknown to me, would fill my father's eyes as Linda grinned so hard it looked as if her dimples hurt. And one by one, the other kids would come. They'd gaze at him shyly a minute, gaining confidence, then fly to his arms. He had kisses and hugs for the girls, and for the boys, little punches struck in playful sparring style—funny, he'd never, ever punched Cliff and me like that.

My father would tell Vinny, who was my age, "Once, when you were a little tyke, you said to me, 'Uncle Gerald, take me to the golfball game!'" Remembering this, he'd grin, so proud; he loved that boy. "Imagine, Vinny," he'd say, "'Take me to the golfball game!' I'll never forget it. You were something, you were."

Before he became second father to the Beeler kids, I had no particularly strong feelings for him in any way. But now I hated this *other* father, the father he was to them. I hated that charm of his, those smiles so detestably genuine. I hated the delight my father took in each and every Beeler kid.

*   *   *

That summer, the summer after Uncle Neil's death, I turned eleven. Something went wrong, and we couldn't afford to rent a cottage at the beach. It was the first time in years that I'd seen the poppies bloom in their boomerang-shaped bed near the front steps of our house. I loved the fluted crimson petals that gave to yellow, then to white, then to black where they narrowed to meet the base of a bulbous centerpiece; but I wasn't sure it was worth staying home all summer just for that.

I had trouble killing time those July days. It was too hot to arm myself with a bow and arrow and go off shooting imaginary game in the Burrs' fields, too buggy and steamy in the woods along the Merrimack for tracking, Indian style. When the poppy petals had fallen off and the pale green inner nodes stood bare (but for their crowns of ink-black seeds), I'd get a broom handle and swing at them as if they were baseballs, send them flying off to the clear ground beneath the spruces, their milky contents splattering in the still summer air.

"Want to go to the park?" my mother said one day, thinking I seemed bored and lonely. She was standing on the porch with her dark glasses on, her car keys in hand. "Come on," she said, "I'll take you both."

There was a fieldstone pavilion at Shedd Park that floated in a sea of yellowed, scuffed-away grass. In the summer, a counselor taught crafts there and organized games to keep the Fayette Street kids out of mischief. Beyond the pavilion was a pool where those who had less informed mothers than I went to catch polio and all sorts of other crippling diseases (I'd make mental note of who the bathers were so as not to let them get too close once they were out of the water—they were the untouchables).

My cousin Vinny was at the park that day. He was wearing a Red Sox cap with its brim bent down at the sides like a mallard's bill, and he carried his flattened baseball glove, folded in upon itself, under his arm.

The counselor was organizing a baseball game as Cliff and I climbed the shaded steps to the pavilion. "You play outfield, Sam," she said, throwing me an oily glove with a shredded lining. Cliff escaped, scurrying off quick to the swings, his hand over his mouth to muffle a nasal laugh. He loved it when bad luck befell me.

I'd never played baseball before in my life. Up at the beach, the few boys I knew lived in bathing suits and never dreamed of traipsing off to the ball field on a hot summer day. When the counselor threw me the glove, I said, "Oh no thanks, I can't. I ... ahm ... I ..." I was ashamed to tell the truth—that I'd never played before, that I hadn't the vaguest idea how the game worked—so I ended up quietly following along to the field, my knees buckling, my heart nervously pounding.

The first part was easy because I just stood there in the outfield wearing that sticky, flat glove and the ball never came my way. But it was a different story when I went up to bat.

I didn't understand then that you don't swing at bad pitches. I didn't know that you're supposed to just stand there and wait with the bat over your shoulder, watching the stray ones pass. I swung, stupidly, at the first wild pitch, missing the ball by the length of a bat, and that's when they all started calling me names. A dozen different voices with contradictory commands cut their way through the dusty, lime-white air, and I didn't know who to listen to, who to trust. At one point I thought I could make out Vinny's voice among the others, but by then not even his seemed friendly.

The next pitch came dead at my face, and as I watched the ball grow big and dark, shutting out the sky, I listened to their shouts. Stepping back, I barely hit the edge of the ball, then right away bolted the way I'd seen them do on television. I ran as fast as I could. When I passed first base, the ball was already in the air on its way to second, and that's where they got me. I was out because I had no idea that you could stop at one of these bases along the way to home plate, that if you got to any of the bases before the ball did, you were safe.

By the time the game broke up, my whole body was quivering; my mouth was chalky and dry, and I knew that if I had to say anything to anyone then, my voice would have sounded faint and sickly with shame.

My cousin Vinny stood waiting for me by the bench. He had the half smile on his face that ran in the Beeler family, a smile that made me conscious of how little I knew about things that figured into most boys' lives.

"Had a rough day?" he said, through a whispered laugh.

"What ever gave you that idea?" I said, barely making myself heard.

That September, my mother checked the pockets of my father's raincoat before taking it to the cleaners, and there it was: the receipt for the Beelers' mortgage payment. Suddenly, she understood why we'd stayed home all summer for the first time in years.

Recently, my mother had talked of moving. "I'm gosh darn sick and tired of this old farmhouse," she'd said, when the side porch caved in or when she cut her finger on the broken brass knob of the back hall door. And it *was* an old farmhouse, this house we lived in; my mother never really liked it—she hadn't even seen the place until the day we moved in when I was a year old and Cliff was two. Uncle Neil had found the house for my parents while they were still in Waterville, where my father was working for Jefferson Stores and couldn't find time to get away and see realtors. My mother always had the feeling that she'd been put in that house by Uncle Neil, almost against her will, never having had any say in the matter, and she blamed him for her unhappiness there. Had she had her way, she'd have bought a house in Belvedere, where she'd have had neighbors who were more like herself, neighbors she could have talked to and befriended instead of the "bunch of old Yankee Baptist buck farmers" who lived in our R.F.D. zone in North Tewksbury.

There were lots of nights when, after I'd gone to bed, I'd hear my parents, feisty with whiskey, arguing in the living room in front of the television set, arguing about moving. My father didn't seem to like change, or so, at least, he insisted. He liked our house far more than he liked this or that other property my mother might have noticed wearing a For Sale sign.

Only once did she get him out to take a look at a house that interested her. It was on Holyrood Avenue, not a farmhouse at all but a house where a professional man and his family might live. For a day or so, it seemed that my father was actually thinking seriously about the idea, but then I learned, listening to them argue one evening after dinner, that he'd never really considered moving at all, that he'd given in and gone to look at that house only because she'd insisted so.

"Well *you* don't have to work in that gosh darn old kitchen!" my mother hollered.

"We'll do it over, if that's your problem," my father said, angrily resigned, "for the love of God ..."

And so the next day, a contractor came by to measure the kitchen with its disintegrating, dog-eared linoleum and twenty-year-old, rusty cabinets with grease-blackened chrome handles.

Later in the week, my parents had another fight. "That bid's ridiculous!" my father said. "What a joker!"

Immediately, my mother's fork clanked down hard. "Nothing is ever going to change around here," she said. "I might as well face it—I'll be stuck in this gosh darn old farmhouse for the rest of my life!"

The next night, she painted the kitchen, all by herself. She'd bought cans of brown enamel, and turpentine and brushes, and after dinner, real drunk, she started in. All night long, my father kept getting up, going to the top of the stairs and calling to her. "Come to bed, Mummy!" he'd say. "For the love of God, can't you do that in the morning?"

But she didn't stop till dawn.

It was the worst paint job I'd ever seen. There were brown drips all over the chrome cabinet handles, all over the edges of the appliances, brown on everything she'd obviously intended not to paint. High above the refrigerator was something shaped like a pie plate; it covered the hole where a stovepipe once disappeared into the wall. Before my mother painted the kitchen, there was a landscape on this platelike thing: a newly cut wheat field with tied sheaves standing up in neat rows. I'd often gazed up at this scene, like a painting, staring at it until I was actually standing, safely, in that landscape. It was brown now. That peaceful, orderly field of wheat was behind a layer of sloppy paint, and I'd never enter into that world again.

But if she thought that this horror would prove a point—that if we couldn't move, then at least she deserved, now more than ever, a new kitchen—she was wrong. That was the kitchen my mother would cook in (and drink secretly in) until the day, when my father was seventy years old and dying of lung cancer, they moved out of our house in North Tewksbury and into a small apartment at Harvest Green in Andover.

And so it was a shock to my mother to learn that my father was paying off the mortgage for the Beelers' house on Curry Street, and paying it off in secret. If he had such a secret as this, my mother wondered, how many other secrets were there? How much money did my father give the Beelers for other things? These were the kinds of questions she asked him that night after discovering the evidence. My bedroom door was open and I could hear what they were saying.

But my father never once admitted to paying off their mortgage. He denied it. When my mother said, "And so how do you explain the receipt in your raincoat pocket?" my father just said, "None of your gosh darn business!"

In a minute came the noise of plates getting handled in a brisk, careless way, and when my mother climbed the stairs moments later, the pattern of her breathing told me she was crying.

It was that Memorial Day I was telling about, the day my mother was madder than I'd ever seen her before, the night Cliff gave my father the finger for turning the channel on him to watch a Ted Williams interview.

My mother had been moody and cross ever since my father left the house early that morning, and she'd tried getting over it by doing special things for Cliff and me. She took us to the Rex Grill for lunch, where Cliff had the "Plank Steak"; then afterward, we went to see *The Student Prince* with Ann Blyth (my mother liked Ann Blyth's teeth).

My mother walked into the living room now with dinners for everybody, but none for herself.

"Where's yours?" my father asked, putting aside the newspaper and his pipe. Tears filled my mother's eyes as she ran off to bed without a word, her feet stomping so hard on the wooden stairs that the rails rang out like harp strings.

I was staring at my portion of boiled cabbage, boiled potatoes, and chicken in clear golden broth with floating ovals of fat. "She's gone to bed," I told my father. "She's mad, you know."

My father went upstairs after her, leaving his dinner to get cold, and a minute later the two of them were screaming.

After a while, my father came back down and ate in silence, watching TV and reading the paper at the same time, his necktie slung back over his shoulder, his glasses balanced on the tip of his nose.

The next morning, my mother didn't speak to him, but he didn't seem to care. He left for work as usual, hardly saying goodbye to anyone.

At lunchtime, he came home with two big boxes in a bag from Rhynn's Sporting Goods. He didn't say anything about what he had in these boxes; he just took them out of the bag and put them down on the living room floor—but in a strange place, way in the back where we usually put the Christmas tree.

I walked over to the two identical red-and-white boxes and read what it said on the side of one of them: it said "Rawlings PRO 3."

My father had left the room, and so I opened the lid. Inside was a baseball glove of new, almost orange leather, and set in its palm was a baseball, wrapped in crispy tissue paper, white as the orchids he gave my mother on Easter.

The two of them were in the kitchen trying to keep their voices down as I put the ball back in the palm of the glove, repacked everything just the way it was, and closed the box so that no one could tell I'd touched it. "Baseball gloves," I said to Cliff, who then made a face.

"But you don't love them," I heard my mother say beyond the kitchen door.

"Shut up!" my father shouted.

"It's the truth," she said. "I swear to God you don't."

"Just shut up," he said, "or I'll give you a backhander you won't forget!" He rushed off through the dining room, then quickly climbed the stairs.

A minute later, my mother appeared in the living room doorway. She was holding a dish towel in her hands, and she stood there in her pale blue Bermuda shorts, looking toward the far end of the room where the picture window was and where the boxes sat at the edge of the rug.

"Who are those for?" I said.

"They're for you and Cliff," she said.

Cliff was looking at a movie magazine. "What did we do to deserve *this?*" he said, a sarcastic smirk on his face.

There was an arc of perspiration on my mother's lip, and she wiped it away with the dishcloth. I was waiting for her to smile at Cliff's joke, but she never did. She was still too mad at my father, so mad, she'd one day tell me, that she was practically ready to divorce him. My father, come to find out, had taken the four Beeler boys to a Red Sox game at Fenway Park.

"You only care about *them!*" was what my mother had yelled at him in the kitchen that afternoon. "I'm so sick of you and those gosh darn Beelers. You've got two boys of your own, you know. When have you ever taken *them* to the ball game? Never, that's when. You don't give a hoot about them. Not a blessed hoot!"

When he came back downstairs a few minutes later, he was wearing a sport shirt and casual shoes. His face was red and dry. As my mother brought in our grilled cheese sandwiches he made his unannounced exit. I listened, thoughtfully, to the engine of his used Cadillac as it lazily awoke, the crackling gravel of the driveway under wheels, as if these sounds would tell me where in the world he was off to now.

"Is he ever coming back again?" I asked.

"I don't know," my mother said, "and I don't care!"

"That makes two of us," said Cliff.

After lunch, I got on my English bike and headed down Mill Hill; it was a long, fast coast that left a tingling sensation in your chest as you had your way with gravity. Deep in the cleft, where Burr Brook passed under the bridge, the air turned cool and freshened me up for the short climb, in first gear, to the flatlands at Wexford's farm: wide fields, along the road, newly planted out with corn.

At the end of our road was an International Harvester dealership, and next to it, a narrow street that led to Brightacre Golf Club. It was starting to rain as I parked my bike by the pro shop and climbed the steep steps to the clubhouse.

Under the eaves of this gray clapboard, barn-roofed building was a narrow terrace with some aluminum chairs facing the ninth and final green. He was sitting there, all alone, in one of them, with his legs crossed, his arms folded, his chin resting in his hand.

This was something he'd never done before, gone off to Brightacre without the idea of playing golf in mind, gone off just to sit alone and stew, far away from my mother, Cliff, and me. Yet something told me he would be there; it was an idea that occurred to me just as it must have occurred to him: we always were, in so many ways, alike, he and I.

"What are you doing?" I said as a waitress brought him a beer and a shot.

He looked surprised to see me, but his face didn't change; his lips stayed set, expressionless. "You can't come up here," he said. "You know that, Sam. You have to be twenty-one."

"Oh never mind," the waitress said, balancing my father's empty on a round, cork-lined tray. "Nobody's around."

My father took up his shot glass of whiskey, belted it down in one go, then chased it with a deep swallow of foamy beer—it gave him a white, pencil-thin mustache that fizzed, then quickly disappeared. I think he was drunk, but with him it was never easy to tell.

"I opened up one of the boxes," I said to him, "the boxes you brought home. Is that O.K.?"

"They're for you and Cliff," he said, softly, not looking back at me. "Course it's O.K."

"Thanks," I said, a faint confusion in my voice.

"You're welcome," he said.

The rain picked up and a foursome with hooded ponchos pulled their carts hurriedly toward the green. My father was staring at their golf balls, which lay at different distances from the pin. In my mind I drew lines between these glossy, white balls, linking them up like the stars of a constellation in whose mythology some deep truth is hidden.

"Do you want a Coke?" my father asked.

"No thanks," I said.

"You're sure?"

"Now, about the gloves," I said. "Maybe we could play catch someday, you and me. Someday when you have time."

He looked at me and smiled.

"That is, if you're planning to come home again," I said. I was watching the golfers putt, but then I turned and faced him. "Do you think you're ever coming home again?" I asked.

"Sure I am," he said. "Home is home, after all."

"We could play catch out on the lawn," I said. "Later on today, even. If you have time, I mean."

"Yes," he said.

"But there's only one problem," I said. "I think there's something wrong with the ball."

"What's that?" he said.

"I don't see how it's ever going to bounce," I said. "That ball's hard as a rock; I think it's petrified."

When I was in high school, I saw my father even less than before. He had a lot of fish to fry in those days.

Neil Beeler, Jr., and his brother Bill were after him day and night; they called him on Saturdays and Sundays, late in the evenings, early in the morning. My father would use their nicknames—Neil was "Gus," Bill was "Biff"—nicknames that my mother, my brother, and I never dared to say, thinking them reserved for the Beelers themselves, and for no one else.

My father didn't keep it a secret that he was helping the boys get started in a business of their own. When he had meetings with them at banks or at the real estate brokerage, he told us exactly where he was going as he put on his hat.

Just prior to this, my father had been talking about making changes in his own business. He wanted to move his package store to what he believed would be a better location, Couples Square, in a more middle-class part of town. He had plans drawn up to show what the new store would look like. He talked about how much better, more modern, and more prosperous it would be. My mother came up with the name "The Little Brown Jug." She thought that would be "cute" for a package store. She was very supportive of this forward step of his because she wanted a new car. She wanted winter vacations in Florida. There were some old beds and other pieces of furniture in the attic that she was saving to put in the beach house she hoped we'd one day buy at Rye, walking distance from the summer houses of their friends.

But just as my father's plans for the move to Couples Square began to take shape, the Beeler boys started setting up their Plymouth dealership in Wilmington. The result was that he never moved his store as he'd dreamed of doing, as he'd promised. It stayed in the same location on Fletcher Street at the corner of Broadway, in the building his stepfather bought when my father was a kid, until he sold it the year they moved to Andover.

As things got rolling in Wilmington my father spent more and more time "out at the garage." Instead of coming home at noon, as he'd always done, he would go to lunch with the Beeler boys at the Towne Inn. Soon he bought a Plymouth for himself, a brand of car he'd always hated; it had the biggest engine available and all the options, and it had an enormous, reflective "Beeler Bros." sticker on the trunk. And he started dressing like the Beeler boys too: blue and white checkered pants, white belt and white shoes. He turned to wide polyester ties with raised silver motifs, as his paisleys and rep stripes got shuffled to the back of his closet along with the serious, dark suits chosen by his former, reserved self. He began to talk like the Beelers. He used all their expressions. If someone was drunk, he'd say they were "on the sauce," or they'd had "a gargle." He acquired their snorting laugh.

And then he began to drive like the Beeler boys. Once he got on the highway, he floored it. We were in the habit then of going to Westminster every Sunday for the buffet at The Old Mill. It was a long trip out Route 3 and my father would race to get there and back. I was very afraid of his driving. Once, when I asked him to slow down, he said, "Muffle it!" then sped along all the faster.

Where did he get "Muffle it!"? I wondered.

Neil junior was seeing a woman named Louise at the time. One Sunday we were all in the living room (which was in its usual messy state), when a car drove up. It was Neil and Louise, paying a surprise visit.

Louise was a wide-eyed girl with glossy cheeks. Her lips seemed to pronounce your words for you as you said them. She and Neil sat side by side on the sectional couch while my mother fixed them drinks.

When everybody was settled, Neil said, "So ... ahm ... Uncle Gerald, we're thinking of taking the plunge." The way he said it, it was clear they wanted my father's blessing. It was understood he was the head of the family.

Their wedding was held at Loon Country Club. Whenever we'd asked my father if we could join Loon, he'd always said that even if our application for membership, by some social miracle, were to be approved by the board, we didn't belong in a fancy club like that. But Neil was a member there now, and so they had a beautiful wedding in an elegant country setting.

As we went through the reception line Louise held my father's hand in hers. "Uncle Gerald," she said, her face very close to his, "I don't know that I'll ever be able to properly thank you for your very, *very* generous gift."

My mother got drunk at the wedding. She knew nothing about such a generous gift. She knew that Louise wasn't referring to the modest set of silver candlesticks they'd bought them, the ones displayed on the gift table with all the other usual items one finds at such weddings. She knew that Louise had to be referring to money.

"And how much money?" my mother asked, on the way home that evening in the car.

"Oh, what's it to *you?*" my father shouted. "Criminy!"

Neil and Louise bought a house on Paddy Lane, one of the prettiest streets in Lowell. It was a house I'd always admired, brick, ivy-covered in the summer, with a richly lacquered front door that displayed a polished brass knocker with an eagle on it. It was a house that made me think of what England must look like, must be like, a country of houses such as these in which proper people lived in a particular refined way. It was, in fact, a house I'd often imagined *us* living in, a house I would have wanted my father to buy for my mother, a house that might have ended the sadness.

And so, one by one, the Beelers married, and my father, in a morning suit, gave the girls away just as if they were really his.

And who paid for the girls' weddings? my mother wondered.

One day, when I was away at college, I received a letter from my mother, and tucked inside this letter was a death notice from the *Lowell Sun* with a photograph of my cousin Vinny, the youngest of the six Beeler kids, the one who was my age. He'd been killed in a car crash (I later learned that he had been drag racing his souped-up Plymouth along the boulevard in Dracut). By the time the news got to me in Vermont, he was already buried. And I thought that this was very weird. Why hadn't they telephoned me to come down for my cousin's funeral?

It was this event that cut me off from the Beelers, created a distance between them and me that would grow broader and deeper as years went by. Suddenly, there was a gap in my knowledge of this family history we shared, a gap made by my not having been there at the time of Vinny's death.

Years later, my mother explained why I wasn't called down for the funeral: "It was just too sad," she said. "And besides, I didn't want you to see Gerald."

Something had apparently happened to my father with Vinny's death. It was as if a minus sign was drawn and Vinny's life was subtracted from his, making a diminished total, leaving him that much closer to his own death. "He got old fast," my mother said. "His heart wasn't good. He got tired and slept long hours." Even in time, it seemed, things never righted themselves.

After college, I didn't go back home to live with my parents, to live, as before, close to Aunt Jenny and my cousins. My mother drank heavily in those years; in the evening, she was never pleasant to be around. And so I chose to make my own life, my own peace, and headed off to graduate school in California. When Neil junior died of a stroke at the age of fifty-one, I didn't attend the funeral. I was three thousand miles away, and nobody expected me to make the trip.

It wasn't until shortly after Neil junior's death that my father admitted to being sick. Lung cancer was the problem, but he didn't know it then; he believed it was just old age slowing him down.

My mother called in the middle of the night to tell me she'd taken him to the hospital. "I think you'd better come home," she said.

I arrived back in Lowell just in time to be with him on the last night of his life.

We were sitting in the waiting room of intensive care, my mother, Cliff, and I. "I know they're all busy with their kids and everything," my mother said, "but this is their last chance to see Gerald. I told them that on the phone. Honest to God," she said, "those Beelers!" She drew blunt lines of red across her lips, then tossed the lipstick, without its cap, into her open bag.

"Yeah, well ..." said Cliff. He was sick of her harping on this Beeler business.

"Where are they, do you suppose?" she said, wiping her eyes with the brown paper napkin she got at the restaurant. "I can't get over this!"

She'd just come out of the unit where she'd spent ten minutes at my father's bedside; a long time to be with a man who can do nothing more than look at you with his tear-filled eyes. He knew he was about to die, yet with the respirator in his mouth, he couldn't tell you how it felt. Earlier, as I watched his chest rise and fall mechanically, I wondered what was on his mind. I wondered what he would say if he could speak, if he were given one last chance.

"It's awful," my mother said, sitting all hunched forward.

"Did you talk to him?" I asked.

This made her break down in sobs. She would never have told us what her last words were; we've always kept such things to ourselves in this family.

"Cliff," she said, "you go in now. Your turn."

"Do I have to?" said Cliff. "I feel faint."

"I know," my mother said. "We all feel just *awful*. But go on though, Cliff. It's getting late."

"I can't," he said. His head fell to his hands.

I thought about the time Cliff told me that he hated our father more than anybody else in the world, and about how hard I'd sometimes fought against those same painful feelings.

Cliff got a chill. He threw his jacket over his shoulders and sat with his arms folded in his lap. Funny that now, as a grown man, he'd taken to wearing a baseball cap; it was sitting right there beside him on the couch—of course, it was just a fashion thing.

My mother didn't push Cliff, insisting he go in. She'd always handled him with tolerance and understanding. She never once pushed him to go to the dentist or to get a polio shot.

She looked at her watch. She couldn't see it without her glasses. "What time is it?" she said.

"Midnight," I said.

She was fiddling with the wad of toilet paper she'd stuffed into her shoe to pad a bunion. "Well, no Beelers," she said, putting the misshapen shoe back on. "Not a blessed one. And after all Daddy did for those kids. Look how rich they are now! Houses in Maine, houses in Arizona, houses all over the place. You'd think they'd want to show Gerald their appreciation, wouldn't you?"

"I'll go in," I said, getting up quick while I still had the courage.

The ward was like a theater-in-the-round. Onstage, nurses and doctors moved about in pulsating light, checking monitors, reading charts, setting dials. The patients were the audience: those who were conscious kept their eyes on the show.

My father saw me coming. He waved his hand as if to say, Don't bother with me anymore. I'm done for. Beat it!

I stood by his side. The white, curling hairs on his naked chest were in the same places as those on mine. I wondered why he was all exposed like that. I pictured myself covering him up, gently, with the sheet.

I wanted to say just the right last things to him. I wanted this in the worst way. But even though I'm O.K. at putting words together in my mind, I'm terrible at saying them out loud.

"We're all here," is what I told him, when the time felt right. It was the strangest thing to say; a few words meaning nothing, meaning everything. "We're all here, all of us ..." I said, "Mum, Cliff, and me ... *all* of us."

And really, why *should* there have been any Beelers at the hospital that night, the last night of my father's life? It made perfect sense to me that there was only this one family by his side, the woman he married and the sons he actually fathered, his own family doing its duty.

My cousins hosted a luncheon after the funeral, and they did justice to the occasion. Everything seemed fitting: the early winter chill, the dusting of fresh snow that covered the backyard, that stuck to the swing set and to the young saplings held straight by stakes and wires. "A memorable, beautiful tribute," is what everyone said about the day. Bill's wife had prepared the food; there was plenty to eat and plenty to drink.

Bill's hair was now white as his mother's had been. He told me of his personal successes: the new Mercedes dealership he'd just bought, the real estate development he was working on. I was happy for him, for all of them.

"I'm very different from your father," Bill said to me at one point. "Gerald was a contented guy. What little he had, it was enough. He lived from day to day. What made him special was that he liked doing things for others, helping people out. He was good at that, you know. I'm a greedy bastard, see. Your father wasn't. That's the last thing anybody could ever say about *him*."

And I know I'll never forget those remarks of his. They were ideas about my father that I myself might never have had, since I'd only looked at him through the eyes of his son, and not through the eyes of a nephew who, no doubt, had the best of uncles.

Somewhere along the way, I learned the rules of baseball. I learned the rules to lots of games, in fact, and I learned them on my own. By now, I've forgiven my father for never having played catch with me out on the lawn.

My father, like most men, was cut from flawed cloth. If he didn't love Cliff and me, he loved his brother's kids at least, and so, he *did* love. Still, those voices, the ones I'd heard that day, long ago, in Shedd Park, the voices of boys who spoke a language I'd never been taught, will always be there for me, no matter how distant and faint, if ever I let myself grow weak enough to listen.

THREE

7

A DARN LONG RIDE

The lands of Gozzini, near Gambassi and Tavarnelle, form a small knob on the western border of Chianti Classico. We're no different, in terms of climate or soil, from valleys to the immediate north and south, yet when the boundaries of Chianti Classico were drawn, we were included while they were not.

The wines of this estate have never been particularly distinguished. We talk about it for days if a stranger turns up unannounced at our direct-sales desk. Our product is indispensable only to Baron Gozzini, my boss.

I'm here applying U.C. Davis high technology to methods unchanged since the Greeks named this land Oenotria. I share a small apartment in the original villa of the estate with Fred, the guy I've been living with for almost six years. We prefer our simple house to the newer, eighteenth-century villa where the baron lives, built, in a flash of prosperity, by his more immediate progenitors.

We're on the tourist route. The American shower curtain we've hung in our guest room bath hardly gets a chance to dry between departures and arrivals. Fred likes the calendar full. He takes great delight in guessing who next season's visitors will be. If bookings don't come in at a regular clip, he worries; in the summertime, he gets gloomy and lonesome if we go for more than a week or two without a guest. Unlike me, he's happy taking three meals a day in company. Unlike me, he never tires of explaining the same Italian cultural ins and outs to newcomers.

This is the day my mother arrives from Boston. It was Fred's idea that we pay her travel expenses as a seventieth-birthday present. Giovanna, the young maid who comes with my job, has prepared our guest room in the converted lemon house, where I've placed a vase of three pale orange roses and a basket of our fresh fruits: white peaches, green summer pears, red table grapes not quite ripe enough to eat but pretty to look at.

We're in the kitchen when the phone rings. Fred answers, then grows quickly pale. His lips are rounded and creased. "No," he says, into the receiver.

I spread my hands wide and flat on the kitchen table, listening.

"Crying?" he says.

"Who is it?" I ask.

"Your brother," he whispers, shifting his weight toward the west. He has on the shirt I wore yesterday. "Why didn't she call *us*?" he says.

"What happened?" I say. "Is she all right?" I look at my hands. The cold marble goes misty around my fingers.

"No," Fred says. "Wait a minute. Talk to Sam." He hands me the receiver.

"Cliff?" I say.

"Hi," says Cliff. "Listen, she's in Rome, but she thinks she's in France. She went to the telephone office and there was a girl there who spoke English. She didn't know where she was going, or why. She was bawling. She wanted to come home. I told her you were meeting her in Pisa and she said, 'Nobody told *me* that.'"

A muted cry comes through the phone; I realize it's mine.

"The telephone office girl said she'd take her to the Pisa flight and put her on the plane," Cliff says, "but I'm not sure."

"I've been worried about this," I say. "She can't seem to keep two facts straight. She called me *every day* before she left and ran through her schedule over and over and over again."

"When I spoke to her the day before yesterday," says Cliff, "she said, 'Pack? For where?' I said, 'You're going to Italy.' She said, 'Well nobody told *me* that!'"

"This was a mistake," I tell him. "She's in no condition to come over here all by herself."

"I think once she's with you, she'll be O.K. It's just that she's nervous and so she gets confused."

"I hope you're right," I say. "I'll call Alitalia and make sure she's on the flight."

"She's wearing a green skirt and a plaid Ralph Lauren shirt," Cliff says. He chuckles a little. "All right?"

As soon as I hang up, I call Alitalia to see if she's boarded the plane. They say that new laws prohibit giving out such information. I raise my voice. "But this is a crisis situation!" I say. "We're talking about a very confused woman. She doesn't even know where she is! She's ill."

They say they can't help me.

Fred phones our travel agent in Florence. She checks and sees that the name Margaret Beeler does not show up on the list of boarded passengers. The plane is scheduled to take off in five minutes.

"We'll have to drive to Rome," Fred says, taking charge.

"You're talking three hours," I say. "What about calling through to the gate? She's wearing a green skirt and a plaid shirt."

"How do you know?"

"Cliff told me."

"How does *he* know?"

"He took her to the airport, Fred. Come on!" I'm sorry to be shouting, but I don't say so.

Fred goes to the phone and picks up the receiver.

"No, wait!" I say. "Fred, it's too late. Look, thanks. But it's too late." I sit down and squint into the palm of my hand.

He hangs up, defeated. Suddenly, he makes a decision. "We're going to Rome!" he says. "Let's have Giovanna throw some stuff together!"

I sit there at the kitchen table in silence, as if I haven't heard him. My mind has to finish painting this portrait of Meg, lost and panicked, against a backdrop of Roman smog and chaos.

The phone rings. It's our travel agent. Meg's name is not on the list of those who boarded because she required special care. She's on a different list. And yes, she's in the air.

Once, over breakfast at Fred's parents' home in Chicago, Fred, following a line of conversation that had to do with parent/child relationships, said, "Sam is ashamed of his mother."

Fred's father's eyes fell disdainfully on mine. He is a man whose devotion to the family is as natural as it is boundless. When he tells stories about his parents, or about his ninety-year-old sister who just bought herself a new Chrysler, you hear the love in his voice, in the way it goes boyishly high. Now, believing I was ashamed of my mother, he saw me as a peerless example of disrespect.

I blushed, angry and humiliated. How could Fred say such a thing, making me explain myself to his parents, forcing me to tell them what it means to grow up with an alcoholic mother? I wasn't ready, then and there, to give them all the history with its humiliating specifics. I was so furious with Fred for putting me on the spot like that I couldn't think. As the three of them sat there with disappointed, scolding looks on their faces, all I could say was, "It's not true."

"Then why is your face all red?" Fred's father said.

"It's not true," I said.

Fred, driving, checks and rechecks his controls like a DC-3 pilot: radio volume, air-conditioning, seat position, side mirrors. Every time he adjusts something, we swerve and I reach out to brace myself against the dashboard. Fred takes these reflex leaps of mine as unreasonable complaints. "Do *you* want to drive?" he says angrily.

A moment ago, before we veered sharply to the guardrail, I was remembering my mother's last visit. It was in September, two years ago. Fred and I took her to Venice and we spent a week there together in a rented apartment on the Grand Canal.

"I've seen a lot of beautiful places," my mother said, "Saint Kitt's and Martinique, but this is the best place I've ever been."

Fred and I took the master bedroom, with its better bath and big double bed, leaving the small room with twin beds for her. Delivering her luggage, I sensed a vague discontent in the way she moved, and in her eyes when she looked at me and said, "Thanks." It left me feeling ill at ease and confused. Had we been selfish? Or had she thought, even after all these years, that Fred and I were just good friends? In a minute she came into our room and looked out the window for the longest time, and I got it: she'd felt cheated out of that view of the left bank, of pretty Palazzo Barbarigo by the mouth of the *rio*. We offered to switch, but she wouldn't hear of it. We would make it up to her somehow.

She would never take a nap after lunch, as was our Italian habit, but sat up in the all-white living room waiting impatiently as Fred and I read and dozed. After dinner, she refused to go to bed, insisting we walk to the Piazza for a drink at the Florian.

One evening, over a sentimental brandy under the arcade, we listened to the orchestra play "September Song" as she told us a story. "When I first got my driver's license," she said, "I thought it would be fun to take my mother and Aunt Ethel on a trip. We went to Mount Vernon, and in the square in the middle of town, I bought Ethel an ice cream cone. Ethel sat there eating her ice cream, looking toward the square, and she said, 'Who'd ever thought I'd be eating an ice cream cone in *Mount Vernon?*' And that's the way I feel right now!"

She's loving it, I thought to myself. She gets Venice. For the first time in years, it seemed like we were really and truly related.

Vaporetto workers were striking in the narrow street outside our window. We listened to their angry demands and rough language till the early hours of the morning. They wanted year-round jobs instead of seasonal ones. Over breakfast, my mother said someone

had been "banging" under her bed all night. "What are they building under there?" she asked.

At high tide, oily, green water crept under the side door of our
palazzo. She told me that water from the canal had found its way
into her room. I went to investigate, and yes, it was true. Her shoes
were standing in a puddle on the floor of her armoire.

"Look at this!" she said, showing me the sleeve of a white crepe de
Chine blouse that hung from a twisted wire hanger. "It's soaking!"

I felt the blouse.

"It's wringing wet," she said.

It was true.

"How come?" I said, looking up at the ceiling of her closet.

"Well, I washed it in the kitchen sink this morning," she said, "but
don't you think it ought to be dry by now?" As she took the wet blouse
off its hanger huge drops fell to the tile floor in cold, spreading puddles.

She's so thin. Her hair falls stiff and dry across her forehead. A
man in uniform has her by the arm. Even from a distance, I see the
fear in her eyes.

I meet up with them. "Are you her son?" the man asks.

I look again. "Yes," I say.

I kiss her and hold her a moment. She doesn't smell so good.

"Oh was I mad!" she says. Her bottom lip is trembling. Her eyes
jerk about in search of familiar images.

"You were?" I say.

"I said, 'This is kidnapping, you know!' They said, 'You get on
that plane!' and they pushed me. Oh I was so mad. 'This isn't funny,'
I said. 'This is what you call kidnapping!'"

"Well, it's all right now," I tell her. "You're here with me." I try to
get her to move more quickly toward the luggage claim, but her
steps are short, unsteady.

"The woman told me you'd been kidnapped," she says.

"She couldn't have," I say. "I think you misunderstood."

"I've never heard such stuff in my life," she says. "Who kidnapped who?"

I take her blue vinyl flight bag. It's covered with smudges of liquid makeup. "Nobody's been kidnapped," I say, guiding her past the closed customs office.

"Oh, but that's what she said. She said you'd been kidnapped. Now are you saying she didn't? I'm not that crazy, am I?"

"I don't know," I say, and then I laugh.

She laughs too, and it feels like a breakthrough. "Oh I was so mad," she says.

"It's O.K. now," I say. "It's all over. You're here with me, and you'll be all right. Nobody's been kidnapped. They were just trying to help you make your flight, that's all."

The bags are up. Fred, still standing behind the glass wall where, by regulation, I too am supposed to be, waves to my mother, smiling.

She waves back. "Who's that?" she asks.

A voice in my mind says, Don't tell me she doesn't remember Fred! "It's Fred," I say.

"Oh," she says, still waving, doubtful.

"Watch for your bags," I tell her. Will she ever recognize them? "How many pieces do you have?"

"I don't know," she says, not at all worried. She laughs. "Well, I can't get over this." She gives me a sharp poke on the arm with her finger. "I'm going to be seventy, you know!"

"This is what we always suggest," Fred says. "Go to bed now, and get up before dinner. After dinner, go to bed when we do, and in the morning, you won't have jet lag!" Fred loves to lay other people's plans.

"I never take naps," Meg says. She won't be pushed around by Fred. I know she hates it when he asks her personal questions, questions about her finances, for instance, or about her doctors, her cancer. He is only looking out for her in this way, as a grown-up son looks out for his widowed mother. He asks these questions because I don't, knowing how she feels when people try to take a guiding role in her life. She's always been suspicious of kindness. When she has the sense of Fred's moving in too close, she tightens up, taking a cold, dismissing tone with him, and then he feels unloved and hurt.

He doesn't understand. He thinks she doesn't approve of him because he's Presbyterian, or because he doesn't drink, or because he doesn't share her daft sense of humor. I tell him he's only half right.

"How about a glass of water?" I say.

"Nope," she says.

Does she want to change her clothes? Wash up? "Nope. Nope." Does she want Giovanna to put a button on her shirt (it's wide open). "No. No."

I call Cliff to tell him that everything's all right, that she's safe with us at last. She takes the phone. "Cliff," she says, "where are you?" The old-fashioned receiver makes her head look small as a little girl's. Her eyes light on things that aren't there. I understand that she's at home now, in Andover, by the upright piano she uses as a telephone table. "Oh I was so mad," she tells Cliff. "I said, 'This is kidnapping, you know!'"

She listens hard, and I wonder what encouragement Cliff has.

"Is Cliff coming here?" she asks me, once she's hung up.

"No," I say. "He was just in Paris a month ago, but he's back in Boston now."

"How far is that?" she says.

"Five thousand miles."

I bring her outside where the air is harsh with smoke; they're burning dried bracken in the upper olive groves. In smoke-filtered light the garden takes on a tawny flatness. I'm disappointed that things aren't quite so beautiful as they usually are, until I remember that my mother has always hated gardens. Our across-the-street neighbor in North Tewksbury, an Italian lady in fact, took great pride in her tulips. Every spring she would lead columns of her Sunday dinner guests through the sloping tulip beds, where they'd happen upon the odd hyacinth or narcissus, and my mother, leaning on the soiled windowsill, would scorn Connie's passion with a series of spiteful slurs. There was a lesson here for Cliff and me: flowers are the business of immigrants and damn fools! I wonder what my mother must think of me now with my roses so methodically deadheaded and my hydrangea beds lined with peat.

One of the farmer's little boys comes skipping through the garden. "This is Emilio," I tell Meg. "You say, *Buon giorno*."

"*Buon giorno*," she says, embarrassed by her good pronunciation.

"*Buon giorno*," Emilio says, loping off.

"He's got the darndest rubber pants on I've ever seen in my life!" she says.

Settled in a wicker chair, she glances at Fred. "Well, this is nice of you, isn't it?" she says.

"Yes, it is," says Fred, smiling.

"I don't have to stay very long, you know. You'd get sick of me. Besides, I miss my cat. I'll stay the night, don't be silly, though I don't even have to do that. It's good seeing you, but I don't want to be a pest."

"'*I'll stay the night*'!" Fred repeats. The two of us are afflicted with a laughter we haven't shared in months. Meg joins in. Are we having a good time?

"You're staying nine days," I say.

"Nine days?"

"Yes."

"So much? How come nobody told me that?" Her squinting expression says, Can I stand it? Will I make it?

Fred holds a watering can under the garden faucet. When normal people come to visit, people who make sense, Fred can't find time to freshen up the gardenias—unopened buds fall to the grass, dead of thirst. But today he waters every pot, and once they've drained, he does it again.

I watch my mother's eyes settle on strange things; she is especially curious about the drainage slots in a high fieldstone retaining wall. She stares, transfixed, like a cat before a mouse hole. Fred insists she hallucinates.

"When does Cliff get here?" she asks.

"He's not coming," I say.

"No?" she says. "I should think he'd drop by, since we're all here and everything."

"He's in Boston," I tell her. "This is Italy. Boston's far away."

"How far?"

"Well, you just came from there. How long did it take you?"

"I don't know," she says, "but it seems to me it was a darn long ride!"

Fred has to practice. He plays violin with the Orchestra del Maggio Musicale Fiorentino. This month he's preparing two operas and a ballet.

I show my mother the way to the lemon house. I'm sorry she can't stay with us in our apartment, but we have only one bedroom. I carry her big soft suitcase. It's packed so full it awakens an old pain beneath my shoulder blade. She has more stuff than Henry James took along for a grand tour of the continent, yet she's forgotten her toothbrush and toothpaste. I wait on the terrace as she changes into shorts and a tight-fitting tennis shirt which reveals her off-balance chest. She owns a proper prosthesis, but gave up using it years ago. I am touched by Fred's belief that this is some kind of statement she is making.

I set her up in a lounge chair under the kiwi by the Gozzinis' pool. A breeze clears the air. Swallows circle high overhead, and a few courageous ones swing low to bathe in turn. I hope she falls asleep; she needs it.

Beverly, an acting teacher on a year's sabbatical from C.C.N.Y., will be joining us for dinner tonight. We see each other a lot. In the morning, she flies to Rome for ten days, so this is her only chance to meet my mother. Meg's confusion will come as no shock to her. I've prepared her for the worst. But I wasn't entirely honest. I probably led her to believe that there had once been a time, before this dementia set in, when my mother understood things as well as anybody, a time when she made intelligent comments which had just the right sound to them, the right ring. But Meg has always been outrageous;

drunk or sober, you never know what she's going to come out with. Once, at my friend Dana's house in Magnolia-by-the-Sea, she looked around his plush living room and said to him, "Ah, rich bitch, hah?" It was the only time I ever saw Dana blush. It's so much easier for me now that we can all call these imprudences of Meg's mere "symptoms."

I consider canceling dinner, thinking her too upset. There in the shade, her head has fallen to the side. Her eyes are closed and she's breathing through her mouth. She's asleep.

I go to Fred's tiny studio. "I can't believe Cliff let her make this trip all by herself," I say. "He sees her all the time. He knows what kind of condition she's in. Didn't he realize this would happen? Why didn't he tell us how bad she is?"

Fred lays down his instrument. "It's amazing," he says. "He should have called and discussed it with you first. But you know what I think? I think he wanted a vacation."

"Maybe he deserves it," I say.

"Maybe?"

"She has exactly what her mother had," I say.

"What?"

"After a while, my grandmother didn't even know her own husband. She'd say, 'Who is that old man sitting there?' It broke his heart. He was a big guy, but boy, he cried his eyes out. She called him 'that old man.'"

"Did she drink too?" asks Fred.

"Not a drop," I say.

"Sam!" She's calling out my name, "Sa...am..."

I walk out, but I don't see her at first. She's up in front of the lemon house, her hands on the wall, leaning out, looking down at me in the garden thirty feet below.

"How do I get down there?" she asks, shouting, mad at me.

"Stay right where you are," I say. "I'll come and get you."

I meet up with her at the pergola. It's only five-thirty, but she's dressed for dinner in a fresh Polo shirt and her fox face earrings with ruby eyes (these are things Cliff buys her). I lead her down the weedy staircase. At each step, she dips, then jumps, landing sideways with deeply bent knees. On the garden path, she sticks to the scarce paving stones, her arms out, the way you ford a brook. "Jeesh," she keeps saying. Our guests never find these separate quarters inconvenient, nor did Meg two years ago, but today it's as if she's sequestered in a faraway parish beyond the rainbow.

I put her in a wicker chair, under the umbrella pine, where she shouts out loud at mosquitoes and swats them against her ankles. She scowls at me as if I arranged this infestation. Her legs are dry and flaky. "Would you like a little moisturizer?" I ask, making a small measure with my fingers.

"No thanks," she says. "I haven't touched a drop in months."

Beverly comes at dusk and we eat in the garden. My mother is impatient, even during easy, general conversation. I have the sense she doesn't like Beverly. Meg has never tolerated smart types; "know-it-alls," she calls them. She asks me when she's scheduled to go home, and I remind her of the date, and the day of the week. "I'm forgetful," she tells us.

"So what do you think of the Italian men?" Beverly asks. She flutters her lashes, having fun with Meg. "I mean, are they gorgeous or what?"

"Why are they always poking at their piticazzuttis?" Meg says.

Beverly, her mouth covered, lets out a nasal burst. I howl. Fred can't stand it either. "The things you notice!" he says.

"And something's bugging me too," Meg says to Beverly. "Did you say you were married?"

"I used to be," Beverly says.

"You're a widow?" says Meg.

Fred laughs.

"Well *I'm* a widow," my mother says.

"I'm divorced," says Beverly. "I'll tell you the story." She looks at Fred and me, winking. "And this is just to prove a point, O.K. Meg? Point is, none of us remember a thing, right? Anything anyone ever tells us goes in one ear, and right out the other, doesn't it? You're not the only one, O.K.? Story goes, I was thinking about marrying this guy Dave, no? He was crazy about me. While I was trying to make up my mind he sent me a letter, this incredible letter listing all his faults. He said he was 'insensitive, egotistical, egocentric, pigheaded, irrational, and dishonest,' and that he just thought I should know all this stuff before I decided to marry him. I read the letter and I was like, What do you mean? This guy is *so* outfront! Straightforward as you can get! Sending me a letter like that? So I married him. Two years later, I couldn't stand him. Couldn't stand the *sight* of him! The guy was off the wall! When I left him, he said, 'What's the problem?' I said, 'You're insensitive, egotistical, egocentric, pigheaded, irrational, and dishonest.' He said, 'Well honey, I spelled all that out to you in a letter before our wedding.' I said, 'You did, Dave? I don't remember that. I don't remember anything about a letter!'"

My laughter gives way to an aching smile.

Obviously Meg hasn't paid attention. "Well, why the heck did you marry the piticazzutti?" she says.

At dessert, she points to a rose in a vase. "What kind of flower is *that?*" she says.

"It's a white rose," says Beverly. She takes it out of the vase, breaks off its prickly stem, and sticks it through the top buttonhole of my mother's Polo shirt. It's as though all evening she's been longing to give her something.

I walk Beverly to her car. "She's adorable, your mother," she says. She kisses me good night on both cheeks, close to the corners of my mouth. "I don't think I'd want her to be *my* mother or anything," she says, "but still, she's...I don't know. Something. You know what I mean, don't you, Sam?"

In the morning, I take the baron's Land Rover and gather grape samples from zones of different exposure. Everywhere, rock buntings, shamefaced, scatter and take to the hills as if they know

I'm the boss. Later, I look at sugar/acid ratios, then order the malvasia harvest to begin at Uccelliera.

After a while, I sneak away to spell Fred, who's keeping my mother company by the swimming pool. I never feel right leaving them alone together for very long. If she had her way, Fred wouldn't be around at all. I know he's not for her; too serious, too rational, too organized in his life. I'm sure she thinks Fred's a lot like Connie, our old neighbor with the flower gardens. Once, over at Connie's, my mother gazed up at her clothesline and saw seven pairs of panties hanging out to dry. "Look, Meg!" Connie said, pointing. "Monday, Tuesday, Wednesday..." Meg told that tale for years, mocking Connie's high, squealy voice. You see, Meg has never owned panties. If I went poking through her luggage right this minute, I wouldn't find a single pair.

I join them at the pool. Meg looks piqued, as Fred, in the shade nearby, reads *Answered Prayers*. At the table, under the pergola, I look at the figures of various recent vintages. Fred slips away to practice. Meg appears bored and restless. I know she's playing it up for attention, and so I don't put down my work; I have my responsibilities to this business, after all. Every time I look up, she's standing in a different place, wearing a different pair of Bermuda shorts, her hands on her hips, her legs spread, looking off toward the valley floor, the pine-covered hills.

"What's that noise?" she asks.

"Cicadas," I say.

Silence. She takes a few steps. "Does Giovanna have a mother?"

"Yes," I say. "And a father."

Silence.

"When am I leaving?"

"Eight more days."

Silence. She makes a half turn. Her eyes seem to settle on the church bell tower where a few of the baron's doves light. "What's that noise?" she says. "Is it a wire?"

"Cicadas," I say. "Just bugs crossing their legs."

*　　*　　*

Before lunch, we move to the cool shade of the garden. She dozes in a lawn chair. Now and then her eyes open by half, then slowly close again.

Fred and I wander off toward the side of the house. "Is everything all right?" I say.

"Sam," he says. "Your mother is *crazy*." This is not the first time he has told me this.

"I know," I say.

"I mean, sure she's demented. Worse than ever. But she's just crazy anyway."

I nod sadly, in agreement.

"You don't mind my saying that, do you?"

"It's O.K.," I say.

"And...another thing," he says, "she doesn't like me." The way he breathes, I see that he's hurt.

"What happened?"

"No particular thing," he says. "She just doesn't like me. I know she doesn't."

"She said something," I say. "I know her. What did she say?"

"I mean, we buy her this ticket, we bring her all the way out here and give her a change and everything, and it's like she hates me for it. She saw the book I was reading and she said, 'Truman Capote! Can't stand him. Damn pantywaist!' And then she looked at me like I'm some kind of a pervert."

"Oh," I say. "Yeah, well...that's her. She's always been mean to Cliff's boyfriends, too."

Abruptly, the cicadas stop their racket. The silence is sudden, arresting. "Your mother's an awful person," he says.

I don't say anything. I stare at a dulled oleander flower, bent before the fall. Do I need to decide whether or not this is true?

"But I love her," Fred says.

I look him in the eye, incredulous.

"I mean...I have a love for her."

I wonder how even this can be possible, and yet I have every reason to believe it's true. I've never known anyone who loves as much as Fred.

"Don't you have a love for my parents?" he asks. "You do, don't you, Sam? You must, by now." Fred's parents are handsome, wise, consistent. They are kind to me, unflaggingly thoughtful. They are the ones who made Fred who he is. They made him a lover. They are everything Meg, without realizing it, without ever having really intended to, taught me to fear and distrust.

I look at Fred and hesitate. I see a hint of despondency, maybe even pain in his eyes. He wants me to be the best human being there is. He wants me to be a lover, wants that more than anything in the world. "I…do," I say, not sure I'm telling the truth: I *am* Meg's son, after all. "Of course I do," I say.

Fred has gone to the butcher, and my mother is asleep under the tree. I risk leaving her alone for a moment. I get a knife and a basket, then go off to pick eggplant.

In the kitchen, I cut the eggplant into paper-thin slices and begin frying them up. All at once, the double doors burst open. I hear my mother's voice. Suddenly, she lunges into the room. Giovanna, worried, has Meg by the arm in respectful attendance. Meg's wide eyes look useless to her. Her mouth is twisted, littered with flakes of yesterday's lipstick. She covers her chest with an open hand. "Oh God," she says, "I've been all over the place. Where have you been? This isn't funny, you know!" She's as white as the walls. Her Polo shirt is wet with perspiration. "I can't find my way around here!" she says. "I've been down at the cars, up in the woods! Why do you need such a big house? How do you get around this place? I'm going home! I'm not kidding either!"

"Why the woods?" I say.

Giovanna listens to this, then looks at me, puzzled. She doesn't know a word of English. "*Cosa?*" she asks.

"*Era persa,*" I say. "She was lost."

"I've had enough of this! Where did you go?" She pushes a few white locks away from her forehead, leans against the wall, and takes a short, gasping breath as though she's about to faint.

"It's all right," I say.

"I want to go home," she says.

"No you don't," I tell her. "It's not so bad."

"Yes I do. I can't believe this!" She's crying, but they're crocodile tears.

"Now just try and relax a minute," I say, taking her hand. "How about a nice cold glass of water? A beer?" Yes, she loves beer, I remind myself. That'll take care of it. She isn't supposed to be drinking, but the doctor says an occasional beer or glass of wine won't do her any harm. I get her the glass of beer and wrap one of those embarrassing paper napkins around it: they bear the inscription "Good times, good friends, Sam and Fred." (Meg gave us a package of them for Christmas, and I've never opened it until now.) I take her back outside where a warm breeze stirs the wisteria and rattles in the low, dry fronds of a palm.

Once she's refreshed with a drink, a certain proud poise returns to her cheeks. "What's *her* name?" she asks, pointing to Giovanna who, in the kitchen, passes by an open window.

"Giovanna," I say.

"Does she have a mother?"

"And a father," I say, nodding.

She drinks up, and in the bottom of her glass I see her front false teeth, set apart from her face, downscaled.

"When am I leaving?" she asks.

"In eight days."

"Not till then?" Her head falls back in self-pity.

"That's nothing," I say. "Eight days. We'll have fun, don't be silly! Want a seafood dinner tonight?"

Silence.

"What's that noise?" she asks. "Some kind of wire?"

"It's nothing," I say. "Listen. Do you mind if I go and fry some eggplant, otherwise we'll never have lunch."

"Go ahead," she says.

After we eat, I show my mother to her room in the lemon house. I close the drapes and they flutter before the wide-open windows. I turn back her sheets. "Everyone takes a nap after lunch," I explain. "Just an hour. O.K.? It's nice." She doesn't seem convinced, but she agrees.

Fred and I steal twenty horizontal minutes from the midday heat. We don't find time to remove the bedspread and take out the nighttime pillows. We take off our shoes and lie side by side, on top of the neat spread and its matching French roll, our hands clasped upon our chests as if ascending to heavenly peace. We try not to squirm and make creases in the dry-clean-only fabric.

Exhausted, I'm fast asleep. My dream takes me, late, to a hot classroom where I'm listening to a lecture on archaeology. Dressed in khaki, we all sweat like pigs as we examine stones carved with cryptic messages. Suddenly, more black, volcanic stones just like the ones before us fall from out of the sky, raising thunderous dust. A woman screams. I open my eyes. She is standing at the foot of our bed. Her wild hair is stiff with fright, or hair spray. Her scream taints the close air around us. Or is that my own shout? I think of Fred there beside me. I see us through Meg's eyes: twins, brothers in licentiousness. She has made her way too deeply into the jungle. She has dealt with ten thousand horrors en route to this inner den of depravity and come to the source of all outrage. "Jesus!" I yell, bolting up, wide awake now, creasing the fake silk. "What do you want?"

Instantly, she's calm. "I just want to know when I'm leaving," she says, "that's all." And then she whispers, "For God sakes, don't have a fit!"

We cut her visit short. The only nonstop flight to Boston is out of Paris. With great sacrifice to Baron Gozzini and to Fred's practice schedule, we decide to take her there, show her around, spend the night, and put her on the plane the next day. She's so excited; she's never been to Paris.

In the taxi between Charles de Gaulle Airport and our hotel at St.

Germain des Prés, she keeps saying, "My mother was born here, you know!"

"But this isn't Montreal," we say. "This is Paris."

"Oh, that's right."

A minute later: "I used to come here a lot with my mother to visit my second cousins."

"But this is Paris," we say.

She hammers her forehead with a white, creased fist. She hates being confused in this way. "Oh, there I go again!" she says, furious with herself.

In the city, she walks *so* slowly. The oddest things catch her eye: a dusty, forgotten stuffed dog in the window of a toy shop, the crack in a curbstone, discarded things, base things.

We pass a homeless woman, sitting on the steps of a government office building, with a two-and-a-half-liter bottle of wine by her side. She is naked from the waist down. My mother stops and stares. Embarrassed, I take her by the hand and urge her on. "She has no pants on," Meg says. "Is she *crazy?*" We take a few steps and she stops suddenly, looking back, her lips parted as if in recognition of an old friend. "Did you see her?" she says. "Is she *crazy* or something?"

I lose all patience. How much of this can I take? All the splendors of Paris around us, and look what we're up to. "Of course she's crazy!" I say, shouting. "What do *you* think? You think she's *normal?* You tell *me!* What do *you* think? Is she crazy or what?"

"Well jeesh!" she says.

"Come on!" I say, and pull her by the hand. I imagine that everyone we pass is aware of Meg's problem, and that they all pity us, that they pity me especially.

In no time, she forgets my lapse of kindness. She's distracted by the charming, cute behavior of old people with small children. "Watch out now, Granny," she says, coaching. Or, "You'd better go sit down, Grampa!" And then she says, "He's probably younger than I am!"

At Vaudeville for dinner, her teeth pop out onto the table, and she laughs as she fishes through her bag for a tube of Fixodent. "I'd better go to the ladies'," she says. Without teeth her lips crease, falling in. Her rippled tube of Fixodent is covered with lipstick stains. "Is anyone looking?" she asks. "What the heck, I'll just stick them back in right here."

The next day is her birthday. Before the flight, we have lunch at Maxim's at the airport, and allow her one glass of champagne, which she chugs down in a single gulp as if it were a dose of Metamucil. "Happy birthday, Meg!" we say, then lean across the table to kiss her on the cheek. Unfortunately, her *noisettes d'agneau* are served on a bed of *tagliorini*.

"I've had enough noodles to last me for the rest of my life," she says.

"Sorry," Fred says.

When we check her bags, Fred asks the clerk if someone could be available to show her to the gate and help her board the plane. I distract Meg as Fred explains the situation. "She gets confused and doesn't know where she is. She forgets what she's doing."

A pretty woman in a uniform appears. She'll meet us near the bottom of the ramp at hall 36, half an hour before the flight.

She's on time. She has a little girl by the hand. "This is Annie," she says. Annie has a ticket pouch around her neck. I wonder if we should have fitted Meg out with one.

Meg bends down to speak to Annie. "Hi there," she says. I can tell she's about to cry. She always cries saying goodbye, but never openly. She fights back the tears, ashamed to have emotions, feeling foolish.

"Now you go along with her," I tell Meg, indicating the woman in uniform. "I promise she's not trying to kidnap you."

She laughs and looks away, unable to control the flow of tears.

We both kiss her. She gathers up her carry-on bags, and says goodbye. The tears fall, as predicted, and she doesn't wipe them, giving herself away. Following the TWA girl, she takes a cautious step onto the escalating ramp conveying passengers to Satellite 2, then bends again to speak to Annie, making friends.

"Sam," Fred says. "I think you did real well."

"You do?" I say, my eyes on Meg.

"I do," he says. "You gave her a wonderful time."

I sort through a collection of memories, and see clips of myself in action: myself, impatient; myself, irritated; myself, embarrassed; myself, unloving—even, maybe, ashamed.

"She's impossible," he says. "I think it's amazing how well you've done. I'm proud of you."

"You are?"

"I am."

The conveyer draws Meg up through a Plexiglas tube. Bright distance opens between us. She has such a sunny look on her face. If anyone were to ask her right now where she is and where she's going, I know she'd answer, respectively, Paris and home, as if there weren't a doubt in her mind.

8

READY

I haven't been in the States in over a year. People ask, "Sam, aren't there things you miss? Fanny Farmer Chocolates? The *CBS Evening News?*"

I eat well in Italy; I get the news. If my mother weren't in the midst of a crisis just now I really wouldn't be coming back at all.

Cliff called the other evening. "They've put her in the hospital," he said. "She doesn't eat. She's dehydrated. She can't do anything for herself anymore. They won't release her until we find a place for her to go. If fact, she's tied up; or at least she tells me she is. She calls ten times a night. I've got my hepatitis back, and it's her fault."

Sometimes I wonder if Cliff doesn't invite these problems that make his life miserable. Maybe he'd actually wanted that rare tropical eye infection he got swimming in Puerto Rico. Maybe he'd actually wanted to have the motorbike accident in Greece when he broke his leg and ended up getting hepatitis from a dirty needle. Maybe he wants this relapse. Some people thrive on troubles; they're made that way. When you say to them, How are things? the last thing they want to tell you is, Couldn't be better!

Five days later, I'm in Boston, standing beside my luggage at Cliff's front door in the South End. Gazing down at sand clogged between sidewalk bricks, I recall how it gets there: orange D.P.W trucks spew the stuff out to icy streets the way a peasant in Tuscany seeds a plowed field.

Cliff comes to the door in sweatpants. He has coarse, coiling hair and a beard of the same short length. He's apparently been to a tanning studio again. The lines that fall from the corners of his nose to his lips are hard and deeply shadowed. He doesn't say hello, he just breathes out and his sallow cheeks shudder. A diminished fall sun shines through a stained-glass fanlight overhead (it shows a brig in high seas) and washes the walls of the entry with pinks, yellows, purples.

I'm afraid to say, "How're you doin', Cliff?" I'm afraid to touch him, shake his hand, kiss him the way brothers in Italy kiss after not seeing each other in a long, long time. Cliff and I don't act out emotions; we're full of attending feelings which, like seas, advance and ebb but always hold themselves just back a bit, minding their place. And Cliff's obvious anger makes me shy. I know that he feels abandoned, left to care for Meg all alone, and that he holds my absence against me and always will.

Inside, upstairs, Danny's in the shower. Alone now in the living room, I hear spraying water; then it stops. The phone rings. Cliff comes back into the room. "Now it starts," he says.

"That's her?" I say.

"Of course it's her."

"How do you know?"

"Who else is it?" he says.

"Well, answer it," I say.

Cliff goes to the phone. "Hi," he says, then listens. "I was at work where I always am!" His voice is brittle, sickly, but its volume expands, gaining wind. I stand there quietly, watching his clouded eyes, and then he hands me the phone. "She's calling from prison," he says.

"Hi," I say.

"Who did this to me?" Meg says.

"Did what?"

"Put me in prison."

"In prison?" I say, laughing.

"In jail!" she says. "I'm in jail and I just want to ask you one thing. Why am I here?"

"You're not in jail," I tell her. "You're in the hospital."

Her speech gets clipped. "I am *not* in the hospital." Her voice picks up with emphasis. "You know damn well I'm not!"

"What language!" I say, winking at Cliff.

"I'm not the same," she says. "Who would be? I don't care. I'm in jail in North Tewksbury and who knows what they'll do. They could bop me over the head and take my money. They have me tied up." She starts to cry. "I can't believe it. I can't believe this is happening to me."

"Tell her to read what it says on the sheets," Cliff says.

"I'm coming to see you tomorrow," I tell her.

"It's written on the sheets," Cliff says. "St. John's Hospital. Just tell her to read it."

I don't want to go through all this stuff about the sheets, build a whole case and work on convincing her that she's in the hospital and not in jail like she thinks. This is Cliff's approach. I'd have my own.

Cliff went to business college in Boston, then settled for a dull, secure job with a big bank. Bow ties make Cliff happy. Dinners at The Whistling Oyster in Ogunquit July nights. Barbara Cook concerts at the North Shore Music Tent. February cruises in the Antilles. I'd always wanted more than that. I studied enology at Davis so I could work in wine country anywhere, get out of Boston once and for all.

"I'll be coming in to see you tomorrow morning," I say. "Can you hold out till then?"

Meg stops crying. "What time?" she asks.

"Early," I say. "Just wait for me there."

"Wait for you!" Meg laughs. "I'm all tied up. Wait for you! Jeesh!"

"How did you do that?" Cliff says, once I've hung up.

"Do what?"

"Get rid of her so fast."

"I don't know," I say. I take off my necktie and sit on the smooth beige couch that goes with the chair Cliff's sitting on, his feet pulled up under him.

Danny comes in. I stand and shake his hand. Danny's from Argentina; he has clear blue eyes going to white at the irises and a tightly trimmed beard just like Cliff's. In the corner of the living room is a wicker daybed, and Danny sits on it with his ankles crossed. "Was that her?" he asks.

"Of course it was her," says Cliff.

"I unplug the phone after a while," says Danny. "Cliff can't handle it. He's been very sick with this hepatitis thing. He needs a rest."

"She brought it on," Cliff says. "She's driving me nuts. I haven't got a moment's peace. I haven't had a vacation in a year and a half because I'm afraid to go away and leave her. My doctor's prescribed Valium..." There's an incantatory rhythm to Cliff's speech, highs and lows on a regular beat. "And now she's in the hospital!"

"Tell me what the doctors are doing," I say.

"Her doctors are all jerks," he says.

"Oh?"

"They had a neurologist in."

"What did he find?"

"Brain damage," he says. "That's all they can tell me. Irreversible brain damage."

"But do they think that cancer is the cause?" asks Danny, whose words are separated by spaces as on a printed page.

"Years of hard drinking is the cause," I say, looking around for reactions. "Last year, her oncologist told me that her liver was injured because she tends to have 'too many cocktails.' That was the way he put it. Because her liver isn't doing its job of purifying the blood, brain cells are getting killed off."

"But she never had a drinking problem," says Danny. "Did she, Cliff?"

"Of course she did," I say. "She's an alcoholic. She's been an alcoholic for thirty years. When we were kids living at home, she was drunk every night."

Danny looks at Cliff as if expecting him to disagree.

"It's true," says Cliff. "She drank in the kitchen. She blocked off the door with a heavy stuffed chair so nobody sitting on the living room couch could look through the hallway and see her drinking by the sink."

"I never knew that," says Danny.

I'm surprised. Danny and Cliff have been together for years. Why doesn't Danny know all there is to know about Meg?

Danny gets up, climbs the stairs to the loft, and turns on the TV. I hear canned laughter and the voice of an American child getting smart with her mother, saying the clever words adults wrote for her.

"I'll start dinner," Cliff says, then goes to the kitchen.

"Want to watch TV?" Danny calls down.

I climb the carpeted wooden stairs, which creak and move under me like a living thing. Danny's lying flat out on the couch in his stocking feet, his arms wrapped up around his head. I duck down under the low ceiling and, feeling as if I've come into a temple, take off my shoes and sink to the floor cross-legged, my eyes on the light of the TV screen.

"This sitcom's one of the biggest hits of the season," Danny says.

I'm not really watching, but pretending. I'm not listening, not following the story. The lacquered stovepipe behind my head heats up and snaps and I smell chicken getting cooked with gas. In a minute Cliff comes upstairs and sits on the floor beside the couch. Danny puts his arm around him, and I wonder if I'm imagining that Cliff's heavy expression changes, just a little, to a lighter one, and that it lingers there at least until the telephone rings and it's Meg again.

It's five-thirty a.m. I slept on a spare bed in the loft. Now I'm up and it's tricky getting dressed all stooped over under the low ceiling.

I find Cliff downstairs in the bedroom ironing a shirt for work. Hung on a closet door behind his back is one of Meg's nightgowns, with a frilly collar and a bow at the throat.

"Will you take that to her?" says Cliff, tossing his head back. "I washed it."

I gaze at the nightgown hanging loose and flat, clean and pressed; how tiny it looks, as if it belongs to a little girl.

Danny's still in bed. He's on sabbatical from his teaching job at Wellesley College and spends his days fixing up a house in Roxbury that he and Cliff just bought. "Hey Cisco," Cliff calls out, saying it the way Poncho always did in the last scene of *The Cisco Kid*. Danny stirs, curling himself up under the dark blue down comforter for a final doze. Cliff finishes pressing his shirt, giving it a stiff, human form like a suit of armor. I'm grateful to be seeing Danny asleep, to be watching Cliff iron his shirt, to have seen more deeply into their things, the insides of their closets stuffed with camping gear, the old toboggan we had as kids that I haven't thought about in years.

"Hey Cisco!" Cliff calls, louder this time.

Volunteers with untidy makeup jobs and pink smocks work the front desk at the hospital. They all know me—Meg started volunteering here when I was in the fifth grade. It's not visiting hours, but the ladies tell me to go on upstairs just the same.

"I *thought* that was you," Meg says as I walk in. "I recognized your footsteps." Her hair is matted and her eyes are wide and outsized like a baby's. She's wearing a robin's-egg-blue robe and white terry slippers that the hospital supplies.

"You know," she says. "I was just looking in my pocketbook. I only have thirty dollars. That's crazy. Supposing the girls come by and want to go out to lunch. I'll feel like two cents if I can't pay."

I notice it. It's like a white vest with only a front, and there are straps at the four corners. The straps go around the back of her chair and then they're tied together with bows like shoelaces. "I don't think you'll be going out to lunch," I say. "You're in the hospital. They don't let patients go trotting off to restaurants with their friends."

"I'm in the hospital?"

"Yes," I say.

"I'm not in North Tewksbury?"

"You're in St. John's Hospital in Lowell."

She looks to the window, then to the door. "Is this my room?"

"Yes," I say.

Something connects in her mind, as if a plug, loose in its outlet, got pushed back in. "Oh of course," she says, and smiles. "Those are my flowers. That's my snowman."

"It's cute, the snowman."

"Cliff gave it to me." She thinks a minute. "Then where are my clothes?"

There are two closets. "In there, I guess," I say, pointing. I get up and open one of them. There's a green linen sport coat and a Polo shirt on a hanger. On the floor is a pair of running shoes, toes facing out, with white cotton socks stuffed inside.

"That's all?" she asks, losing patience.

"That's all *here*," I say.

"Then where are the rest of them?" she says.

"At home."

"In North Tewksbury?"

"You live in Andover," I explain.

"*I* know I live in Andover," she says, offended. "Jeesh! Don't you think I know things?"

I sit.

"That's all I hear from Cliff," she says. "'You don't remember anything! Your mind is gone!' I'm forgetful, that's all. So what of it?"

A girl in white comes in with a menu for tomorrow's meals and a yellow half-sized pencil. "Oh *there* you are!" says Meg. She looks back at me, a smile coming to the left side of her face. "They hate me, these girls," she says. The girl's legs are as big around as Meg's waist (I can't get over the fat in the States). "You all hate me," Meg says, "don't you?"

The girl laughs and makes some little remark in an understanding tone.

Meg puts her hand to the side of her mouth. "Well, they're apt to tie you up, you know," she whispers.

The girl leaves, smiling.

style hammock leaning against the wall by his side. Meg, on the other hand, always looked content there, as if she were on vacation in a rented condo in Florida.

In the hall I meet a neighbor, Mrs. Drake. "How's your mother?" she asks.

"Not so well," I say.

"We've been so worried about her," says Mrs. Drake. She's wearing a black raincoat and carries an electric heating pad and a bunch of other things under her arm.

The Drakes are my mother's age and yet their minds run smoothly. They go to Florida five months out of the year. They drive to Michigan together to visit their daughter. Seeing Mrs. Drake now, I ask myself, Why couldn't Meg have lived differently, been sober and minded her health so that things might be better for her now? I'm angry that Meg isn't like this woman who's taken careful, dignified steps along her route to old age.

"You're putting her in a home, your brother tells me," she says.

"I think she's beginning to realize herself that it's the only answer," I say. "Daily life is tough."

"Well, it's a good thing she feels that way," Mrs. Drake tells me. "I had to *force* my mother to go. I took her to the home myself and I left her there. I could hear her screaming as I drove out of the parking lot, and I can still hear her screaming, in my mind, right this very minute. But there comes a time—maybe it will happen to you, maybe it won't—when you have to walk away and leave them there. And I want to tell you, Sam, when that moment comes, you'd just better be ready for it, that's all."

Meg always says that her cat, Beatrice, hates men. When a man walks into her apartment, the cat hides and doesn't come out until he's gone. But I made friends with Beatrice during my last visit, coaxing her out from under one of the draped end tables beside the couch. I even got her to purr beneath my hand, and roll over playfully.

I can't believe the smell when I open the door to Meg's apartment. Cliff has been coming in to feed Beatrice, but he hasn't cleaned out her box. If her box is soiled, she goes in the bathroom sink or on the living room chairs. But even if the cat behaved herself and went in her cat box, the apartment would still be filthy, the air used up and close. For security, there are broom handles in the tracks of Meg's sliding glass doors. She lacks the agility to bend down, the dexterity to take the broom handles out so she could slide open the doors and let in fresh air.

Sitting on the wobbly piano bench, I look around and see this apartment in a new, different way. No longer my mother's home, it is the unlivable space in which a disaster has occurred; it is the dead center of all my hurt. I see these furnishings of hers not as a collection of still-good, functional things which might serve human needs in daily life, but as negated objects, soiled by a dreadful accident, which have to be disposed of.

In the afternoon, I visit two other nursing homes, better, more expensive ones, and decide that the second is the one I like best. Is it just because the social services director is so attractive, so well dressed, someone I know Meg would find cute and so might be happy to see every day? Maybe. But still, it seems like a good place, family run, spotless, with pink tablecloths in the dining rooms and waiters in bow ties.

At five I go back to the hospital to see Meg, who's now angry and even more confused. "Where have you been?" she shouts, furious to have been left alone for the afternoon.

"I've been visiting ..." I don't want to say "nursing homes." "I've been looking at places for you to go to," I say.

"Do you know what I think?" she whispers, onto something. "I think Cliff is up to no good. I just heard that he's always off in Boston with my cancer doctor. Someone from here told me. They're thick as mud, the two of them. And here I am in jail. You think about this for a minute. What are they up to anyway? Oh I *hate* Dr. Field. Honest to God, I hate that man for doing this to me."

"For doing what to you?" I say.

"I'm old now," she shouts. "You don't do this to old people."

"But this is a hospital," I explain, "not a jail."

"Oh don't you tell me such nonsense. I'm in jail in North Tewksbury and I'm fed up with it." Her chin crimps up and reddens, and she starts to cry again.

I have an idea. Wouldn't she understand she was in a hospital if she could step out into the corridors she knew so well as a volunteer?

"Let's take a little walk," I say, getting up.

Meg looks at her feet, then searches for her bag. I untie the restraint and it falls to the floor. "What's that?" she says.

"Nothing," I say, tossing it on the bed.

I help her into the robe my cousin Mary brought in—it's so long it drags on the floor behind her like a train. She hooks her Gucci bag over her arm, picks up a black wooden cane (I have no idea where it came from), then takes my arm. As the two of us step out of her room, tears, caught in the folds beneath Meg's eyes, reflect the bright overhead lights, and her cheeks rise in a poised smile like the one she must have worn as a volunteer delivering newspapers from ward to ward on Friday mornings. Suddenly, she is the woman everybody looked forward to seeing as she made her rounds: patients, nuns, orderlies, candy stripers.

Meg and I turn the corner, heading out of the ward, and pass three old men, restrained in wheelchairs. "Off for a little gallivant," says Meg to their gray, stone faces.

But after a few steps, she's sad again. "I never thought it would come to this," she says. "Oh gee ..."

"To what?" I ask.

"Going into a nursing home." She sighs, stepping on. "Oh well! I suppose I just have to face it, don't I?"

Did she really say that? I wonder. Does she really feel this way?

"I wish I'd known," she says. "I would have said goodbye to my cat, at least given her a last hug." Her face draws in.

There's something under my foot. I stop and bend down. It's a nurse's aide's plasticized ID with a photograph on it. I show it to Meg. "Do you know her?"

"No," she says.

"She lost her ID," I say, then invent a mission to distract Meg. "This is terrible! Without her ID, she might not know who she is. We'd better see if we can find her. Study this image well!"

Meg laughs and moves faster. She holds the cane under her arm as if it were an umbrella she'd made the mistake of carrying on a sunny day. We come to the station of the next ward, where there are two nurses whose faces are white-blue in computer light. I look at the ID, show it to Meg, then look at the nurses. "Is she there?" I whisper.

Meg laughs. "Course not," she says. The nurses are watching. "He's silly," she says, and gives me a little shove.

There's an old woman in a wheelchair beyond, and as we pass she reaches out to me. Her open palm is shriveled and flaked; I start to go to her and give her my hand, but I don't. I stay back.

"She wants you," says Meg, nudging me.

I hold up the ID to give Meg a look. "Is it her?" I say.

Meg laughs.

Down the hall we meet a patient, a woman, much younger than Meg, with dyed blond hair and traces of old makeup around her anxious eyes.

"Good evening," says Meg, her smile expanding.

"Greet'ns," says the woman.

"When are *you* going home?" asks Meg.

"Tamorrah," says the woman. She wears a floor-length white robe, as if she were already at home, en route from the bedroom to the kitchen for a glass of milk. "And you?" she says.

"Oh I'm not going home," Meg tells her, confidently. "I'm going into a nursing home."

The woman steps back and frowns at me. Her face grows small and fierce. I feel despotic, ashamed to hold this ugly power over the small lives of others. "Nursin' home!" she says. "Holy Mother o' Gawd! Nobody's evah gonna put me in a gawddamn nursin' home. They'll have to chain me up first!"

I look at Meg, whose smile is all but gone. I want to get her away from this woman before she ruins everything. I take Meg by the arm. "We have to go along," I say. "Important job to do." I slip the lost ID into her hand. "Bye for now," I say, "O.K.? Bye-bye!"

"Nevah say goodbye," the woman says. "Say so long."

"Goodbye," Meg says.

A few steps later, I feel confident that Meg isn't at all affected by the woman's feelings about nursing homes. Who knows what she's thinking about, but it isn't that, I'm sure.

All of a sudden, Meg laughs. "Imagine," she says, "'so long.' I've never said 'so long' in my entire life. I'm not about to start now."

I go to dinner at a trendy new place in Andover. At the bar, I read the menu and nothing appeals to me; not the two enchiladas, not the blackened red fish, not the junior steak. I overhear people using expressions Cliff and I used as kids: "Whattaya, weird?" and "Whattaya, soft o' somethin'?" and in a moment I find myself alone with Cliff on a hot spring day, beyond the Gazecks' mown field, down at the bottom of Mill Hill where we skied in the winter, across the Garabedians' broad cornfield, and down, down a fern-covered, steep slope, bathing in Burr Brook, in its cold water, bending to dunk our elbows beside slippery black stones. Suddenly, someone else is there, way off there in the woods where we know no one ever goes. I see a shadow on the water which isn't Cliff's, isn't mine. I look up. It's Meg, so far away from the house, with a watermelon under her arm, with plates and napkins and knives and forks, standing, in shorts, with her legs spread wide apart (like a wrestler, my father always said).

The waitress lays out a paper place mat in front of me, gives me a glass of ice with a little water in it. "Yes?" she says.

I feel the way I felt when I first went to Italy and didn't know the language. I don't understand the customs anymore; I don't know what's expected of me. Across the bar a businessman, all alone, raises his beer and, looking at me, says, "Cheers," but I think he must be toasting someone else, someone behind me, in the scant reddish light. I don't dare turn around and look.

*   *   *

In the morning, I search for the impossible, the one-of-a-kind pre-chain, pre-big-business diner where I might find a fresh pot of coffee and a homemade bun, but have to settle instead for a microwaved muffin at Pewter Pot.

Back at my mother's place, the phone rings. It's Cliff. "Where have you been?" he says. "That guy Simon from Andover Manor has been trying to get you. They have an opening. They can take her on Monday morning."

I'm thrilled. No one at these homes seemed very confident about finding Meg an empty bed. "That's fantastic," I say.

"It is?" says Cliff. "What's the place like?"

"It's the best I've seen," I tell him. "It's very airy and has a pretty setting."

"Does she get a room of her own?"

"Ah…no," I say. "They're all doubles."

"You mean she'd have a roommate?"

"I'm afraid so."

"Oh great," he says, laughing. "She's gonna love that."

"But her problem is loneliness, Cliff," I say. "No one to talk to. How do you know? She might love the other gal."

A silence.

"Well, I want to check it out," he says. "Call and see if you can get an appointment for tomorrow morning."

"Sure," I say.

It's Sunday. I put on a suit and tie for Mr. Simon. Cliff turns up on schedule with Danny, and they're both dressed in hunting outfits. Cliff, in a thickly stuffed, signal-orange quilted pullover, looks ruffled and bushed. Whenever he's with me, he seems to hold his mouth in a narrow, sour frown, but I can tell he's feeling this hepatitis relapse. He doesn't want to put Meg in a home any more than I do, and this, too, has him down.

Look Cliff, I want to say to him. It's not your fault, not our fault, but just the fault of time, nothing more. And I do say something like this, but the words that come out don't seem to sound so good as the ones I put together in my mind, words like: Hours and days go by, Cliff, years and years. None of us can go ahead at the same pace forever. We tire somewhere along the way, all of us do.

Cliff isn't cordial to Mr. Simon. He barely looks him in the face, doesn't speak to him, doesn't ask questions the way Danny does, questions about the home's obligations to the "guest," legal points. Mr. Simon leaves us in the conference room to fill out the application.

When the door closes, Cliff says, "He's nothing but a shyster!"

"Shush," I say.

"I don't care," says Cliff. "He's just a moneygrubbing—"

"Shut up!" I shout. My echoing voice in the bare room sounds like that of a child.

We're all silent now, reading the prospectus. Cliff gets his calculator and starts figuring out whether or not Meg can afford this.

"Well?" I say. "Do we do it or not?"

Looking off, Cliff considers. "Yes," he finally says, softly.

I nod. "O.K.," I say.

We have lunch together at The 99. I pick at my cheeseburger, knowing I can't digest all that fat. Cliff eats quickly, dutifully, in silence, now and then setting a crumpled paper napkin to his lips, and looking to the side at Danny. "You know, we're supposed to be in London on vacation," Cliff says. "But how can I go on vacation? What if something happened?"

"We're doing this, in part, for you, Cliff," I say. "With people looking after her, you don't have to worry anymore. Go next week. Go ahead. Make your reservations now."

"You don't know what I've been going through."

"He's really pretty sick," Danny says.

"Eventually, you have to decide that this can't destroy you, Cliff. We do our duty. We do all we can, but we have our own lives to lead, and the fact that we go on with these lives of ours has nothing to do with the scope of our love for Meg—"

Cliff pounces. "Oh that's easy for you to say! You go off to Italy and I'm the one who's stuck here with the abuse!"

I don't snap back like I always did as a kid, or like I might have done up until just a few years ago. Instead, I look at Cliff and nod as if to say, Yes, you're right. Go on, Cliff. I deserve it.

"Want another beer?" Danny asks.

"No thanks," I say. I begin to think of all the things that have to be done: Meg's clothes to be gone through, her apartment to be broken up. And the cat? "You won't take the cat?" I say.

"We can't live with shredded furniture," says Danny.

"I don't blame you," I say. "But let's try to find her a home. Couldn't we?"

At the apartment, Danny and Cliff go through Meg's things. They take the silver plate flatware and linens. I gaze at a photograph of Meg on a boat in Acapulco, a picture I've always hated because it shows a woman whose mind is nearing death. Cliff had a rough trip with her there two years ago. In the photo, a mustached pirate holds an old Spanish pistol to Meg's head and threatens to shoot as she, grotesquely, crooks down the corners of her lips. When Cliff and Danny go, I'll destroy it.

On Monday morning I select, from Meg's immense wardrobe which contains doubles of everything, a warm outfit for her to wear: a tweed jacket with suede patches at the elbows, a cotton shirt with a bow at the neck, a forest-green woolen skirt. Cliff said it ought to be my job to take Meg to the nursing home, and I figured that seemed fair since I'd done so little for Meg over the years. Cliff is no good at times like these; he can't block out sorrow the way I block things out.

Meg, already dressed in the clothes she arrived in two weeks ago, is sitting in a chair waiting for me as I come in. Her bed is stripped. Her snowman is tucked in a plastic bag beside her chair.

"But you can't go out like that," I say.

"Like what?"

"A linen jacket and a short-sleeved shirt? It's cold now. Look at me. I've got a coat on, see? It's fall."

I have her change into the outfit I brought, but let her keep on the running shoes.

"And what is this place you're taking me to?" she says.

"Andover Manor," I tell her.

"What kind of a house is it?" she asks. "Are you sure about this? I'm happy to stay *here*, you know. This is a nice place, fixed up cute. Is this my room?"

"This *was* your room," I say. "But you're leaving now."

Jean Young, one of Meg's friends, a fellow volunteer, comes in to say goodbye, and Meg looks up and brightens.

"I think it's the best thing for you, to go over there," Jean says. "I've heard nothing but good about it. We'll come and see you, take you out to lunch." She looks at me. "Your mother loves the lunches, you know."

Meg tries to cover up her sadness with a quick change of subject. "Oh, you know who just came in, Jean?" she says. "That high-society gal, you know? Always in the paper." Her voice wavers and tears rush down her cheeks.

"High society?" says Jean. "I didn't know we had any high society in Lowell." She glances at me and winks.

I carry Meg's flowers; from out of a plastic bag marked "Personal Items" their blossoms unfurl. Jean, with the snowman, will come with us to the car, walking beside the girl who pushes Meg in a wheelchair. As we pass the desk, nurses go to Meg one at a time. Their puffy, bare arms engulf her and they kiss her on the cheek. They are sad to see her go. No doubt Meg will always have a way of pulling people into her life.

"Bye-bye," says Meg with a sort of laugh. "I knew I was going to cry. I'm going into a nursing home, you know! Goodbye," she cries.

"No one will ever find me here," says Meg, "surrounded by woods. What's through *there*, anyway?"

"It's a bird sanctuary," I explain, knowing, of course, that Meg has always thought of birds as nothing more than dinner for her cats. "You can take nature walks."

"With who?" she says. "I have no one to take walks with."

"With the other people who live here," I say.

We're met at the door by a young woman with a clipboard, not the attractive girl who took me through on my first visit but another one—"I'm Audrey"—who isn't Meg's type of person at all, too big and strong, high-shouldered and chinless.

A group of people, all with snow-white hair, sit in the lobby in wing-back chairs, and Meg studies them as we're led past to the room she will share with Mrs. Forbes, who, Audrey explains, "comes from a very fine old Andover family."

Mrs. Forbes is much older than Meg. She is well dressed and handsomely groomed. Graciously, she receives her new roommate, then takes my hand and looks into my eyes. "How lovely!" she says. "Oh, how lovely to see you!"

Meg stays back in the doorway, just managing a smile.

"And you'll, of course, be doing this for all of us, won't you?" says Mrs. Forbes.

"Doing this?" I say. I glance at Audrey for help.

"Forget it," Audrey whispers. "She's confused."

We leave our coats on the chair to take a walk. In the hallway, Meg grabs my arm and pulls me back. "Oh, I don't like this place," she says. "Do you? Do you like this?"

"Well...I think it's very nice," I tell her. "You haven't seen it yet. Let's have a look around before you decide whether or not you like it."

Meg, wrought up, struggles to modulate her shout. *"Did you see those people in the lobby?"* she says. "Oh Sam, I've *had* a look around."

Audrey falls back and listens in. Meg speaks to her politely. "You have a beautiful place here," she says, "but I'm old. I can't just throw myself into something like this. I'm going to have to think about it for a while. It was very nice to have met you."

"Well," says Audrey, "the best way to think about it is by spending the night." She's employing a trusted argument. "Then you'll have a better idea about what it's like. Come, let me take you around."

We walk, Audrey out ahead. Meg pulls me back. "I'm not spend-ing the night here with that old lady," she says, whispering forcefully. "Are you crazy? Oh, I don't like it. This is an awful house! Come on now. I've seen it. O.K. Let's go." She gives me a quick-before-any-body-sees-us look.

My confidence breaks. The situation is out of my control. Blood seems to abound in my system, then suddenly go cold in my veins. Drops of perspiration fall away from my underarms and skitter down my sides. I never expected this, never dreamed she'd refuse to stay, refuse care, companionship, things she seemed to understand she needed. I expected to have trouble with her cat. I've been preparing myself for that morning when, before the movers arrive to take the furniture off to Cliff and Danny's rental property in Roxbury, I'd have to coax Beatrice out from under the tented end table and, gradually taming her, take her up in my arms—hoping she won't sense the terrified beat of my heart—then quickly slip her into the Cat Caddy. I've been preparing myself for that struggle, for that painful refusal, but not for this one.

Meg stands with her legs spread, ready to go forward or back according to the strength of my insistence, taking short, frightened breaths, her small, unsteady hand against her forehead. All at once, I'm struck by a different kind of grief, one that has nothing at all to do with sentiment: it's about the struggle against mortality.

"Aren't you coming?" says Audrey.

"Where are my car keys?" says Meg, desperately. "Where's my coat? I'm getting out of here."

"But they were going to give us lunch," I say.

She bursts. "O.K.," she shouts, "then *you* stay! If you like this so much, *you* stay here in this damn place!"

"Weren't you going to introduce us to some of the guests?" I say to Audrey with a weakened voice.

Two women pass on their way to the dining room. Meg pulls herself together.

"Ladies," says Audrey. "Just a moment. This is a new resident." She gestures with her clipboard to Meg, then to the others. "This is Mrs. O'Neill, Mrs. Dillon."

"Oh, I'm not staying," says Meg with a quivering smile. "I'm just looking. It's a beautiful place, this one. But I've got some others in mind. I have to look around for the right house. I'm old now, and this is the rest of my life."

The ladies walk off chatting in lowered tones, looking back.

"I'd like to take you now to one of our visiting rooms," says Audrey, "where we can talk about this in private." As we turn a corner and head up a ramp Meg bows her head and climbs.

Audrey gets me aside. "I think you should leave," she whispers.

"When?" I say.

"Like *now!*" she says.

I'm thrown off. I'd never considered this: just leaving her there, disappearing the way Mrs. Drake did with her mother, leaving her there like a package dropped at the right address. I want to set Meg free, bring her through electronic barriers, sirens bellowing, attendants rushing, help her young heart escape to what passion or conquest there is left in this dwindling life of hers. I want to take her, now, into my arms, the way Italian sons embrace their mothers, and press my cheek against hers, and hug and hold her and keep her near, always. But I can't.

In the visiting room, Meg, trembling, holds her head and breathes feverishly. "Oh Sam," she repeats. "Can't I go home? I still have a home, don't I?"

Another young woman, wearing a gray suit, comes in followed by a waitress carrying lunch: a cake of glutinous scrambled eggs with ham bits inside, cut in the shape of a pound of butter.

"Why don't you give us a chance?" says the woman in gray. "Let us show you what we can do."

Meg's shaking hand breaks the geometry of her eggs with the side of her fork.

I excuse myself to go to the bathroom, but instead, want to find a telephone, want to call Cliff. Audrey, following me out, takes me to her office.

The fumes of business coffee, reduced to sediment, bore a hole in the wall of my stomach. Nausea sets in. Audrey picks up her phone and presses 9 for an outside line, then pushes it in front of me.

I will say something like, "We have to make a decision, you and me, Cliff. We have to decide something together, the two of us, right now."

Audrey, sitting across the desk from me, looks into my eyes. "You can still leave, you understand," she says. "We're professionals. We're used to taking care of these things."

I pick up the phone and dial. Cliff comes on the line. "Cliff," I say, "we're here at Andover Manor…" I'm crying and my voice shows it; it weakens and snaps back in the middle of words, a disconcerting sudden burst of volume like bad TV reception.

"And?" says Cliff. There's a trace of hope in his low tone.

I gaze out the window behind Audrey's head. In a bit of walled-off ground, a maple tree stands on a round carpet of its own crimson leaves. I see something of myself in the lone migratory bird paying a call here en route to its winter home. My whole life with Meg is contained within this landscape, contained in this moment, a moment I am all at once ready for.

"They just gave us lunch," I tell Cliff, "and…everything's fine. Don't worry," I say. "I think she'll be happy here. Really, Cliff, I couldn't be more sure of it."

9

THE QUIET ROOM

My first morning home, I went through the odd scraps of paper I'd been carrying around in the left pocket of my pants for the past three weeks. Dr. Bishop: 956-7080. Danny in Wellesley: 536-2393. CCU, Floating: 956-6575. Wellesley Cemetery: 536-0200.

A little later, I unpacked my address book and erased Cliff's name.

All this began a few weeks ago. I called Cliff, and for the first time ever, it was his own voice on the answering machine, not Danny's. "Oh, I'm probably in the shower, or taking the dog for a walk, or doing any number of other exciting things ..."

I left my message. Cliff didn't call back, but there was nothing strange in that. He never called me. It wasn't that he didn't want to spend the money; he had a decent-paying job; he could afford an occasional transatlantic call. Whenever we spoke, his bad feelings toward me sallied out of their deep hiding places, making him angry not only with me, I'm sure, but with himself. I never wanted to torture Cliff, but I needed to hear his voice once in a while, find out how he was doing, especially during these last months when he was so sick.

I decided to try him at six-thirty a.m. his time, Saturday, when I'd be sure to find somebody at home. Danny answered. "Cliff?" I said.

"No. Danny," he said, seeming, in his tone, to object to the confusion, or maybe just the inconvenience of my early call. He'd always had a chip on his shoulder dealing with me.

"It's Sam," I said. "Did I wake you?"

"Ah...yeah."

"Is Cliff there?"

"Nope," he said.

I waited a minute for the explanation that never came. "Where is he?"

"He's...in the hospital," he said, with a full stop.

I got, by now, that Danny was resentful, if that's what he wanted me to get. He was bitter and grudging, just like Cliff. Cliff always wanted his friends to dislike me as much as he did; sometimes he succeeded in poisoning me for them, sometimes he didn't.

"How long has he been in the hospital?" I asked.

"Almost two weeks."

"With what?"

"Pneumonia."

I got angry. "*Why didn't you tell me?*" I said.

"Cliff doesn't want anybody to know," he said.

"Danny," I said, invoking all my courage. "Does Cliff have AIDS?"

For the longest time, he didn't answer me, but I would have waited for that answer forever if I'd had to.

"Sam," he finally said, "when Cliff gets better, maybe the two of you should sit down together and talk this over then, just the two of you, O.K.?"

I felt as if I'd just hit the ground after a fall. "O.K.," I said, with more breath than voice.

I found Fred in our room, on our bed, and sat down on the chair beside him. "I asked him if it was AIDS," I said, "and he wouldn't tell me." Shivering, I cried as I told Fred this. I couldn't remember when I last cried this hard. Fred, crying too, moved closer, but I didn't want to be touched just then.

"What did Danny say?" Fred asked. "I want to hear everything."

"He didn't say a thing," I said. "Danny's weird."

Five years ago, Cliff and Danny came to visit us here in Italy. It was Cliff's first time abroad. Though well into their thirties, the two of them had set out on their trip to Europe like a couple of college kids, with backpacks, short shorts, faded T-shirts.

At first, Danny did most of the talking as Cliff, maybe listening, maybe not, struggled to maintain a worldly pose.

A friend of ours, meeting him for the first time, asked Cliff what he did. Cliff puffed up. "I'm a banker," he said. Somehow I doubted that the term "banker" aptly described his role at the enormous bank where he'd worked for years as supervisor of a busywork department. Why didn't he just say, "I'm with Shawmut Bank," offer our friend a genial smile, then get on with it? When I'm around, he tries too hard. My mother always used to explain, "He's jealous, Sam. Let's face it. He thinks you ended up with everything. He can't stand it that you always get what you want, have more money than he does, travel the world. He's like a little jealous kid, Sam. He'll never grow up."

Cliff must have been enraged by the magnificent scenery all around. He must have hated the idea that such landscapes, streaked with cypresses and dotted with olive trees, are mine to enjoy always, not just for a few special hours out of a whole lifetime.

On the second day, Cliff, looking for some sort of rise out of Danny, broke through his weak guard. "When I get home," he said, "I'm going to the opera with him." All at once, he was his awkward self again, showing where his mind had been as Danny lectured us on the distinctions between Romanesque and Gothic architecture.

"Going to the opera with who?" I asked.

Cliff pulled out a cigarette and held it between his creased, thick lips. Trying to light a stubborn wax match, he reddened and beamed at Danny over the secret the two of them shared.

in their apartment, holding a birthday cake. Only its top was covered with pink, too-liquid frosting which had dripped down, sloppily, along its swirling creases. Something about the cake's clumsiness informed the sadness I felt. I recognized it as Cliff's culinary work.

The nurse picked up Cliff's greenish, swollen arm and rubbed it as if to stimulate circulation. She looked at me, smiling. "Come," she said. I went to her and stood at Cliff's bedside. His face was jaundiced. His eyes were not quite shut, and what showed through the slits was yellowed and faceted like old pearls. I was told there were seven tubes going into his body.

The nurse left us alone with him. Danny broke down. He put his hand on the top of Cliff's head and ran his fingers through his hair.

The CCU intensive care unit had automatic double doors. You pushed a square-shaped aluminum plaque, and they opened fast, toward you, with a loud hydraulic whoosh. There was a small waiting room beside a window with a view to the Southeast Expressway, and this was where the three of us always sat, Danny, Fred, and I. Soon we knew by sight everyone who came and went—for the most part, wives visiting husbands who'd just suffered massive heart attacks. Cliff was the only AIDS patient in the ward, and this was quite unusual, we were told.

"I'm getting tested on Wednesday," Danny said, "but I have no great hopes. I'm sure I'm positive."

"But how are you feeling?" asked Fred. "Have you had any symptoms?"

"No," he said. "Nothing. Although right this minute I think I've got a sore throat coming on. I'm such a hypochondriac." He looked down and sighed. His face was ruddy and slack. I couldn't imagine how it must feel to know that the person you love the most in the world would be gone any day now, and that before long you, too, would be sick.

"We're all hypochondriacs, at this point," I said, having tried this theory out in my mind beforehand. I hated the way I sounded, so cautious, so discreet, yet something about Danny made me terrified of talking off the top of my head. "All we have to do is get a new pimple," I said, "and we freak out. That's how we all live these days, isn't it?"

"Have you guys taken the test?" Danny asked, raising his chin and peering at us beneath his swollen eyelids.

"No," said Fred. "When I asked our doctor if we should, he said, 'Don't bother.' Really, we've been together for years. Not only that, neither one of us has had the slightest symptom."

"We haven't had the flu," I said. "We don't even get colds."

Danny laughed reprovingly, almost spitting as his lips parted. "That's the worst sign," he said.

Suddenly, I felt a fleet pounding at my temples as cool moisture collected on my upper lip. My body heat rose. I grew light-headed and queasy as all my worries about Fred and myself came back, worries I'd done my best to suppress ever since I'd first learned of this disease. "What's the worst sign?" I said.

"Not getting colds or the flu," Danny said. His eyes were steely. "It means your antibodies are working overtime, fighting a losing battle. It's the worst sign there is."

For the next few days, Fred and I were sure we had it too.

Every morning Fred and I drove up from Newton to spend an hour or so with Meg in the nursing home. One time, we brought her a cup of ice cream from Rose Glen; another time, a stuffed tiger. The nurses knew we were in town, and dressed her up for company in clothes my aunt Kathy had bought her: permanently creased, synthetic-fiber pants, floral-print blouses, and colored glass beads like the ones little girls wear playing mommy. Meg's style has gone the way of her mind. She doesn't know where she is. She doesn't know who, in her life, is alive or dead. "What's Pepe doing this morning?" she said, asking for my great-grandfather.

On the wall of her room is a bulletin board where someone had pinned up a Mother's Day card. It said, "See you soon, Love, Cliff," and it made me think of all Cliff had done for her over the years, all the time he gave her, all the personal gifts that only someone close to her could have known how to buy: Polo shirts, espadrilles in hot pastels. Cliff guided Meg through a dozen fashion phases. Her favorite outfits were the ones he picked out. I always wondered if he didn't feel just a little silly in Filene's dress department browsing through the size fourteen racks, composing ensembles in his imagination, laying items out on the sofa by the changing room door. He dressed her the way he himself would have dressed had he been a woman. How many times had they shown up for a date together in embarrassingly similar outfits: the same pastel-colored Ralph Lauren Shetland sweater, his pants and her skirt of the same forest-green corduroy? Cliff loved Meg. He made up for my lack of attendance. He did more than both of us together could have done. He stayed with her through the worst of times, throughout the seventies even, when she was rarely sober—I remember Cliff telling me she was up to a size sixteen.

Our first day there, Fred and I got to the nursing home by ten. It was sunny and we wheeled her out into the courtyard where there were tables with umbrellas. I found a pair of dusty, lavender sunglasses in her bag, slipped them on her face, and positioned her in the sun. I could tell she thought she was at the beach. She pushed with her feet and set herself rolling off backward, doing a quarter turn, a girlish grin on her face.

We took her inside just as they'd begun distributing lunch trays. I spoon-fed Meg her ground breast of chicken, mashed potatoes, squash. I held the glass of milk to her lips as she drank. She looked forward to the ice cream we brought her. After each mouthful of whipped potato, she asked, "Where's the ice cream, Cliff? Is it still here?"

There was no point in correcting her when she called me Cliff. "It's right here, Meg," I said. "Don't worry."

"Well, where is it then?" she said, getting short, employing the familiar irritable tone she often took with Cliff, though never with me—I've always been too much of a stranger to her. "Show me where it is, Cliff!" she said, looking at her roommate's empty bed. "I don't trust that one!"

*   *   *

In the afternoon, Fred and I went in to visit Cliff—this was Fred's first time, and he cried as if he'd walked in on *me* dying there. Fred feels a deep closeness to everyone in my family, a natural sense of responsibility to them. "Call your mother," he always tells me, when he notices I haven't done it lately. "Call Cliff!" he used to say, every fifteen minutes, until I couldn't stand it anymore and called.

While Fred gazed at Cliff, silently, his hands clasped together, his head tipped as if in prayer, I went through the photo album Danny had left out on a table near the foot of Cliff's bed in order to show the doctors and nurses that "Cliff once had a life, that he isn't just another case, a medical statistic." It was all travel shots. There were pictures of the two of them posing before various famous landmarks in Rome, in Venice, in Florence, all taken when they visited Italy five years ago. But strangely, there were no pictures of Fred and me. There were no pictures of the farm where I work, or of the house Fred and I live in. But come to think of it, the whole time Cliff and Danny were with us, neither one of them ever pulled out a camera.

One afternoon, as Fred and I sat in the CCU waiting room—Danny was off getting a complete physical—a woman appeared. "I'm looking for the Beeler family," she said. She had neatly combed gray hair, and a blithe, public personality. When I told her I was Cliff's brother, she asked me to sign something. "Unless this information is released to your brother's insurance company," she said, "they will not be responsible for the bills."

I took the paper and read it over carefully. Fred read it too. My signature was to give hospital administrators the right to reveal the results of Cliff's HIV test, showing AIDS infection, to his insurance company. We agreed that this all sounded reasonable, and I signed. The woman thanked us and went into the unit.

"Let's not even tell Danny," Fred said. "He's upset enough without having to deal with things like this."

Danny arrived, weary and bent. His face was full of shadows. His shirt was wet with perspiration.

The double doors of CCU sprang open, and the woman we'd just seen came back out, heading to her office. She looked at Danny. "Are you a relative of Cliff's?" she asked.

"I'm his partner," Danny said.

"It's a legal matter," the woman said, holding up the paper I'd signed.

"I have power of attorney," Danny said.

She handed him the document. "Then you should see this too."

Danny read. His hands trembled. "But this is not true," he shouted. Angry, he tore the paper up. "This test can't be given without the patient's authorization, and no one has ever had that. Cliff has not taken any such test, and therefore, there are no such results. If the insurance company needs to know Cliff's condition, it is pneumonia. Pneumonia is the diagnosis, and nothing else. If you care to prepare a document with that on it, I'll be happy to sign, but this one, I'm afraid, is out of the question!"

The woman took the torn-up bits of paper and struggled to tear them up herself, into even smaller bits. "I'm sorry," she said, flustered, yielding. "I'm only the messenger, you see, doing what they've asked me to do. I'm so sorry."

I was thinking about the damage I'd almost done, and felt a great sense of relief that Danny had shown up just in time to stop it. He was doing a good job for Cliff, and he had a right to that job. We had no business going around him.

"You'd better wake up, Sam!" Danny said, once the woman was gone. His hands were open in his lap, and he wore a Band-Aid on each forearm. Veins darkened at his temples as he raised his voice. "You obviously don't know what's going on with the insurance companies and AIDS. After the first bout with something serious, they cancel, the fuckers. You should know this stuff." His hands grasped the chair arms and squeezed. His lips were purple. "There's a war going on out there, Sam," he said. "You'd better inform yourself, or you'll end up on the losing side."

"I really don't think he's going to make it," I told my aunt Kathy, who sometimes looks after my mother. "No one I've spoken to so far seems very optimistic."

She wept into the phone, and when she could, apologized for it. "I really don't think your mother needs to know," she said. "I think it would only set her back. Does she ask you where Cliff is?"

"Once in a while," I said. "But I change the subject, and she forgets she ever mentioned it. Besides, at this point, I think I represent both of us to her. She's put Cliff and me together in her mind and made us one son."

After hanging up, I wondered if Meg now attributed to me all of Cliff's kindness, the wraparound skirts, the birthday parties and Bundt cakes. I hoped not. I really didn't deserve this legacy of his.

The next day, I went to CCU alone as Fred did a few errands for the two of us.

Danny looked so small sitting there on the vinyl couch, his legs crossed knee over knee. "Sam," he said, "I've been meaning to talk to you about something." His voice was cracked and throaty.

"What's that?" I said.

He fortified himself with a full breath. "I just wanted to say I'm sorry," he said. His words seemed tapped out, staccato. For the first time ever, I sensed what must have been his inherent fondness for me, Cliff's brother.

"Sorry for what?" I asked.

"For jumping on you yesterday afternoon about that insurance thing." His voice was soft, new to me.

"Forget it," I said. "I forgot it."

"I'm sorry I was so tough," he said. "I'm all stressed out. Last night, lying awake, I realized I haven't been treating you very well and it made me feel like shit."

"Don't be silly," I said. "I made a dumb mistake."

"Well, it was an easy mistake to make," he said.

"I won't make it again," I told him. "Don't worry."

He got up to throw his cigarette butt in the men's room toilet, and when he came back, his eyes were full of deep thought. "You know," he said, "Cliff always believed he got the rotten end of the deal. Did you know that about him?"

"In a way," I said. "Maybe."

"He always wanted to compare his own life to yours, Sam. As far as he was concerned, your life was fabulous, while his was miserable. He always said your mother and father loved you more; everything they did was for you. If you wanted to go skiing, the whole family went skiing. Stuff like that. He'd always tell me I was the only good thing that ever happened to him. Imagine that? *Bullshit!* He had a *great* life. He really did. We had something special, your brother and I, something like what you and Fred obviously have. Cliff was happy." His eyes filled up. "He just didn't realize it, that's all."

Danny went into the unit to rewind the tape in Cliff's cassette player, and while he was gone I remembered something I hadn't thought about in years. When I was twelve and Cliff was fourteen, I got thrown out of a variety store for browsing through a little booklet of men in posing straps, or with their backs turned to the camera, completely nude and oiled. "I'm telling," Cliff said, once we got outside. "No, Cliff. Please," I said. "I'm telling," he said. "No. *Don't!*" I said. "All right then," he said, "but you're going to have to do everything I tell you to do. Everything. Otherwise I'm telling. Whenever I tell you to do something and you refuse, I'll say 'FBK,' Fact Be Known. All right? If you don't do what I say, I'll tell. You'd better get familiar with the term 'FBK,' Sam, 'cause you'll be hearing it a lot from now on."

Cliff held me in terror for a whole year as I took out the garbage on his nights, raked and mowed the lawn when it was his turn as well as my own, walked the dog in below-zero temperatures when he should have done it, put up the Christmas tree without his help, relinquished all rights to TV time, and let him take the best of everything. At least once a day, I heard him say "FBK," and at least once a day, I did what I was told.

Danny was gone a long time; he'd exceeded the ten-minute limit. He was the only visitor who walked right into CCU without announcing himself first. In the entire hospital, he was the only one who smoked; the doctors and nurses caught him in the act all the time, yet they let him get away with it.

A few minutes later, he came out. "He's listening to Barbara Cook," he said. "That is, Barbara Cook is singing in his ears." He sat down and smiled, reflecting. "You know what they said when I first went in there to see him? They said, 'Oh, here comes his father!' Can you imagine that? Even on his deathbed Cliff looks younger than I do, the son of a bitch!"

On the night table beside my mother's bed was a letter, written in pencil but not in her handwriting. A nurse must have helped her with it. It was written to her brother Brian, who died more than fifteen years ago.

"Dear Brian," it said. "We are all fine, mummy and pop. We miss you very much. Things are no fun when you're not here with us. Where are you? Are you still at the Point? I can't wait to have you home again, you and Sam..."

Dr. Bishop, the head man, showed up with Cliff's nurse, a young platinum blonde (an ingénue, Cliff would have said). Danny and I went with them to a place called the Quiet Room where we could talk in private.

The doctor spoke with easy clarity, and never once looked at his watch as he described Cliff's condition. They had made two unsuccessful attempts to "wean Cliff from the respirator." He was heavily sedated. They couldn't begin decreasing the respirator's function unless he was conscious, but both times they allowed him to come to, he panicked to see the condition he was in and ripped off tubes, even one sewn to his chest.

The biggest problem was Cliff's perforated lungs. Even if the doctors could get him off the respirator, which in itself seemed doubtful, it was clear his lungs would never heal.

"There is a decision which is going to have to be made," Dr. Bishop said, "and that decision is this: either we leave him as he is, attached to the respirator, and he goes on getting sicker and sicker until he just can't stay alive anymore—a week, ten days—or we heavily sedate him, remove the respirator, and just let him go off peacefully, making very sure he doesn't suffer in any way."

The nurse's eyes seemed to ache with the same sadness Danny and I felt. She had grown fond of Danny, and this was much less a professional duty she was doing than it was an offering of personal care. Her voice was low and steady. "We could do it in the evening," she said, "after visiting hours, when no one else is around. We'll bring some chairs into Cliff's room, and those of you who are close to him can gather there, and be with him as he goes."

I was crying now, and so was Danny, and there were tears in the nurse's eyes as she spoke.

"This is a decision I can't make," said Dr. Bishop. "Only you can do it. But keep in mind, it isn't a true decision at all. Not really. Don't give it too much significance. The outcome is a given here, and no decision any of us could ever make will change the circumstances as they are. There is nothing more we can do for Cliff, and what we have done, I assure you, is state of the art. Now I want you both to take your time and think this over, and when you're ready, we'll meet here again and you can tell me how you feel."

Danny and I joined up with Fred where he'd been waiting at CCU, and the three of us walked slowly to the elevators. I knew Fred had guessed what was going on. Danny was crying, but he struggled to keep silent. Fred put his arm around him. Danny made a choking sound. "Fred...please!" he said. "Please don't!"

The next day, Fred came with me to the Quiet Room. The two of us had thought hard, talked it over endlessly, and made our decision. We hoped Danny's decision was the same as ours.

Danny arrived with Dr. Bishop, the head nurse who met with us yesterday, and a friend of Danny's, a Jesuit in plain clothes. His presence seemed to make this moment a solemn one. A rite of passage had begun.

"First I will describe how I would like to see it happen," said Danny. "Then you can tell me your feelings, Sam." He had his briefcase on his lap, a notebook open on top of it, a pen in hand. "I would like to do it on Friday night. And then I would like to have his body cremated. In about a week's time, Father Bill here will say a memorial Mass at Wellesley, in the chapel. We'll invite everyone who loved Cliff to come and celebrate that with us. Cliff never wanted a wake or a funeral. We'll give him a celebration instead." Danny looked at me. "But there is something else," he said, "something very important to me, Sam. I just want you to feel that I have done the right thing, that's all. I want you to be able to go home feeling that I've done it right. O.K.?"

Out in the courtyard, in the sun, my mother asked me, "Where's Cliff?"

I thought for a minute. "I'll be seeing him tonight," I said. I would never lie to her.

"He brought me ice cream on Sunday," she told me. "He had the other one with him. What's his name? Oh I can't remember," she said. "I forget things at times."

"But there are lots of things you remember," said Fred, "aren't there?"

"Yup," she said, with confidence.

"Do you remember how to spell?" I asked.

"Course," she said.

"How do you spell *rhythm?*"

"R-h-y-t-h-m," she said.

"How do you spell *kerosene?*"

"K-e-r-o-s-e-n-e," she said. "Kerosene."

I was thinking, How can I keep her son's death from her?

"That's enough spelling," she said. "What's for lunch?"

"You just had lunch," I told her.

"I did?"

"Just a minute ago," I said.

"Funny," she said, "I don't remember that."

It was Friday night. Fred and I had an early dinner out, then showed up at CCU at about eight, as scheduled. Several of Cliff's friends were seated with Danny in Cliff's room, and had been there since four in the afternoon, "telling Cliff stories," as Danny said, "laughing and making a party out of it." A woman who worked with Cliff at the bank was there, two girls who once took a Caribbean cruise with Danny and him, the guy Cliff lived with before he met Danny nine years ago, Father Bill, and a few others. These were loyal friends; they loved Cliff. When Fred and I showed up, they all offered their condolences to me, before the fact, and some of them kissed Cliff on the forehead and said, "Goodbye, Cliff," before going down to the main lobby where they would wait until it was over.

Danny, Father Bill, Fred, and I stood just outside Cliff's door as Dr. Bishop removed the respirator; then we all went to Cliff's bedside.

Above Cliff's head was a monitor which showed the rate of his pulse. It was strong because he was young. Though deep, his breaths were uneven, since only one lung worked. Beside the regularly curving line shown on the monitor was the number 80. "When it gets down to sixty," the nurse explained, "it'll fall fast."

Danny held Cliff. For a while, he even lay beside him on the bed, and spoke to him, softly, as if Cliff understood.

At eleven, Cliff was still alive, but they assured us he wouldn't last long. I went out to the men's room, and on my way back into the unit, I found Danny just outside the double doors, taking a cigarette break. "He won't give up," he said, "the son of a bitch. You know, one thing you can say about your brother, he sure is a stubborn bastard."

I laughed. "Always was," I said.

As if to hide tears, he turned and looked out the window to the Expressway and the bumper-to-bumper traffic heading north for Memorial Day weekend. Beyond, in the carbon-blue sky over Logan Airport, planes lined up, descending. "Tell me, Sam," he said, his back to me. "Did you love him?"

I didn't hesitate to answer. "I did love Cliff," I said. Of course I did. Always.

"I'm glad you did," Danny said. "Because he loved you, Sam. He really did."

"I know," I said.

He fumbled for another cigarette. "I want to say something else," he said, "just one other thing. I want to say that I'm sorry, Sam."

"It's all right," I said. "It really is, Danny."

"No," he said, "I owe you an apology. I had this idea about you and Fred that was really all wrong. You two are damn decent guys. I'm sorry, I really am."

"Never mind," I said. "Come on, let's go back."

At quarter to twelve, Cliff's pulse rate fell to sixty. Danny picked up Cliff's head and held it in his arms, and wept with his whole body as he said Cliff's name.

Fifty. Forty. Twenty. Father Bill put his hand on Danny's shoulder, and bowed his head in prayer. My head was splitting from all the tears I'd cried. I watched the monitor, and so did Fred: 15, it said, and then, 00. The line of green light was flat now but for a few tiny bumps, like straggling foothills where the ground levels out to plain.

Dr. Bishop came in and put his stethoscope to Cliff's wrist. "He's passed away," he said, in the softest voice. "There is a trace of heartbeat, but it isn't doing anything. He has no pulse." He turned off the monitor, and it went dark.

When Danny let go of Cliff's body, his weeping stopped. He stood up, and I went to him. I threw my arms around him—it wasn't only Danny I held there; it was Cliff, too. As I lay my head against his he brought me close with his own arms. When he loosened his hold on me to break away, I didn't let go.

My mother admired our suits. But she didn't ask where we were going so dressed up, and I didn't tell her we were on our way to her son's memorial Mass.

We'd walked in on the "Feeding Program": the nurses and order-lies bring a bunch of the patients to a sunny reception room at the end of the corridor, and spoon-feed them their lunches there. Meg seemed to like this arrangement. One day, after giving her lunch myself in her room, I took her for a little spin. "What's going on in there?" she said, when we got to the end of the hall.

10

AMONG THE SAVED

I'm finally getting around to the pile of mail we found on the kitchen table when we got in. Tearing the ends off envelopes, I'm eating raspberries one by one. Two years ago, Fred and I put in our own personal raspberry patch, and it's full of fruit this June, fruit that Fred can't pick because he's color blind; *daltonico,* the Italians say, referring to John Dalton—as if he were the first man in history who couldn't see reds against greens. On the flight back from Boston, when I wasn't thinking about Cliff's death and all we'd just been through, I thought about our raspberries. I pictured their millions of tiny drupelets ripened crimson. I couldn't wait to get to them.

Fred is on the phone to the Istituto dei Fanciulli, an orphanage in Florence. "I was given your number by the archdiocese," he says, in Italian. "I'd like to help out the kids. I'm a music teacher, and I have a couple of free afternoons a week. Do you need a volunteer?"

Fred's been talking for months about getting involved in something like this. Years ago, while studying in Chicago, he taught violin to underprivileged kids. Last fall, we went to a recital given by one of his former students; it was an inspiring night for all of us. Fred is not a real career musician; playing the violin is a job he does, and does well, but he doesn't have dreams of becoming a great soloist, he seldom talks of furthering his studies, and he doesn't practice any harder than he has to. He misses teaching, though mostly he misses kids and that unique kind of affection only kids can give.

"English?" he says. "No, I've never taught English. But maybe I could manage. I mean, I don't see why not."

I'm holding a letter from a friend who lives in San Francisco. Attached to it is the obituary of an acquaintance, a well-known architect. These deaths are routine in our lives now; we stopped counting at fifty. When we learn of them, we're sad, then angry, then accepting, then resolute. The newspaper article from the *Chronicle* says he "passed away, at the age of 47, after a long illness." They don't say AIDS had anything to do with it—everyone is still so reserved about that. At my brother's memorial service the other day, a friend of his made this announcement: "We're asking that contributions be sent to a fund set up in Cliff's name at the New England Conservatory of Music." I glanced over at Fred when she said that, and there was a look of total disbelief in his eyes, just as I knew there would be—Fred had been boldly telling everyone to give to AmFAR.

He's off the phone now. "News?" he says, going for the berries, then bending to read over my shoulder.

"Charlie Laird died," I tell him, handing him the obituary with Charlie's picture, the smiling face we hardly knew.

"Yeah. Well, we saw that coming." He nods and shrugs, chewing. "Tart one," he says. "Do you like them like that?"

"So what did they tell you at the Istituto?" I say.

He seems to want to check his smile, as if I'd object to his feeling good. For some reason, he thinks I *disapprove* of his helping out the orphans. That's not exactly right. I approve of it for him, but not for me. If he wants to work with kids, that's fine. It's just that I don't want to work with kids, and I don't want Fred pushing me into it.

"I'm going there Monday afternoon before rehearsal," he says. "They're real interested. They don't have anybody. In fact, they've been looking for a volunteer to give the kids a hand with their English homework. I don't have to teach violin; I don't care. I just want to be with them." His face takes on a thoughtful cast. "I want to change their lives," he says, nodding (Fred's a nodder). "That's what I really want to do."

"Well great," I say, picking up the phone bill.

"I'm pleased," he says, setting free his smile: it's a wide one. "You're not, though, are you, Sam?"

"Sure I am," I say.

"I can tell you're not," he says. "It's written all over your face."

"Do we have to talk about it now?" I say, my good mood gone less good—I can't bear his telling me I feel one way when I'm sure I feel another.

"No," he says, "we don't have to talk about it now." He bows his head in silence, then carefully opens a letter from his parents.

One thing Fred and I do not have in common is this fondness for children. When I was a small boy, I felt at ease in their company, but this security of mine was as short-lived as summer. I was particularly outgoing then, like my mother, always ready to ham it up, put on a one-man show. I liked mugging, singing made-up songs, doing imitations of everyone around me, entertaining.

But then things changed.

One day in the third grade, Sister Saint Edmund had a few minutes to kill before the bell and she said, "Does anyone want to get up in front of the class and tell a story?" They all looked at each other for a while, shrugging, till I rose. "Master Beeler?" Sister said, her right arm curling out ceremoniously. I had on a three-button sleeveless sport coat, white shirt, and pretied bow tie mounted on an elastic strap. My face was still brown from the beach, and my shaved head was a golden burr. Facing fifty kids who, as far as I knew, loved me as much as my mother did—what reason did they have not to?— I told them about a dream I'd had.

I remember, even today, what that dream was all about: my visit with a witch, a good witch who had a white castle on a hilltop. I remember describing the misty, humid atmosphere of her kingdom where puffy racks of color sailed through the air like clouds. I showed the class how her body moved, draped in cumbersome velvets. I imitated her voice, her odd accent, and I told them what she'd said to me word for word—I'd had that dream only the night before and I remembered it as precisely as I would have a movie I'd just seen. But halfway into the story, I saw that my audience's response wasn't quite what I'd expected it to be. Some of the boys were mocking me, ridiculing. A wave of hatred turned quickly over the class, and by the time it crested and broke in my face, I'd made close to thirty enemies, the most aggressive of whom would torment me right up until graduation day five years later. "Fairy," "fruit," and "Dilla Marie" were the names they had for me as they yanked out my bow tie and let it snap back so it smacked me in the throat like a karate chop. I can still see their mean young faces now. "What a *fruit* you are, Beeler!" they'd say, circling clear of me in the schoolyard as if I were a leper. Kids are cruel; in my book, they have very little to recommend them.

I put in a few hours of work this afternoon and accept condolences all around, from the cellar manager, from the men who tend the vines, from the women in the bottling plant, from Baron Gozzini's thirteen-year-old son, Carlo, who, in Day-Glo spandex, washes his mountain bike by the farm shed. It's hard to know how to respond when these people say they're sorry. I just say, "*Grazie*," and lower my eyes. My lips open to an ironic smile, that of patient acquiescence, universally understood.

Baron Gozzini is in Milan tending to the business that keeps us all in groceries here, but his wife is in residence. She calls the *cantina*, looking for me: "Can you come at six? For a drink?"

There are workmen all over the villa: plumbers, electricians, carpenters. The Gozzinis' New York cousins will be paying their biennial visit this summer and the baronessa, who prefers to be called Elena, is renovating a bedroom for them. "Americans have to have everything just so," she says, "don't they?"

She has a houseguest at the moment, her elderly aunt who lives in Crans-sur-Sierre. The aunt speaks to me in English. "Where are you from?" she says—I'm not sure if she really has the language, or if this is just a phrasebook line so often repeated she's got it down pat.

"*É di Boston,*" Elena says, making a Brahmin of me with her high tone.

"A lovely town," says the aunt. "I haven't been there in thirty-five years. How must it be like nowaday?"

"Changed," I say, "like everyplace."

The three of us go into a small sitting room off the great hall. Generations of Gozzinis have spent countless hours of leisure here. There's a backgammon board set up on a baroque card table by the window. There are magazines and gardening books, in different languages, arranged in neat stacks on a console. Dozens of cigarette packs, every brand imaginable, are displayed in a porcelain bowl as if they were a prized collection of shells. The room has a painted ceiling, cracked all over like parched soil: fantasy birds, against a mauve sky, dive at red apples and yellow pears blown free of their trees in an autumn wind.

"Will you have a whiskey?" Elena asks. Her hand is on the ice bucket she obviously brings out whenever there are Anglos around—Italians don't drink cocktails.

"Whiskey, no," I say. "A glass of wine?"

She opens a tepid bottle of our own Sauvignon. It is pearly in color and has a fresh, living taste. "We owe this quality to Sam," Elena says, offering a glass to her aunt, who sips, savors it contemplatively, then nods her approval.

"I understand you lost your brother," says the aunt.

"Yes," I say.

"I am sorry," she says. "Was it quite sudden?"

"Yes and no," I say. "He'd been ill for some time."

"And he was very young," says Elena, "wasn't he?" She is leaning against the marble mantel, a portrait of her husband's great-grandfather in a snug blue military uniform high above her blond head. "And what was the cause of it, Sam? I don't believe I know."

I have the sense that Elena can handle the truth. We've had many frank conversations since I took this job five years ago. She reads *La Repubblica* every day, and I imagine she shares their nonaccusatory point of view about AIDS. "Well," I say, "he…it was AIDS, actually."

She lifts her chin and her lips part. It's as if, in a dark room, her eyes have suddenly adjusted and she sees what she already knew to be there. But I'm sure this is the closest AIDS has come to her. She sits down in a velvet chair across from me, leaning out, then looks me in the eye. "I'm very sorry, Sam," she says. The way she says my name, it sounds like "some."

I nod, and glance at the aunt. She wears a fixed, dignified smile; an aristocrat, nothing will shock or disturb her.

"I've lost dear ones too," Elena says. "My little sister, when she was in her twenties. We emerge very changed afterward, don't we? When someone we love passes on, it brings us closer to God." I've often looked out my bedroom window at nine o'clock on Sunday morning, as the bells in the tower peal out their last frenzied call, to see Elena rushing, sometimes with her son, sometimes alone, across the bridge to Mass. "Isn't it true, Sam?" she asks me. "We know more now, don't we?"

"I've been thinking a lot about faith these days," I say. "We have to believe that this life comes to something in the end, don't we? If not, then what? It's all so pointless." I sit back and gaze into the radiator's dusty rungs, then briefly lose consciousness of Elena and her aunt, of where I am. My mind is on Fred's idea that "life is a dirty trick; you have it, then it's gone." For him, the only hereafter is what you leave behind on earth.

"*I* have faith," Elena says, as if to summon me back. Her eyes are distorted beyond thick glasses; they seem to have a patina to them.

"Yes," I say, "I know. That's why I'm telling you this now."

"Nothing is more stupid," Elena says, almost angry, "than the atheist point of view, the idea that there is no more to life than this table"—she touches the table—"this chair"—she touches the chair—"this box of cheese snaps." She opens it and offers me one.

A couple of years ago, on an overcast fall morning, Fred came to me in the garden with this: "Sam," he said, "can we adopt a kid?"

I wasn't looking at him; I was troweling over the dirt around a kumquat in a terra-cotta pot. All at once, I went tense, consumed by a kind of hopelessness.

Fred would stand there as long as it took for some reasonable reply. I went to the next potted plant in silence, then, digging, glanced down at his feet shod in those funny-looking Dr. Scholl's wooden clogs that help his bad back.

"Well?" he said.

"Oh come on, Fred," I finally said.

"Come on, what?" he said. "What do you mean *come on?*"

"Fred," I said, "who's going to give a child to two men? Think of all the eligible childless couples out there who want to adopt kids and can't because they just can't get them. Where do you think *we're* going to get one?"

"They're giving babies to men nowadays," he said. "Ever hear of the actor Davie Dancer? He's important in this movement. He's adopted a baby."

"And so who takes care of it?" I said. "A baby with no mother? Babies need mothers, Fred."

"He'd have something better than a mother," Fred said. "He'd have two fathers; two fathers who could give him a lot. How many people are capable of giving a kid as happy a home as we've got? This is a beautiful place we live in. Think of what a good job we'd do educating him. We'd send him to college in the States."

"And for parents' weekend?" I said. "What do you think about that? How do you think a college kid is going to feel when his parents show up for parents' weekend and it's us? Don't you think that's something a college kid might have trouble with?"

"Why?"

"Why?" I said. "Because everybody else has regular parents, and this kid's got *us!*"

"And so what's wrong with us?" Fred said. "I think we're pretty great myself. I don't think there's anything wrong with us—"

"I don't want to adopt a kid," I said, impatient.

He hung back, pacing, his palms spread flat on the small of his back, his elbows out. "Is it that you don't want to *adopt* a kid," he said, "or that you don't want a kid, *period?*"

"Well, if I wanted a kid," I said, "I'd want my own, not somebody else's. Even though you bring it up and you educate it and whatnot, it's never really yours."

"So why don't we have a kid of our own?"

"How can you stand there and ask me a question like that?" I said. "Have a kid of our own! Do you know what you're saying, Fred?"

"We could find a mother," he said. "People are doing that now. Don't you read the papers? Women who need the money will carry and deliver. It's a service. The child is your own because you've supplied the sperm."

I walked away at this point, exhausted by these bizarre ideas of his. I took my trowel back to the garden shed, then found some other mindless chore with which to angrily pass the remaining hours of the morning.

At lunchtime, I looked into the sitting room and saw Fred reading there by the light of a tall converted church candlestick. I wondered how angry he was with me, how depressed and lonely he was. As I stood there in the doorway he raised his eyes from the pages of his book, but there wasn't a clue in his face as to how he felt, or what was on his mind.

Later, in the kitchen, as I filled a pot of water for pasta he handed me a piece of blue stationery covered with his awkward, childlike script. "I've written to Davie Dancer," he said. "Maybe he can help. Do you want to read it?"

"Not right now," I said. "Do you mind?"

"No, I don't mind," he said, licking the envelope and sealing it.

Days went by, and I didn't hear another word about adoption; it seemed as if he'd finally come to his senses and given up the idea. He got busy with a spate of concerts at the Teatro Comunale, and then a friend of his from the University of Chicago visited with his new wife, and we had a dinner party for them. A group of East European musicians came to town on tour and Fred spent a week showing them around. He brought them out here to the *fattoria* and

we had a pleasant evening with them drinking wine and eating typi-
cal food in a local restaurant, then sitting around our kitchen table
chatting for hours. But then one day we suddenly found ourselves
alone—no dinner invitations, no parties, friends out of town. Adoption talk started up again as Fred longingly awaited the mail, hoping
for that response from Davie Dancer with tips on how to become a
father, the letter that never came.

On Sundays Fred and I often take a drive. We go to some country
village, new to us, where there's an Early Christian church to visit, or
a monastery with baroque frescoes, open to the public, or a villa
with a famous garden, marble statuary in a parterre, and gravity-
driven waterworks. I'm drawn to these dream settings in which Fred
and I move silently about, briefly exalted; I'm assembling, in my
memory, a collection of moments spent in such places which seem to
take the form of episodes in our lives.

Today I want to find this old monastery we've been hearing
about—a tiny one, where no more than six or eight monks once
lived. It was purchased a year or so ago (as a total ruin) by two men
from London. After several months of construction, and a lot of
money spent, they've apparently changed their minds about living
abroad and want to sell. I'm interested. The furnished apartment we
live in comes with my job; it's not ours and never will be. It's small,
we have very little privacy, and it's a long commute to Florence for
Fred. For months now, we've talked about buying a place of our
own, but something always gets in the way of our looking.

The monastery isn't too far from here; it's in Colinetta, midway
between our two jobs, near Carmignano, in the hills west of Florence. We have a vague idea as to how to get there, since an electri-
cian friend of ours who worked on the place, and who's very
impressed with it, has described its setting to us in detail.

Fred agrees that this is how we should spend our first Sunday
back, yet I somehow have the sense that he'd rather do something
else (who knows what?), that he's going along with my plan just to
make me happy. I don't let on that I suspect he feels this way, maybe

because I'm afraid he'll say, "You're right, I don't want to go out," and then I'd have to say, "O. K,. let's stay in." After the sadness of Cliff's death, I want us to reward ourselves with a nice lunch at Da Delfina, with the short, idyllic drive back, and then a nap. I need to feel the road air in my face. I want to reaffirm the promise Fred and I made to each other flying home the other day: to enjoy life, unremittingly.

We're on a steep, unpaved road, making our way through a pine wood; cooler air, left behind by the night, still lingers in trees where white-winged moths dive and rise, drawing graphlike waves. Once in a while, we pass a stone farmhouse where a mama, dressed for Sunday (but with an apron on), straightens up, curious, to watch us pass, her arms around a basket of bitter greens.

We have a few new tapes Fred picked up in Boston: Joni Mitchell; Joan Baez; Peter, Paul and Mary. He's nostalgic for his Chicago "coffeehouse days," for Tom Rush and Tim Buckley, whose tapes he couldn't find. He puts on Tim Harden and breaks the silence of his gloomy mood: "Bought myself a red balloon, got a blue surprise. Hidden in the red balloon ..." He sings along, sotto voce.

Higher up, the road splinters off into capillaries. I choose a direction that feels right. Coming to a spring where an old man in a beret fills his straw-covered demijohn, I stick my head out. "Colinetta?" I ask. "The Englishmen's convent?"

"Yes, yes," the man says, "*più avanti*."

We round a curve, then pass through a dark cleft in the hillside. Fred presses his hands together between his knees. He's been moody ever since he called the orphanage on Friday. He's convinced that I, above all, stand in the way of his having kids. Sometimes, when the parenting urge hits, he airs this grievance, blaming me that he's unfulfilled, but other times, like today, he just falls silent, turned in upon his loneliness.

"Why is it, Fred," I say, "that when I'm driving, you're my passenger? You're my passenger in every sense of the word. But when *you're* driving, I'm not yours."

"I'll always be your passenger," Fred says. "Even if I drive. That's the way it is because that's the way you have to have it." He feels I rule our lives with an iron fist. He calls me "the colonel."

"But that's not really the way I want it," I say. "I don't want you to be my passenger. I want us to be copilots."

"We only do the things you want to do," he says. "We always have."

"Well, *you* never have any ideas for things," I say, not accusingly; playfully.

He snickers. He's familiar with this joke of mine.

"I'm the one with the ideas," I say. "And you like the ideas I have. Like the trip to Naples, for instance. You didn't want to go, remember? I had to force you every step of the way. But then once we got there, you loved it. You loved it even when those cute kids stole the sunglasses right off your face. You hated to leave."

He's silent, bouncing as we dip in and out of deep potholes. I wonder if he thinks it's me shaking him up, not the bumps in the road, that I have him by the shoulders and I'm jouncing him for all he's worth. I want to reach over and touch him gently, but I know he's not in the mood for that. He'd probably say, "There you go petting me again like an old pooch. Sit! Stay! Be good!"

We spot the monastery high up on a green promontory—its four windows across, the apse of its chapel, its medieval bell tower—and after a short drive along a weedy lane, we're there.

The site is littered with construction debris, empty paper sacks, piles of rubble, broken bricks, fractured stones. There's a sky-blue cement mixer and a skid of antique floor tiles, freshly cleaned.

No one's around, so we park and get out. Serins chirp and flutter in an ivy-choked cherry tree. Distant Vinci shimmers in the rising heat, and we can make out San Miniato through the haze.

By an arched stone portal is a *Vietato Accesso* sign, but we ignore the order and walk right into a walled courtyard where there's a persimmon tree, an electric cord entwined in its lower branches. Looking around, I see what this garden could be, not what it is in its current messy state. I imagine geometric shapes drawn out with box hedges encircling a fountain that must have once been here. I imagine santolina, lavender, flowering rosemary alive with bees. I imagine Fred and myself living in this monastery as if on permanent retreat, all worldly goods, but for a few essentials, left behind with the rest of life's weary loads.

Fred is a few steps ahead. He turns around to face me, his hands in his pockets. "I want it," he says.

I was about to climb into the house through an open window, but I stop, one leg in the air. "You want it?" I say.

"Yes," he says.

"Funny you're thinking that," I say. "So do I. It's fantastic, this place!"

"I don't even have to see the rest," he says, excited. "It's perfect! Not too big. Not too small."

I know his imagination is busy converting monks' cells into bedrooms for those several adopted sons and daughters we'd one day have.

It's seven-thirty in the morning and we're picking raspberries before I go off to work. Fred has a ceramic bowl and I have a colander. My colander is twice as full as Fred's bowl, yet I pick only from the sections he's already covered. It must be weird not to be able to see red against green. I wonder if Fred has ever seen red at all, if he has any idea what red really is, or any other color for that matter. His chromatic perception is so confused that he sees all human skin as green, just as he does my sandy blond hair. Fred has red hair. Once, when I said to him, "How you doin', Red?" he said, "Fine, Green." We were out in the car one day driving past a familiar farmhouse as two painters busily brushed an uninteresting shade of green over its faded ocher facade. "Oh what a shame," Fred said. "I'd always loved that pink!"

"They've been remodeling," he says, talking about the Istituto, which he visited for the first time yesterday afternoon. "They're moving walls, bricking up windows. There's dust everywhere, and nobody to clean it up. It's the filthiest place I've ever seen in my

life. The floors are black in the corners. Conditions are unbelievable.
They don't have any toilet seats. There's only one shower."

"For how many orphans?" I ask, my mouth full of fruit.

"Eleven."

"Gosh," I say.

"They're not really *orphans*," he says. "Most of them have parents,
but they're either drug addicts or nuts or prostitutes; stuff like that.
Some of them are even in jail. But it's amazing—these are nice kids.
They're nice-looking, and they're smart."

"So you've met them already," I say. A scarab beetle, couched on
the berry I go for, takes to the air heavy as a cargo helicopter.

"I met with four of them," he says. "I helped them with their
English homework for an hour or so before rehearsal. One of them is
this boy from Parma who's in hiding. His name is Ennio. Isn't that a
nice name?"

"Hiding from what?"

"From his father."

"How come?"

"He's a drug addict. He used to make Ennio steal for him so
he could buy drugs. They say that if Ennio went back there, his
father would probably kill him. He's killed before, this guy. Incredible, isn't it?"

"Boy," I say. I picture Fred hunched over, blood-spattered, and
dead in the back seat of our Fiat Uno, four bullet-riddled doors gap-
ing. "Think of it!" I say. "What's he like, the boy?"

"He's really nice," he says. "He's about fourteen." He grins; he's
finally got kids to be with, and he's thrilled.

"Nice age," I say.

He watches me pull six or eight deep red beauties out from
behind a leaf. "You mean I missed all those?" he says. "I don't
believe it. I give up."

In the kitchen, we cover our muesli with huge piles of raspberries,
then pour on the milk. "You know," I say, "that's about twenty thousand lira worth of fruit right there. What luxury!"

"We can bring cuttings of these bushes up to Colinetta," Fred says—we've already contacted the sellers in London and made a verbal offer. There's a deal in the works; we're sure of it.

Fred sips his tea. "It's perfect," he says. "It's just what I wanted."

"Colinetta?" I say.

"That too," he says. "But I'm talking about the orphanage—I mean the foster care center. I'm working there two afternoons a week to start, but I'd like to spend a little time with them on weekends, too. Ennio hasn't been out in eight months, except to go to school. Nobody cares about him. Nobody cares about any of them. It makes me very sad to think of it." His eyes go instantly heavy with unshed tears. We both cry so easily now after Cliff's death; we cry for no reason at all, at least once a day; anything provokes it.

This is precisely what I was afraid of: weekends with the kids. I like our weekends as they are. I like the drives the two of us take; I like having a few friends in for lunch. There's a big change in the air with this new activity of Fred's. "Weekends?" I say, making a face. "You want to bring them around on weekends?"

"Well of course I do," he says. "I don't want to just see them in that filthy place. Of course I want to bring them around here. Kids love the country."

I can't believe this. The absurdity of such an idea. "Wait a minute, Fred," I say. "I'm sorry, but I don't want any part of this stuff. You don't seem to understand. I'm just not the type to adopt orphans."

"I'm not talking about *adopting* them," he says, getting angry.

"Well, spending time with kids, then; you know what I mean. It takes a certain personality. You have that personality, Fred. That's fine. O.K.? But I don't. I just don't, and that's that."

"You do too," he says. "Kids love you, Sam."

"They do not," I say. "They hate me."

He laughs. "Come on, Sam," he says. "You could show them around the *cantina*, explain how wine is made. They'd be fascinated. It'd be great for them."

I draw in a deep, equalizing breath. "Look, Fred," I say. "Can't you just do this on your own? Put in your two afternoons a week and be happy? Why do you have to bring me into it?"

"Because you're here," he says, giving me a warm look of appreciation for the generous thing I haven't done and will never do.

I spend the morning supervising the installation of our new cold-stabilization plant. When I get back to the apartment, Fred's at the kitchen table thumbing through a small paperback book with the word "*Inglese*" on its cover in red, white, and blue print.

He reads aloud. "'My lady cousin came to see me yesterday in the country with her little boy, who was delighted to see so many birds and other animals: the oxen, the dogs, the geese, the cart horses, and my little gray ass on which I ride.'" He screws up his face.

I laugh. "What *is* that anyway?" I say.

"I'm learning how to teach English," he says. "Very successful book. It's the eighth edition." He reads on. "'Today is such a fine day; let us go with all the children for a long walk. We shall take the road leading for the woods; it is still early and we have time enough to go till the top of the hill before noon.'" He looks at me, smiling.

"Do we *have* to?" I say.

Ennio has grown fond of Fred. On Thursday Fred took him out to a pharmacy and bought him dental floss. "Is this a weird thing to be doing?" he asked himself en route. Ennio apparently has beautiful teeth but he doesn't take care of them; he never brushes and they're always stuffed with wads of bread and jots of parsley. Back at the Istituto, Fred gave several of the kids a lesson in dental hygiene, showing them how to slip the floss down around the base of a tooth, drawing it back and forth "the way you dry your bum with a towel."

"You'd like Ennio," Fred says. "He plays the piano by ear: Debussy and Ravel, things he's heard on the radio. There's this fantastic old organ in the chapel that has to be hand-pumped. A little boy who looks like one of the Marx brothers stands there and pumps the thing while Ennio plays. Can you picture that? I want to start Ennio on some piano lessons soon. He's ready."

Yesterday afternoon, Ennio opened up to Fred. He's miserable at the Istituto. He has no friends at the nearby school he goes to, because he's short, talks with a Parma accent, and to make matters worse, lives in a home. The boys in his class never invite him to play soccer with them. They don't invite him to their birthday parties or to their homes for visits. He's lonely and depressed. He spends weekends in bed, only getting up to eat. He lives in constant fear of his father—he's sure he's going to find him and take him out of school. His life is useless, pointless, he feels. He cried when he told Fred these things. Instinctively, Fred wants to save him. "He's my favorite," Fred says.

Even before breakfast, Fred's on the phone to everyone we know who has kids Ennio's age; he wants to find him friends. He calls Vivian, an Englishwoman who has three daughters and a son. "The poor boy," Fred explains, "these young Florentines won't give him the time of day. You know how closed they are. Ennio wants to learn English. I think he'd learn fast. I think your Jamie would like him." A lot of silent nodding ensues. "*Ciao,*" Fred finally says, and hangs up.

"What did she say?" I ask.

"She said, 'You mustn't forget, Fred, my kids are *very* sophisticated!'"

"What's that supposed to mean?" I say.

"It's supposed to mean no, I guess," he says, taking the rejection personally.

He walks to work with me today, as he occasionally does—he likes the people on my staff, and hasn't seen them since we got back. I want to show him the impressive new equipment Baron Gozzini has just purchased, the refrigerated vats that will make all the difference in the world to our whites.

Elena, wearing a linen suit and a pair of Wellingtons, is in the vegetable garden out by the *cantina.* She stops what she's doing and comes to us, clutching a bunch of radishes like a bride's nosegay. "A double pleasure," she says.

In a minute Fred's telling her about the Istituto.

"I think it's a wonderful thing you're doing," Elena says. "You'll see, the rewards will be far greater than the effort you make."

"The rewards are coming in already," Fred says. "These kids have so much love to give, and they're giving it to *me*. It's wonderful."

"I think you should be very proud," Elena tells him. "Don't you think so, Sam?"

"Yes, I do," I say. I imagine Fred sees this as a social lie.

"We should *all* be so charitable," Elena says. "The world is full of people who need help, of souls to be saved. I admire you."

Fred tells her Ennio's story. "He's a nice boy," he says, "very gentle and well-mannered. He needs friends who understand. I was wondering about your Carlo. They're the same age. I don't know how to ask this. Do you think Carlo would like a friend?"

He's put Elena on the spot. Her courtly smile collapses with a faint quiver, and she looks away. "It's a difficult moment for Carlo, just now," she says. "He's studying for exams. He already has tennis, then football practice three days a week. And now he's just joined this mountain bike club."

Fred nods. "Oh," he says, quietly disappointed.

Elena looks at me, then back at Fred. "Carlo's far too busy," she says, guiltily. "It's a *momentaccio*. I'm afraid your boy will have to look elsewhere for this companionship."

I glance over at Fred. It seems to me that his eyes are filling up again, but I'm not sure. Perhaps it's just a trick of morning glare; or are his eyes just generally more liquid now after Cliff's death, after all the tears we shed at his bedside? I wonder when this fragile period of ours will pass, or if it ever will.

"I told him, Cut it the way you want. Give me something crazy." He turns around to show me the back, how it's shaved up the neck, then gets long, abruptly, at the crown. It's the haircut lots of kids are getting these days, but not too many men Fred's age. "What do you think?" he says.

"It's neat," I say. "It's nuts."

"Is it awful?" he asks. "No, really."

"It's awfully crazy," I say. "It's weird. It's lunatic. I like it."

"Oh thanks," he says. "I wasn't sure you would."

"Turn around again," I say.

He turns around. His nape is whiskery below a wide tuft that falls like a droopy paintbrush. I'm not so sure I like it, after all. I don't understand why Fred would want such a haircut. "*Mamma mia*," I say.

"You think it's silly," he says.

"I think it's kinky," I say. "Kinky and...kinky."

He's poking his fingers through his scalp, scratching. "Do I have cooties?" he says.

"Of course you don't have cooties," I say.

"Well, I might," he says. "This boy Sauro goes home every weekend to his father who beats the shit out of him, and when he comes back, he's got head lice. They have to wash him with this medicinal shampoo, but it doesn't do any good. The kid goes home a few days later, and he's back on Monday with cooties and a black eye."

"Well, why do they send him home?" I ask. "Can't they keep him there?"

"I guess not," he says. "They turn him over to the old bastard every Friday afternoon. You should see this boy. His face is all wrinkles. Wrinkly skin. I asked the director about it; I said, How come all the wrinkles on the kid's face? I mean, he's ten years old. She said that he was a new arrival and that's the way they all look when they first get there."

"Wrinkly faces?" I say.

"Apparently," he says. "Don't ask *me!* But that's what she said."

The phone rings. I answer, and it's Vivian, the Englishwoman with the "sophisticated" kids. This call is for Fred, but she doesn't ask to speak to him; she talks to him through me. "I thought Fred should bring his children up to my apartment Saturday night to see a video," she says. "My two girls will be there, but I won't; I'll be in Paris with Jamie. I've invited my three nephews to join you, so I think you should all have a lovely time watching *To Have and Have Not* and making friends. Just tell Fred to show up with them at seven, would you, Sam. I'll have it all arranged. Little things to eat, tea and what have you. O.K.?"

It's Saturday morning and we're at the monastery. Word got to us, through an agent, that the sellers will accept our offer (with a few modified terms), so it looks as though we'll be making our *compromesso* soon, taking the first formal step toward a final purchase agreement. Fred and I are excited and a bit unnerved; neither of us has ever owned a home before.

We're sitting in the car waiting for the agent who's meeting us here for a final viewing.

"They were all mad as hell yesterday," Fred says (his mind is only on the Istituto these days). "Sauro peed into the bottle of distilled water in the laundry room, and the laundress ironed the dishcloths with it."

"He's the boy with the wrinkly face?" I ask.

"Yeah," Fred says. "You should see him *now*. Patrizia, the one girl there, got a hold of this black hair dye. First she dyed her own hair, then she did three of the boys. They all look ridiculous. I told her, 'Patrizia, I really don't like your hair like that.' I had to be honest. And now Sauro's got this wrinkly face and dyed black hair—can you picture it?"

"No," I say.

"He's a weird boy. He wants to be a goat. All his drawings have goats. They had a state psychologist in to check him out. After his interview, the psychologist went to the director and said, 'What's this with all the goats?' She said, 'Don't ask me, you're the psychologist!' Took *me* to find out his father's a goatherd. Sauro grew up sleeping with them. Used them as pillows."

"No wonder he's got a wrinkly face," I say.

"Anyway," Fred says, "you'll be meeting him tonight."

We've been arguing this point for the past three days. I don't want to go to Vivian's video thing; this is not my idea of a Saturday evening well spent. "No I *won't* be meeting him tonight," I say. "I don't know what I'll be doing, but I *won't* be meeting Sauro."

All at once he's angry. "Sam!" he shouts. "*Why?*" He pounds his open palms on the steering wheel and it rings through the dash, a plangent plea. "*Why* do you have to be like this?"

I open my door and feel a rush of cool air on my ankles. "Why do you force me to do things I don't want to do?" I say. I hear my speech take on those pissed-off tones that irritate the hell out of Fred. I've become so furious now, I just want to go home. I stew for a minute in silence, then gush: "I don't want to get involved with the kids, Fred! I've told you this time and time again. Why do you have to put such pressure on me? Why do you push and push? Why can't this be something you do on your own? Why do you have to drag *me* into it?"

I get out of the car, slam the door, and make my way to the house. My arms folded, my head bent, I see only the square yard of ground where my next step falls upon shards of terra-cotta, rusted screws, the frail running stems of morning glories and their pathetic, pale flowers.

In the walled courtyard, I'm waist-deep in weeds that weren't quite calf height two weeks ago when we first came here: ensnaring weeds, blue-flowered thistle, bending, grasping. I'm planning my escape from Fred, from the children, from the stratagem of family life. I see myself standing at the threshold of an arched stone portal, looking into the unfamiliar space beyond that is absolute solitude, black and beckoning. I brace myself, close my eyes so hard they're buried deep inside my skull, set my teeth, and take a step …

I sense Fred standing beside me. I open my eyes and look at him. He's been crying. He's been crying for three weeks now, with tears and without, and there is an indelible redness in the shallow, patterned creases of his face: those of his brow, those that comment on his eyes the way rays do the sun, those that fall away from his poised, high cheeks. When our eyes meet, we both experience an odd moment of embarrassment; we're like two strangers on a train catching each other in the act of impertinent, mutual scrutiny.

"I had a dream last night," he says. His low voice is the one he'd use if we were on the phone together.

I nod and look away.

"Do you want to hear about it?"

"O.K.," I say.

"We were in bed in the middle of the night," he says. "It was the house we live in, but at the same time, it wasn't; the shape of our room was different and the windows were smaller, narrower. I had the sense that there was water nearby, that the house was on a river, near falls maybe. Something woke me up: a noise. I lay there with my eyes open, looking from left to right in the dark. I could hear footsteps on the stairs, slow scuffing ones. Still dreaming, I said to myself, I'm having a nightmare and I want to wake up. But I didn't wake up; I kept on dreaming. The footsteps grew louder, coming from the hall now. I reached over and woke you, and you got mad and said, 'What do you want?'—like that. I said, 'There's someone in the house.' The two of us sat up in bed, listening. Suddenly, someone opened the bedroom door and light filled the room. I saw his hand on the doorknob, his arm outstretched, his foot crossing the threshold. It was a man, a small man with short hair and a short beard, yet it wasn't until he got to the foot of the bed that I recognized him: it was Cliff, Sam. 'I just wanted to say goodbye,' he said. He stood there looking at us for a minute, smiling, and then he said, 'I never got a chance to say goodbye, so I'm doing it now. Goodbye, you two,' he said, and then he waved, like this, just once."

I'm on the phone to one of Meg's nurses at Andover Manor. "How's she doing?" I ask.

"Oh, she's just peachy," she says. "Would you like to speak to her?"

"Sure," I say.

I hear Meg in the distance. "Sam ..." she says, calling to me from her wheelchair, her faintly excited voice resounding in the hollow corridor.

"Here he is," says the nurse. "Speak up now, dear." Meg hates it when people call her "dear."

"Hello?" says Meg, in a guarded tone; she's already forgotten who's calling.

"Hi, it's Sam," I say.

"Sam," she says, surprised. "I thought you were coming to the fair today."

"What fair?" I say.

"Oh, they have some cheese and crackers. But don't you dare bring the dog, they say. What nerve! Honest to God. I'm not going. It's not such a nice day anyway, so I'll just stay in. I've got enough groceries."

I can never think of anything to say to her, commenting on her imagined activities, so these calls of mine get rarer and briefer as time goes by. Sometimes, when I need its convenient help, a technical disturbance fouls the line, filling in the silence, and then I say, I can't hear you anymore, Meg. I'll try you later on, O.K.?

"How's the weather," I ask her now.

"When are you coming home?" she says, talking over me.

"I was just there," I say. "A few weeks ago. Don't you remember?"

"That's right too," she says, doubtfully.

"But I'll be back," I tell her, "one of these days. I'll come and see you and we'll do some things together, O.K.? How does that sound?"

"Oh, that'll be nice," she says, "I need that. I'm lonesome, you know, with the kids all grown up and living on their own." And then she says the strangest thing. "I love you, Sam," she says, so easy with those words—it's as if she's always said them, and always will.

"I love you too," I say, telling her that for the first time in my life.

Fred told me, "Be there at seven-thirty," but just as I was getting in the car the blacksmith showed up with a bill for the work he'd done this afternoon on the bottling yard gate, and I had to go over it with him and inspect the job. So here I am now with a dripping umbrella, forty-five minutes late, climbing Vivian's five flights of medieval steps, thinking, Fred'll kill me!

The door is ajar, so I push it and go in. This is Vivian's new apartment, but it's very similar to the last one she had. The foyer is stuffed with the same items she stored in the foyer of her previous home: an old steamer trunk with a crinkled Simplon Pass sticker, and the folded Victorian Oriental rug her mother left her, too big for any room Vivian would ever have.

Fred and the kids are sitting around a wooden table in a mostly glass breakfast room converted from a dying loft. Beyond their heads is a moving panorama of wet, red-tiled roofs, Giotto's campanile, Brunelleschi's cupola, and as I stare off, losing myself in this display of precious objects, Fred and his three kids become mere silhouettes.

"This is Patrizia," Fred says in clear English. "That's Ennio and that's Sauro." He gestures to me. "This is my friend Sam."

I run my eyes nervously past theirs, all trained on mine, and wonder how much they know about me. Do they know that I live with Fred? Have they heard the story of how we met, nine years ago at a bar in Boston while I was visiting my family and Fred was working with Boston Musica Viva? Do they know that just a few weeks ago we were with my brother at the moment of his AIDS-related death? Do they know that this week Fred and I are contracting to buy a house where we intend to live together, forever perhaps? And if they don't know these things, how would they feel if they did? Would they feel any differently about Fred, whom they now consult with their glances, searching for the wise, fatherly directives they're confident he has?

"What do you say?" Fred says. "Do you say, How do you do? Let's see what you've learned. Don't embarrass me in front of my friend."

The kids squirm. They bow their heads, cross and uncross their legs. Patrizia's arms are folded tight against her well-developed chest. "Let's drop it for now, Federico," she says in Italian. Fred told me that as a little girl she'd been badly beaten by her father, who eventually wound up in jail where he belonged. With her hair dyed black she looks fast, but I wonder how fast she'd be if she had a regular family who loved her and gave her a happy home.

Vivian's two daughters come into the kitchen. They go to English public schools but are in town this week for holidays. I don't understand why Vivian chose to go away to Paris with her son, while the two girls are here, but Vivian is passionately unconventional. Her two pretty blond daughters wear droopy, loose-knit sweaters and Arab shawls tied around their necks. "We're busy packing," they say.

"I love that accent," Patrizia says, in rough dialect.

"Packing for what?" I ask.

"We're going to Torino to visit Father," the younger, more Italian one says. "We have to get the train at nine twenty-eight. But don't you worry; the house is yours. Just pull the door shut when you leave and switch off the lights."

"And your cousins?" I say. "Aren't they coming?"

"Mummy invited them," says the older girl, "but no."

This isn't at all the kind of evening Fred wanted it to be: an encounter between lonely, foster-cared-for kids and potential friends from the outside world.

This is how the privileged classes ward off subversion, I suppose. Cardinal rule number one: Keep clear of the downtrodden and their infectious handicaps. I, too, have had a taste of oppression, be it ever so minor and weird. Ultimately, I line up with the subjugated; I guess I always will. I feel this rejection the way Fred does, the way the kids must.

Vivian's girls have prepared a pot of black tea, which fills the room with crude, medicinal vapors—this is a macrobiotic kitchen. They present it to Fred's kids in mugs of assorted raku noncolors, and the kids sit there for the longest time, quietly astonished, staring down into the queer liquid darkness.

"At least say, Thank you," Fred says.

"Tanka you," they all say.

"Tongue between the teeth," Fred says, in Italian. "Like this, thh…"

Sauro's tongue comes out way too far, but he achieves a stiff, comprehensible theta and Fred's satisfied. I think about the fact that this boy was raised in a hut with a dirt floor, that his parents live by begging, that they own no knives and forks and eat with their hands, and that his father's goats have the run of the place.

Ennio wears a denim vest and has an American flag plastered across the right knee of his jeans. He has a smart bearing, and there's an articulate depth to his Parmigiano eyes. This is no ordinary boy; I can see why he's Fred's favorite.

We all rise and head to Vivian's "studio." I lag behind like a camp counselor bringing up the rear. Ennio is one step ahead of me. He's wearing bright green Gore-Tex hiking boots. *"Bei scarponi,"* I say. "Nice boots."

"Got them with my allowance," he says, watching his feet. "They're good in the rain."

"Do you ever go hiking?" I ask, and then I remember that he never leaves the Istituto except to go to school.

"I'd like to go," he says. "I want to go walking in the mountains; that's what I want to do."

I picture him, and a few others, trailing Fred and me as we cut across the shoulder of Cimone in the Apuan Alps. Then I think of Maria Trapp and her kids, and a little laugh escapes. "Maybe you'd like to take a hike with us one day," I say. Fred and I make frequent trips to the mountains. "Could you go for that? You and some of your friends?"

He stops, looks at me, and smiles—Fred's done a nice job on his teeth. "Sure," he says. "I'll beat you to the top, all of you."

"Wanna bet?" I say.

"I'll bet you, Sam," he says. I'm impressed that he's retained my name; he has more social grace than many people twice his age.

"Va bene," I say. "You're on."

Vivian's studio is set up like a classroom with folding chairs and metal-framed tables; it's where she gives her English lessons to Italian businessmen. One of her girls starts the tape, turns off the light, and takes a seat near the door. Her sister's in the room overhead; we hear her hurried footsteps as she gathers essentials for the trip.

Fred is sitting directly behind the kids, and when the action starts he leans in close to explain, in Italian, what Humphrey Bogart is doing with that fishing boat in the port of Martinique.

Right away, Vivian's daughter is up and out the door; her presence, as the titles rolled, was a token participation. I feel sorry for Fred's kids.

I've seen *To Have and Have Not* several times, and the thought of sitting here for close to two hours in this hard metal chair, in this strange dark room, gives me a brief anxiety attack. Instead of watching the movie, I watch the kids. I evaluate their haircuts, their faint personal odors, their shoes and socks, the structure of their necks, their posture, and I apply this information to all Fred has told me of them, all the stories I've heard.

As the movie ends I think about where I've been for the last ninety minutes. I recall, as we do half-forgotten dreams, a few mental pictures, double- and triple-exposed: Cliff, in shorts and a baseball cap, at Disney World, giving his old friend Minnie Mouse a bear hug; Fred and me posed against the backdrop of our new home which is also every home we've ever had together; some settings for human drama that have vaguely to do with dark, stormy seas like the one our hero navigates in this movie; some familiar, tiresome images out of my childhood I'd best forget once and for all.

And I recall a question that ran, repeatedly, through my mind as the tape played itself out oblivious to my disregard: How do I express thanks that Fred and I have made it, that we're on the lifeboat, among the saved? Perhaps it's enough just to give and to celebrate the promise, to rock peacefully, while I can, in the bosom of the sea, and not to bitch about the brand of canned beans we're served, or the dinner company I'm forced to keep.

Sauro, the goat-boy, turns on the light. My gaze falls to the back of Fred's head, which looks like the bobbed tail of a strawberry roan; from behind, with his scruff shorn clean, he could pass for a kid himself. All of a sudden, I like this crazy haircut. I nod my delayed approval, and laugh a little, under my breath. When we get home, later on, and it's just the two of us again, I'll tell him how cool I think it is.

PAUL GERVAIS was born in Maine, and spent his childhood in Massachusetts. He holds a Master of Fine Arts degree from the San Francisco Art Institute. Since 1982 he has lived in Italy, near the Tuscan city of Lucca.